continued . . .

A Killer Read

"This is a terrific debut! I want to join this book club, eat those cheese sticks, keep an eye on those romances and wander around Ashton Corners. But most of all, I'd love to have Lizzie Turner as my friend. Especially if another body turns up."

—Mary Jane Maffini, author of
the Charlotte Adams Mysteries

"Who can't love a debut novel filled with mystery references and a pair of cats named Edam and Brie? And who can't adore dedicated, saucy Lizzie Turner, a literacy teacher with high hopes for her students? Readers should have high hopes for this series. And thanks to the author's fine research, readers just might find a delicious assortment of new authors to browse."

—Avery Aames, Agatha Award–winner and national
bestselling author of the Cheese Shop Mysteries

"Book a date with *A Killer Read*. Mystery-loving book club members will keep readers guessing as they page through clues to prevent themselves from being booked for murder."

—Janet Bolin, author of
the Threadville Mysteries

Book Fair and Foul

ERIKA CHASE

BERKLEY PRIME CRIME, NEW YORK

THE BERKLEY PUBLISHING GROUP
Published by the Penguin Group
Penguin Group (USA) LLC
375 Hudson Street, New York, New York 10014

USA • Canada • UK • Ireland • Australia • New Zealand • India • South Africa • China

penguin.com

A Penguin Random House Company

BOOK FAIR AND FOUL

A Berkley Prime Crime Book / published by arrangement with the author

Berkley Prime Crime Books are published by The Berkley Publishing Group.
BERKLEY® PRIME CRIME and the PRIME CRIME logo are trademarks of
Penguin Group (USA) LLC.

For information, address: The Berkley Publishing Group,
a division of Penguin Group (USA) LLC,
375 Hudson Street, New York, New York 10014.

ISBN: 978-0-425-27149-0

PUBLISHING HISTORY
Berkley Prime Crime mass-market edition / August 2014

PRINTED IN THE UNITED STATES OF AMERICA

10 9 8 7 6 5 4 3 2 1

Cover illustration by Griesbach/Martucci.
Interior text design by Laura K. Corless.

Acknowledgments

As always, my heartfelt thank-you to the entire team at Berkley Prime Crime, especially my editor, the amazing Kate Seaver, and editorial assistant Katherine Pelz. Many thanks also to my terrific agent, Kim Lionetti of BookEnds Literary Agency.

But let's not forget that it's the ground crew who provide a smooth takeoff and landing for any new book. I readily admit I couldn't do it without the support of Lee McNeilly, my eagle-eyed sister, and Mary Jane Maffini, my dear friend and author extraordinaire.

Many thanks also to Sylvia Braithwaite for her friendship, reading and querying skills. And to Randy Williams for being Southern and so willing to share. I also value the support of my writing group, The Ladies' Killing Circle, for many, many years of projects and fun!

Also, thank you to all my friends who believe writing is a serious business and treat it with due respect, especially for knowing when not to phone.

Readers are the other invaluable part of the equation, and writers would be nowhere without them. Thank you for reading and commenting. Please help keep mysteries around for a long time!

Chapter One

◇◇◇

"What are we waiting for?" I said. "Let's go."

GRACE TAKES OFF—JULIE HYZY

"I know we are here to celebrate Stephanie's birthday, and I do not want to take any of the shine away from your day, honey, but I was wondering if we could take a few minutes to go over the final plans for next weekend." Molly Mathews looked around the table at the other three women, Lizzie Turner, Sally-Jo Baker and Stephanie Lowe, and they all nodded their agreement.

"Good. But first off, a most happy birthday to you, Stephanie. You have had quite the year and, I say this truly, I am so happy you have become part of our book club. No, it is more than that. I am happy you are our friend. I hope this coming year will bring you true happiness." Molly lifted her wineglass in a toast. "To Stephanie."

Stephanie's grin covered most of her face. Lizzie hadn't seen her so excited since her baby, Wendy, was born the previous Christmas. Once again she looked so much younger than her now twenty years. Her shoulder-length brown hair was pulled back in a ponytail showing off her new dangly red earrings, a gift from Lizzie; she'd started wearing more colorful eye makeup after the birth; and her figure had quickly gone back to a size six, as emphasized by the clingy white tunic top and black stretch pants she was wearing.

"To Stephanie," Lizzie repeated. "I can't imagine the Ashton Corners Mystery Readers and Cheese Straws Society without you."

"Nor A Novel Plot," Molly added. "You are my star bookseller."

"Oh, stop it all now. Y'all are going to make me start crying. I don't know what I did to deserve such wonderful friends." Stephanie swiped at the corner of her eye before a tear could fall.

Sally-Jo clinked her glass against Stephanie's. "It's all true. However, I'd be cautious if I were you. Never know what extra duties might flow your way next weekend once we have you good and buttered up," she added with a chuckle.

Stephanie waited until the server had placed the three-tier cake stand filled with fancy tea sandwiches and scones in the center of the table. "I've always wanted to come to the high tea here at the Jefferson Hotel. It's all so elegant and"— she spied the dessert tray at the next table—"fattening."

They all laughed. "But I gotta tell y'all," Stephanie continued, "I'm so excited about the mystery fair that I'm starting to lose sleep. It will be such fun meeting big-name authors and spending the whole day just talking mysteries. I'm sure glad you decided to do it, Molly."

"It was not my decision entirely. I would not have taken it on if the entire book club had not been so enthusiastic. Even with everyone pitching in, I had no idea how much work it would be." She said it with a smile but Lizzie felt concerned that the oldest member was the one doing the most work.

"Is there something else we can be doing, Molly?" Lizzie asked. Not that Molly couldn't handle it. At seventy, she could match even Andie Mason, the youngest member of the book club, in the stamina department any day. Of that, Lizzie was certain.

Molly shuffled through the papers on the table next to her place setting. Lizzie could hear the clatter of teacups threaded with the soft din of voices. One didn't want to speak too loudly in the hotel's Echo Lounge.

"I don't think so," Molly finally answered, having found the page she was searching for. "You will be able to stop by the Quilt Patch Bed and Breakfast on Thursday after school? I'll try to get there by about two P.M. I can't imagine that Margaret Farrow and her husband will arrive any earlier. They said they would be leaving Columbus after lunch and just take a leisurely drive over."

"I'll be there. You can just text me when they arrive." She grinned as Molly frowned. Although Molly was resisting learning to text, Lizzie had a feeling that she was also secretly intrigued by the idea. Lizzie would get her on board sooner than later. "When did you say the other authors are arriving?"

"Well, A.J. Pruitt said in the evening and Lorelie Oliver won't be there until Friday afternoon. I sure hope she arrives in plenty of time for the evening dinner I have planned. Gigi Briggs should also be arriving early Friday afternoon. That's the four of them. I can't imagine keeping track of any more authors than that." Molly sipped her tea.

Sally-Jo moved the sandwiches closer to Stephanie and, after she'd chosen a smoked salmon pinwheel, helped herself to one of the same before passing the tiered stand over to Lizzie. "I've heard there's often a bit of tension between

Lorelie Oliver and Margaret Farrow, or Caroline Cummings as she's known in the mystery world."

"Really?" Molly asked. "I hadn't heard that. Oh dear. Let's hope we do not have a couple of divas on our hands."

"Well they both have series with a Southern belle as protagonist," Lizzie said. "That could put them in competition, don't you think?"

"They do, but Lorelie Oliver has a fashionista and Caroline Cummings writes about a caterer. You'd think that would provide enough distinction between the two," Sally-Jo ventured. "I understand they're pretty much Southern belles themselves."

"Now that could make things mighty interesting," Molly reflected. "Does anyone know anything about A.J. Pruitt?"

"Only that Bob is extremely happy that we've got one writer on the list who has a police procedural. I haven't heard any gossip about him," Sally-Jo added as she tucked a stray strand of auburn hair behind her ear. She'd started growing out her pixie cut but constantly complained about it getting in the way. Lizzie secretly hoped she'd go back to the shorter style, which totally suited her small build and large green eyes and hot pink glasses frames.

"According to their promotional flyer, the three of them have appeared together before, so it seems to me that they should be able to cope. I just hope Gigi Briggs doesn't get lost in the fray." Lizzie had worried about adding the much younger author to the guest list but it had been hard to turn down an enthusiastic writer who made such an earnest appeal to be included.

"Well, we'll all see that that does not happen. Isabel Fox is moderating their panel on Saturday morning and she will just have to keep them under control. Perhaps you could give her a heads-up, Lizzie?" Molly suggested.

"Yes'm," Lizzie managed to say, her mouth full of goat

cheese and watercress sandwich. She glanced around the room as she ate. She was lucky to have been able to schedule all her appointments for the morning, which proved easy enough to do since most people, she realized, have an aversion to Friday afternoon commitments. Except if they involve food. As the reading specialist with the Ashton Corners Elementary School, her days consisted mainly of meetings with students, parents and teachers. A far cry from the very chic lounge where they now sat, enjoying the ever-so-special high tea.

Trust Molly to choose something so beyond Stephanie's usual activities as a birthday treat. In fact, Molly had insisted on treating them all. The room was full even on this Friday afternoon and the variety in ages spoke to the fact that gracious rituals still appealed to a wide range of women. The crisp white linen tablecloths, edged in a taupe trim, the plush taupe chairs, the crystal chandeliers and the expanse of window overlooking the back gardens made the setting idyllic. Lizzie realized how happy she felt to be in this place, at this time, and with her close friends.

"The food arrangements are all confirmed, Sally-Jo?" Molly asked, pulling Lizzie out of her reverie.

"They are. The Ladies' Guild of St. John's will prepare a salad and cold cuts buffet for lunch for the participants, and the Baptist Women's Group at Bethany Church have a yummy menu for the afternoon tea break."

"Now, try to visualize it," she continued. "You're in the Picton Hall at the Eagles Center. We'll have the authors sitting onstage and the audience seated theater-style facing them. That should take up about half the floor space. At the opposite end of the room, we'll set up the tables for lunch and leave them up for the break, too. It's really spacious, so nobody should be crowded."

"That's excellent. And both groups will attend to cleanup?"

"They will. And they'll supply all the dishes and linens. I think we really lucked out here."

Lizzie snagged another sandwich before the serving plate was removed and a bone china tray filled with squares, cookies and cakes put in its place. "I managed to get some great donated items for our gift basket draw at the end of the day. And, I confirmed with George Havers at the *Colonist* that he'll have both a reporter and a photographer at the hall first thing next Saturday morning. We'll do a photo op with the authors to start and then he'll wander around and take pictures of the attendees for a couple of hours. If there's space, George will devote about half a page to the event in the following Thursday's newspaper."

"The authors should be very pleased," Molly said, adding, "not to mention that it's great publicity for the bookstore." Since Molly had bought the closed store several months before, she and Lizzie had been working on rebranding the store away from the former owner and her misdeeds. It even had a new name, A Novel Plot. The fact that almost everyone in Ashton Corners knew Molly and thought well of her for her many philanthropic ventures made the task easier than it might otherwise have been.

Stephanie let out a low moan. "Oops, I'm so sorry," she whispered, looking sheepishly at them. "It's this chocolate thingy. It's just the most delicious treat I've ever tasted. I had no idea. What's it called?"

Lizzie looked at the menu. "That must be the Viennese Chocolate Sable. I'll have to try some, too."

Molly reached over and snagged the final mini vanilla meringue and placed it on Stephanie's plate. "Enjoy this, too, my dear. In fact, all of you enjoy today because come next Thursday, we are headed for a weekend of mystery and mayhem."

Chapter Two

◇◇◇

The important thing was I wouldn't have to do it
alone.

ARSENIC AND OLD CAKE—JACKLYN BRADY

Lizzie pushed herself from a yoga-style sitting position
on the floor, where she'd been reading off book titles to
Sally-Jo, who perched on a wicker chair with the master list
in hand. "What a difference a day or two makes," she said
with a grin. "Friday we're taking tea, all posh and gentle,
today we're taking inventory in Molly's store, dressed in
jeans and T-shirts."

Sally-Jo laughed. "We can't do glam every day, Lizzie."

"I hear you gals. I might remind you that the men in the
book club were not included in Friday's outing," Bob Miller
said with an exaggerated air of aggrievement.

"Am I to believe you would have actually enjoyed high
tea at the Jefferson Hotel, Bob Miller?" Molly asked as she
walked past the girls on her way to the front desk, her arms
filled with books.

"That would be carrying togetherness a bit too far," Bob

said quickly. "Now, this here is more my style. Where would you like this box deposited?"

Molly took a moment to brush back a stray strand of gray hair that had escaped the French roll that had been a tidy hairdo earlier that morning. "I guess right by the back door, Bob. I think I'll end up with several boxes to be tossed. I thought I'd donate some to the Bargain Bin. I like that their profits go to help the food bank. The rest will go to the library. It seems their budget is never quite elastic enough."

"Great idea, Molly," said Jacob Smith, from his perch on top of the ladder. He'd been busy dusting off the top of the shelves, a task that needed to be done on a more regular basis, Molly always said, though she could never quite follow through on it.

"Well, y'all know how grateful I am to you for giving up your Sunday to help with this inventory. Lizzie and I did it when I bought the store but I guess it does make sense to do it twice a year. That way, I can keep better track of inventory changes."

"Uh, you mean losses, don't you?" Stephanie asked. She and Andie had just finished with the children's section and she presented the paperwork to Molly. "I just can't get my head around the fact that people really do swipe books. I mean, they're books, for crumbs' sake. Aren't all readers honest people?"

Molly patted her arm. "I'd like to think so, honey, but you never know what some people will do." She looked around at the store walls. "It looks like we're making good progress here. How about if I send you two across the street to the deli to pick up the lunch and drinks I've ordered? Then we'll all take a much-deserved break."

By the time the girls arrived back, bags of food in hand, Molly had cleared off the worktable in the back room. They set the dishes of food out along with paper plates and plastic cutlery.

"This is just like a picnic," Andie exclaimed, spooning some pasta and artichoke salad onto her plate.

Molly laughed. "Without the blanket and the ants. Just grab a seat anywhere and enjoy your meals. Sally-Jo, maybe while you are eating you could fill the boys in on our plans for the book fair."

"Happy to, Molly." She filled her plate, grabbed a can of cranberry juice and sat on the wicker love seat in the rear of the store. "You do know it's in the Picton Hall at the Eagles Center, which has a stage, a large floor space and a kitchen at the opposite end of the room. We'll have chairs set up onstage for the morning panel portion of the day, along with theater seating for the audience. And it should be easy to switch it up to an intimate setting with two easy chairs, one for the author and one for the interviewer, for the afternoon program."

She scanned the faces of the members of the Ashton Corners Mystery Readers and Cheese Straws Society to make sure they were all in agreement.

"What about someplace to sell the books?" asked Lizzie.

"I'm thinking along the right-hand wall. There's plenty of room for a few tables and chairs for Stephanie and Andie. They'll want to sit down in between dealing with customers. And the signing tables can be on the opposite wall, the one with the entry door. We'll also set up the registration desk along that wall, too. Does that sound about right?"

"I think that will work out perfectly," Molly enthused. "Do you foresee any problems, Bob? You are our logistics person, after all."

He took a while to answer, looking like he was enjoying his food. "Nope. I think it'll be an easy setup, which is good

since it's only Jacob and me doing the heavyweight stuff."
He grinned. "The chairs will take the longest but I'm sure
we can get it all done if we get there, say, an hour before the
doors open." He looked over at Jacob, who nodded.

"Good."

"Will all those heavy book boxes be here at the store for
pickup?"

Molly shook her head. "No, I had them delivered to my
home. They're in the garage. That worked out well for
Teensy Coldicutt's launch, except for the initial glitch." She
smiled ruefully. "The back room here is so crowded already,
as you can see."

This was Molly's first big event as new owner of the only
independent bookstore in town. Molly had spent the last few
months doing some rejiggering of the floor plan and redeco-
rating the store while the book club members had been
delighted with their various new roles. Bob Miller handled
the bookkeeping end of it; Stephanie Lowe took on the role
of manager and worked in the store most weekdays;
seventeen-year-old Andrea Mason worked part-time, mainly
on weekends and a couple of days after school; Jacob kept
his eyes on all things legal; and Lizzie handled the promotional end of things and enjoyed doing the occasional shift
selling books.

The Ashton Corners reading community had embraced
the store in all its newness, especially the fact that Molly
was the new owner. And now, she was venturing a bit further
afield with her first major daylong event.

Sally-Jo was anxious to continue when it looked like
they'd finished processing those details. "Now, remember I
said there's a kitchen at one end of the room? The luncheon
will be held in that area. That makes it easier to set up the
food that will be offered buffet style. We can leave the tables

at the ready all day and it won't interfere with the author events. How does that sound to y'all?"

Andie finished off her can of root beer and set it down on the floor. "I can't believe it's almost here. One more week," she beat a pair of invisible drumsticks in the air, "and we're holding our very first mystery conference."

Lizzie nodded. "It's not really a conference, more like a festival, but since the authors are coming directly from the Readers and Riters Festival in Atlanta, we've decided to call it a fair."

Andie waved her hand. "Conference, festival, fair . . . doesn't matter. I can hardly wait. Aren't ya just bursting?"

Lizzie grinned, happy that Andie seemed ready to dive into another new project. The book club had been Lizzie's method of turning her former tutoree onto reading. And although the club presented a variety of reading tastes and opinions, it seemed like they had also bonded as a fairly effective gang of sleuths, too. She just hoped this latest venture wouldn't end up with another dead body count.

"I once again have to thank y'all for embracing yet another of my pet projects," Molly said, helping herself to some more green salad. "When I took over the store I had no idea how much work it would be but it is because of you that I can try out something as ambitious as a daylong mystery fair. I'm also truly amazed that we have gotten such a good response from the authors."

"Well, why in tarnation wouldn't we?" Bob Miller asked, huffing up as he spoke. "We're a legitimate mystery book club and you own a very popular bookstore."

Molly gave him a warm smile. "You really do put the best spin on everything, Bob. Especially things to do with the store. Of course, we're not paying them, but have put together a nice little package for them as a thank-you."

"Such as?" Bob asked.

"Well, we've booked them at the Quilt Patch for an extra couple of nights after the book fair so they can take in the sights of our wonderful town. And while canvassing for items for our big draw at the end of the day, Lizzie managed to get extra contributions for the authors such as gift certificates for meals and the like. Plus, we have guest passes to the local museums. I think we're treating our authors quite nicely."

Lizzie jumped in. "The merchants are all delighted to help out. They're in favor of anything new in town that might grow into a yearly event and bring in some tourists."

Molly groaned. "Grow? Yearly? One event at a time, please. I'm really in such a tizzy about this fair, you would think it was a whole week long rather than just one day."

"That's understandable, Molly," said Lizzie, reaching over to touch her hand. "It's the first time you've put on an event like this. You've had so many firsts since buying the bookstore and you've handled them all so professionally. I'm sure this event will be every bit as successful."

"That's nice of you to say, honey. I really did jump in with both feet and not much in the way of eyeglasses, buying that store. But you know, I have loved every minute of it and so much more having y'all involved in it. The little book club that could."

"Do you need help with anything besides the bookselling, Molly?" Stephanie asked. "Mrs. Sanchez is staying over at my house for the Friday night and Saturday so that I can attend. I'm really looking forward to it. It'll be the first time in a long time that I'm out at something other than work or a book club meeting. Not that I don't enjoy being here with y'all today," she added quickly.

Bob chuckled. "Even if you don't, you know you can't get out of it. You're part of our book club, little lady."

"And Stephanie, I do not know what I would do without you running the store. You have turned out to be an amazing manager," Molly said.

Stephanie turned a bright pink and grinned from ear to ear. "So, what's the agenda for the fair, Molly?" she asked.

"Well, I went and asked Teensy Coldicutt to be the emcee for the day."

"I thought she was busy house hunting," Sally-Jo said. "She might not have time for us."

"Pshaw. Teensy's a social butterfly at heart and she'll have fun meeting the authors. Who knows, she may get some publicity out of it. After the huge amount of sales her book had in the summer when it came out, it is just languishing on the shelves these days. Not that Teensy is not trying her best to promote it, but there are not many more opportunities here in Ashton Corners and she is not very keen on doing any touring herself."

"Maybe these authors will just sweep her up with them," Stephanie suggested. "Didn't you say they often do events together?"

Molly looked thoughtful. "You are right, my dear. They do and she just might find them to her liking. But as you said, she is busy looking for a house, so we will see."

Jacob sat down beside Sally-Jo on the wicker love seat that resided in the travel section of the store. He took one of two pecan balls from his plate and placed it on hers. She flashed him a smile that made Lizzie feel like she was intruding on a special moment, even in the midst of the entire Ashton Corners Mystery Readers and Cheese Straws Society. Sally-Jo and Jacob had met at the first meeting of the book club and had quickly become an item, much to the delight of all. Nothing like a romance right in their midst.

Molly gave Lizzie a smile that said she felt the same way, before she continued. "As Lizzie suggested, I also asked

Isabel Fox from the library to be the moderator of the morning panel and she is thrilled. I have left the questions she'll ask them entirely in her hands."

"In the FYI department," Molly continued, "Caroline Cummings, whose real name is Margaret Farrow, by the way, and her husband are arriving at the bed and breakfast next Thursday. And, as Margaret Farrow, she has a very popular romance series."

"That's that woman who writes a cozy or something, isn't it?" Bob asked. Bob's nose actually crinkled as he said it.

"It is. She has a Southern belle who is a caterer as her amateur sleuth. Bob, you are more than welcome to be part of the welcoming party, too."

Bob guffawed. "Not on your life, Molly. I'll wait until that fella who writes about the sheriff gets here. What's his name?"

"A.J. Pruitt."

"That's the one. Now he's writing what I want to read. I'll be mighty pleased to make his acquaintance." Bob winked at her.

Molly grimaced. "Continuing. A.J. Pruitt," she looked pointedly over at Bob, "will arrive after supper on Thursday, he said. Lorelie Oliver will come in on Friday and Gigi Briggs will be flying in from Boston the same day. Bob, would you be able to pick her up at the airport? I think her plane comes in at three."

"Sure thing."

"That's all of them then, and we will have dinner at my place, of course. I'm having it catered by Food Lovers' Delight, so it will be an easy evening. Now, have I missed anything?"

Bob shrugged and the others just looked at one another, saying nothing.

"Good. Then, I guess we're all set. Oh yes, I wanted to

remind everyone that even though this mystery fair has been a lot of work, we have all agreed to still hold our regular book club meeting. Bob has chosen *Shoot the Dog* by Brad Smith, which is now out in trade paperback and on our shelves, although you should have finished reading it by now," she said with a smile.

Lizzie stood and stretched. "I'll gather up all the dirty dishes, since they don't have to be washed," she added with a grin, "and the rest of you can resume inventorying."

"Inventorying? Huh. Well, you see what working in a bookstore will do for you?" Bob joked, pulling a garbage bag off one of the shelves in back. "It'll help expand your vocabulary."

Lizzie laughed. "That may be, Bob, but I know one thing that works even better. Reading. I've got my eye on the latest Cookbook Nook mystery, *Inherit the Word*, by Daryl Wood Gerber, and I'll be taking her home with me today."

Her "to be read" pile was getting much too low these days.

Chapter Three

◇◇◇

Now what?

HOW THE LIGHT GETS IN—LOUISE PENNY

The following Thursday, Lizzie tapped the steering wheel of her Mazda 3 as she waited for the traffic light to change. An instrumental version of a song by Christina Aguilera that was popular in the mid-nineties played on the radio and she realized she was humming along. She'd recently watched the DVD of *Burlesque* for about the fifth time, loving the music and her once-favorite singer. She slowed to make a right onto Tay Street. Molly had given her a quick call a couple of hours earlier but had to leave a message since Lizzie was in a meeting with the teaching staff at the Ashton Corners Elementary School, where she was a reading specialist. A phone call, Lizzie noted. No texting yet.

Her message had been brief. The Farrows had arrived and now Lizzie was headed to the Quilt Patch Bed and Breakfast to help welcome them, as Molly had asked. She'd spent the previous evening reading the bios of all four authors who had been invited to the mystery fair, wanting to sound knowledgeable when she talked to them. As she remembered, Margaret Farrow wrote several romance series over the years but switched to her pen name, Caroline Cummings, for her mysteries. Lizzie had noted that the Southern Caterer Mysteries were popular enough to have won a couple of Silver Teaspoon Awards for Best Novel over the years at the CozyCon conference.

Also arriving in town today, A.J. Pruitt had a prolific career writing police procedurals, as Bob so often told anyone who would listen. Lizzie wondered if he realized they weren't the edgy Dirty Harry type he so enjoyed, but rather were heavier on the humor and the puzzle to qualify as a cozy. Probably not.

Lorelie Oliver, another Southerner with a belle protagonist, this one the Southern Fashionista series, seemed to attend every conference going on; and Gigi Briggs was a travel agent by day with the third book in her series, the Big Top Mysteries, featuring a circus trapeze artist, just out. An interesting mix, for sure.

Lizzie parked on the street in front of the B and B and noticed an older, silver-haired man standing on the large wraparound porch smoking a cigar. He watched as she approached the stairs and then stuck out his hand as she drew level to him.

"Carter Farrow, ma'am, at your service. I'm assuming you are the Lizzie Turner we keep hearing so much about." His smile was warm and friendly.

Lizzie shook his hand. "That depends on what you hear. If it's good, then that's me."

Carter guffawed. "I think this will be a very delightful weekend indeed." He gave her a wink, and Lizzie thought his hand was aiming at her backside as she hurried past into the hall.

Patsy Kindall, owner of the Quilt Patch, stepped out of the kitchen and greeted her. "Hey, Lizzie. They're in the front room enjoying a sherry, if you'd like to join them."

"Thanks, Patsy. How are things?"

"Getting busy. I don't want to complain as we're getting into the low season, but I'll be hopping all weekend." She sighed as she pulled back a stray lock of light brown hair that had fallen across her cheek. Her smile looked forced as she added, "Now that Sarah has moved away, I'm going to have to hire someone, I think."

"How is Sarah? Enjoying her new job?" Lizzie knew that Patsy missed her daughter for many reasons, among them the invaluable help she provided at the B and B.

The phone rang before Patsy had a chance to answer. She waved Lizzie into the room to the right and scurried back down the hall.

"Lizzie, I'm so glad you're here," Molly said, rising to greet her. She hooked an arm around Lizzie's waist and introduced her to Margaret Farrow.

"I'm very pleased to meet you and we're grateful you could work our new fair into your schedule," Lizzie said.

Margaret was just what Lizzie had expected. In fact, she looked surprisingly like the photo on the jacket cover of her book. Her dark brown hair, showing no hints of graying even though she was well into middle age, had been swept up in a French roll, the top obviously backcombed, and a fringe of wavy bangs. She wore a powder blue knee-length dress in a jersey material that clung to her lean body.

"I'm the one who's just tickled pink to have been sought out like this. Y'all know how to make a struggling writer feel special." Margaret punctuated the sentence with a giggle, which seemed to surprise her. "And, I prefer to be called Caroline while I'm here, please. It helps me stay in character."

The front screen door slammed and Carter Farrow

brushed past Lizzie, although Lizzie noted there was lots of space in the room. "I've already met this charming young lady outside. Can I pour you some sherry?" He looked at Lizzie. She noticed he held a glass of something else in his left hand. Obviously not a sherry drinker.

"No, not right now. I'm fine, thanks."

"Oh, I don't doubt that," Carter answered.

Embarrassed, Lizzie glanced over at Caroline in time to see the look of disgust on her face. It quickly changed into a benign smile as Carter settled himself on a Queen Anne chair at the far side of the room.

Caroline cleared her throat. "I wonder what time A.J. will be joining us. When we left the conference in Atlanta last Sunday, he said he was planning a long drive and stop-overs on his way here. It seems he used to live in the area and wants to try to track down some old friends."

"Why, I did not know that," Molly said. "I hope he will be able to find them, although not much changes around these parts. Where are you from, Caroline?"

"Why, I'm a Louisiana girl, through and through."

"Hence the Southern belle part of your series," Lizzie threw in.

Caroline gave her a genuine smile this time. "How lovely that you know it. Of course, I'm writing about what I know, as they say. I've been considered quite the chef in my time."

Molly nodded. "I'm sure."

"It's a winning combination," Caroline continued, almost as if Molly hadn't spoken. "My latest book won a Silver Teaspoon earlier this year, you know."

"Yes," Lizzie assured her. "I did know that. For Best Contemporary Novel, wasn't it? And your romance novels are also award winners, aren't they?"

Caroline was positively beaming by this time. "You are so right, my dear. I'm so happy you're a fan of my work."

Not what I'd said. Uh-oh. Better change the subject.
"How long have you known A.J. Pruitt?"

"Oh, the better part of twenty years, I'd say. You know, when I started out writing, we were an awfully small, tightly knit group. Now look at all the authors who turn up for CozyCon. They had so many, to hear the organizers tell it, that some didn't even get on panels. I think there were some who were mighty upset by that. Of course, I also go to the National Romantic Writers annual conference, as myself, and have won two Heart and Dagger Awards over the years."

"My goodness, you certainly keep yourselves busy with all these conferences and festivals and such," Molly enthused. "How did the one in Atlanta turn out?"

"It's always such a popular event with readers. They're sold out for weeks in advance. And it's well worth an author's time attending. The book sales are phenomenal."

Patsy entered with a tray of thimble cookies and short-bread. "I thought you'd like some sweets with your sherry. Now, did you want me to make those dinner reservations for you and Mr. Farrow at the Black Tomato tonight?"

Caroline nodded. "Yes, please do. For six o'clock."

They all looked toward the front door as heavy footsteps crossed the porch and the door buzzer rang. Patsy scurried from the room.

"Oh my, that's A.J.'s voice," Caroline said. "A.J., dear . . . we're in here," she called out.

Molly and Lizzie exchanged glances.

A few minutes and some muffled words later, the door-frame filled with a large male, salt-and-pepper hair on the long side, round face with a very pleasant smile on it. He looked to be big-boned rather than fat, Lizzie realized. And she would never have taken him to be the sixty-six years attributed to him in his biography.

He went over to Caroline and engulfed her in a bear hug. He next turned to Molly, who introduced herself and Lizzie.

"Why, I'm mighty pleased to make your acquaintance, Ms. Mathews, and you, too, Ms. Turner." He gripped their hands in his large bear paws.

"It's Lizzie, please," she said when she'd found her voice.

"And I am A.J." He looked to Molly.

"Molly will do me just fine."

His smile showed real warmth and humor. "I hope I arrived at a good moment. I've been driving all around the countryside and didn't have any idea as to how long it would take to arrive here." He plunked himself down on the settee next to Caroline.

"Have you and Carter had an enjoyable few days since I last saw you?" he asked her.

"Of course. It's such a rarity for us to just take some time and see the sights. My writing schedule is so busy and I find there's one deadline after the other. I keep telling poor Carter that he should just go on a holiday on his own. But the poor dear says he'd be lost without me."

She glanced over at Carter.

"Huh," was all he said. He topped off his glass and helped himself to a couple of shortbread then took a seat at the far end of the room. He turned to A.J. "How's that car of yours for touring?"

"Loving it. It just purrs along. Worth every single penny." A.J. looked over at Molly and Lizzie and explained. "I just made the biggest splurge in my life and bought myself a 1971 911 T Targa Porsche in mint condition. Makes me feel like a million bucks when I drive it."

Lizzie smiled politely, not having a clue as to anything he'd said other than Porsche.

"Oh, men and their cars," Molly interjected. "My dear

departed husband, Claydon, had himself a 1956 Corvette that he just babied like he was a proud papa."

Carter whistled. "I feel really out of place in this company, me and my 2008 Chrysler Sebring. But it does us just fine, doesn't it, sugar cakes?" All eyes turned to Caroline, whom Lizzie rightly assumed must be sugar cakes. She shrugged but there was a sour look on her face.

"I'm really not all that much into cars, as you know, Carter. As long as it gets me from signing to signing."

"Huh," Carter said again.

"So what does Caroline Cummings have on the go at the moment?" Lizzie asked, hoping to relieve the increasing tension in the room. She couldn't quite figure out what brought it on . . . cars, books or men.

Obviously the right topic, Lizzie thought as Caroline's face lit up.

"Why, I'm on the eighth Southern Caterer mystery, which will be coming out next June. Which reminds me, I really must get back to my editor on that. I've asked that the publication date be pushed up at least a month so it's available for the CozyCon conference at the beginning of June. Have you ever been to it, either of you?"

Both Lizzie and Molly shook their heads.

"Well, if you're going to be in the business of cozies, you really must attend." She looked directly at Molly as she said this.

Molly smiled sweetly. "That is good advice. However, my bookstore is not a specialty shop. There are so many different types of books and conferences, I could spend all my time attending them and none running the shop."

Lizzie swallowed a smile. The thought of Molly spending all her time at A Novel Plot just didn't fly. She relied on Stephanie and the others stopping by whenever they were needed but not necessarily every day. However, Lizzie had to admit that Molly did have her fingers on the pulse of the store and knew everything about it.

"Well, yes," said Caroline, leaning over to pat Molly on the hand. "It's much like what I face as a writer. I have to be on top of all my series, writing all the time to meet deadlines, and yet, I also have to get out there and meet my public. The fans demand it of an author and there's all that promotion that needs to take place, too."

Caroline glanced at her watch. "My goodness, look at that. It's four thirty already and I just have to go and have a short nap before getting ready to go out. It's part of my regimen and what gives me the energy to attend to everything."

"When is Lorelie expected?" A.J. asked as he reached over for a cookie.

Caroline's smile slid into a scowl. "Soon enough, I'm sure. Now, if you'll just excuse me. It was charming meeting you both. I guess I'll be seeing you tomorrow."

"Yes, you surely will," Molly answered. "I have left my phone number in your rooms, along with directions to my house, where I will be hosting the welcoming dinner. Now, if you have any questions, just give me a call."

Carter sauntered slowly out of the room behind Caroline. When they were out of earshot, A.J. said, "You're in for a real show tomorrow night, let me assure you. The two divas around one table? Priceless." He left them with a big wink.

Chapter Four

◇◇◇

The next day brought its own set of unpleasant surprises.

THE ETRUSCAN CHIMERA—LYN HAMILTON

L izzie had just finished her cup of peppermint tea after supper and was settling back to her book, *A Fashionable Death*, when the phone rang. She had four chapters left to go in Lorelie Oliver's latest book before meeting her at the author dinner the next evening.

She'd already finished the books of the other three involved in the mystery fair. She'd left Lorelie's for last, knowing it was more romancey than the others, thinking it would be a faster read. It had proven not to be and, in fact, was so complex in some scenes that Lizzie had to reread entire paragraphs. The phone was not a welcome interruption.

"Lizzie, it's Patsy Kindall over here at the Quilt Patch. I've been trying to reach Molly but I guess she's not at home. I've got a bit of a situation here and I was hoping, as part of the fair committee, you could come over and tend to it."

"Sure, Patsy. What's the problem?"

"Well, Miss High-and-Mighty Lorelie Oliver has arrived, early, I might add, and in talking with the Farrows, realized her room is much smaller than theirs and demands another, large, comparable room. I just don't have it." Lizzie could picture Patsy throwing up her hands in despair. "I've tried to explain I have only the one suite, but she says I'm insulting her by offering her a small one. I don't need this, believe me."

"No, and you don't deserve it. I'll be right over, Patsy. Give her a glass of sherry or something and sit her down to wait for me."

Lizzie sighed as she set the book aside, slipped her Keds runners back on and grabbed her denim jacket and handbag. She yelled out a good-bye to her cats, Brie and Edam, the only other living things in her tiny house, and left.

The B and B was only three blocks away and Lizzie didn't even have time to come up with a plan on the drive over. She noted the Cape Cod house was ablaze in lights. She could hear a woman's loud voice, dripping in Southern sarcasm, as she opened the front door.

"Apparently popularity and book sales are not factors taken into consideration by these fair people when allocating rooms."

Lizzie cringed and took a minute to take a calming breath before entering the sitting room. Patsy spotted her instantly. "Ah, Lizzie Turner. So glad to see you. This is one of the women organizing the fair. And this"—she pointed out a tall, well-endowed woman to Lizzie—"is Lorelie Oliver."

Lorelie ignored Lizzie's outstretched hand and launched into a tirade. "I do not appreciate being snubbed like this, Ms. Turner. I have three Heart and Daggers and a Silver Teaspoon. My books are always on the bestseller lists and, really, I'm doing ya'll a big favor by even being here." She stopped for a breath and straightened her red and white tunic top that had ridden up on one hip. Her flowing red pants looked festive. She wore her platinum blonde hair in a page-boy, swept over to one side.

"I do know that this little event of yours is sold out," she continued, "and I dare say that's due in large part to my books."

Lizzie thought to herself, it's because it's a unique event, first time it's been tried in this town. That's why.

Caroline struggled to push her way out of the soft-cushioned love seat. She stood a good three inches shorter than Lorelie and lacked the girth. *Gaunt, as Mama used to say.* "As usual, you are way too full of yourself, Lorelie."

Lizzie couldn't think of a thing to say. She spotted A.J. seated in a leather La-Z-Boy chair over in a far corner, a big grin on his face. He's thoroughly enjoying this spectacle, Lizzie realized. Carter Farrow sat in the shadows beside the front window, the light shining around him rather than on him. She couldn't figure out what his expression meant. Definitely not mirth. Maybe even a little bit scared?

"Now ladies," Lizzie said, realizing she had to take charge. "You can't imagine just how pleased we are to have you both with us, and room allocation has nothing whatso-ever to do with anything other than . . ." she glanced help-lessly at Patsy.

"The suite is for the Farrows because there are two of them," she offered, and added under her breath, "as I'd already mentioned."

"Yes, that's right. Two people get the larger room and the others are allocated according to whomever arrives first." She hoped it didn't sound too much like a question. Since Molly had handled booking the rooms, Lizzie wasn't too sure how things had been arranged. Patsy nodded as Lizzie's eyes sought her out.

Lizzie took a deep breath. "We did choose the Quilt Patch

because it's our finest bed and breakfast in town and we know Patsy, as host, will treat you just royally. And you must take the time to have a look at all her wonderful quilts on display. She's also a multi–award winner, you know." It's also close to the Eagles Center, Lizzie thought, but didn't want to confuse them with too many details. "Now, we do so much appreciate you joining us here and we have planned a wonderful fair with lots of adoring fans. I'm certain you'll feel the love of those fans."

Was she laying it on too thick?

All eyes were on Lorelie. After a few short moments of silence, which felt like an hour to Lizzie, she smiled and said, "That will be just fine then."

What had that been about? Lizzie glanced at A.J., who gave her a big wink. She noticed Patsy serving the tray of sherry, her hands shaking ever so slightly, and decided she could definitely do with one. Lizzie took a sip and turned back to face the room, at which point Lorelie sat down on the love seat and pulled Caroline down beside her. They seemed in deep discussion.

Patsy nudged Lizzie out into the hallway. "See what I mean? They're like two cats hissing and fighting one minute, and the next, they're cozying up and making merry. I'm not sure I can handle this weekend."

"They'll be fine, I'm sure. What else could go wrong?" Lizzie asked, hopefully.

"Well thank you so much for coming over and handling it, Lizzie."

"Have you heard from the fourth author? She's still arriv-ing tomorrow midafternoon?"

"Yes, and I hope she's not going to give me grief over the size of her room. It's a single bed, which is what she wanted, but who knows with this gang? Oh, and I got a call asking for another room. Fortunately, I've just had the back bedroom redecorated, so that's available, although I hadn't planned on renting it out just yet."

"I thought you were keeping the B and B strictly for the authors this weekend."

"Oh, she's part of this, she says, just not an author. Something to do with publicity. From the publisher. She said the authors invited her and she'll be here a couple of nights."

Lizzie shrugged. "That's interesting. It can't hurt to get extra publicity, in case we decide to do it again next year. When is she arriving?"

"Tomorrow, late afternoon. I left Molly a message about it, knowing she's planning that supper tomorrow night for the authors. I'd expect this young lady would be attending it also. She sounds like a very vivacious young woman."

"Maybe she's used to handling the divas. Let's hope so anyway."

"Well, I can tell you this Ashley Dixon sounded real efficient on the phone."

Lizzie's heart skipped a beat. She was sure she felt it do so, physically. She gave herself a mental shake. There must be tons of Ashley Dixons on the planet. Surely it wasn't the same one.

It couldn't be.

Chapter Five

◇◇◇

Those words would eventually turn up on a plate served with sides of fear and regret, and I'd be forced to swallow them whole.

BATTERED TO DEATH—GAYLE TRENT

Lizzie stepped out her front door and took a deep breath. Another glorious day about to begin. It felt more like spring than fall if there was a discernable difference beyond the hours the sun rose and set, and the colors of the flowers.

She set off at a slow jog along Sidcup Street until she came to the corner. She'd planned a run toward the far side of town for a change but the promise of a spectacular sunrise along the Tallapoosa River drew her in that direction. By the time she reached the turnoff into Glendale Park, the sky had gone through a pattern of pinks into a clear blue. She slowed her pace slightly along the path in the woods, always on the lookout for stray sticks that eager dogs had dropped without concern for the runners.

She came upon a large one and rather than jump it, she

stopped and threw it aside. Someone else might not be so observant and could easily trip over it.

Coming out of the park, she exchanged waves with another early morning jogger, an older man who Lizzie saw on occasion, and thought she'd also spotted him behind the counter in the Walgreens pharmacy. She crossed the street before the two approaching golden retrievers and their walkers reached her. She knew these two were frisky young things and quite given to jumping up on passing bodies, even trying to follow a runner.

For the final half mile of the run, she organized her day in her mind. Two meetings with parents at the Ashton Corners Elementary School followed by lunch that was really a school staff mini-meeting. The afternoon she'd set aside for starting to plan the next term's goals for liaising with the primary-grade teachers. And then, to Molly's and what promised to be an entertaining evening.

She was looking forward to meeting Gigi Briggs and seeing how she fit in the current mix of authors. Plus, who knew what a meeting between Teensy Coldicutt, Caroline Cummings and Lorelie Oliver would bring? Lizzie's money was on Teensy.

But what about Ashley Dixon? She'd convinced herself before drifting off to sleep that it wasn't the same woman. How could it be? That would be too much of a cruel coincidence. This Ashley Dixon was part of the publishing industry. The one she'd known at college had planned a career in the art world, and the fact that she knew nothing about art history wouldn't stand in her way. That's where the money was, she believed, so that's where Ashley Dixon was headed. No way it was the same person. She turned up the pathway to her house.

Her cats, Brie and Edam, met her at the kitchen door. As Lizzie did a few cooldown stretches, Brie wound through her legs while Edam had jumped up onto her back, making a quick leap to the countertop as Lizzie righted herself. She grabbed the cat comb when she'd finished and gave them each a thorough session. That was obviously what they'd been waiting for because they both wandered off while she ate her breakfast of granola with fresh blueberries.

They were sitting on her bed, in various stages of their own attempts at grooming, when she entered the room to strip for her shower. Refreshed and redressed in a dark green sweater set with camel pants, Lizzie grabbed her tote bag with her new iPad and a couple of reference books in it, and headed out the door to her day at work.

Her first stop once in the school was at the vice principal's office. This September, the school had been assigned a new principal and vice principal, an unusual move to have both brought in at the same time. Even after a month back in school, the staff was still trying to get a feel for the new team. The new principal, Charles Benton, looked to be close to retirement and, from what he'd told them the first day, was a stickler for protocol and appearances. Kim Lafferty, the new vice principal, seemed more the quiet, laid-back type in her early forties. Lizzie had yet to see her get mad but had the feeling everyone would be aware when it happened.

Sure enough, a new schedule had been posted on Lafferty's door, showing when Lizzie would be allowed to use the office for interviews. Those were the times the vice principal would be teaching in a classroom. Lizzie would have to try to schedule meetings with parents during those hours or meet with them in a small office in the library. That space was adequate in size but lacked walls up to the ceiling. She was concerned about privacy, but more often than not, the library was unused, so chances were it would seldom be a problem.

Lizzie's first meeting was with parents of a second-grade

student, Kyle Jones, who had a lot of trouble focusing on reading when so much was happening around him in the classroom. She'd spent the last couple of days putting together a package of reading materials and aids for his parents to use with him, much to their delight. They left with assurances from Lizzie that young Kyle could overcome this and move forward to a productive school year.

The rest of the day went by quickly. By the time the final school bell rang, Lizzie felt ready for the weekend and whatever mystery that might hold. She rushed home and freshened up, and after spending too much time deciding what to wear, changed into a paisley wrap dress in blues and greens that she'd bought at Chico's the last time she'd been to Montgomery. She thought about the plans for tomorrow's fair, wondering if there'd been anything missed, but she felt that between all the book club members working on it, everything should be on track. She felt just a moment's guilt at skipping her usual Friday night choir practice. But there were still many weeks and rehearsals before the Christmas concert, so she'd have time to get up to speed.

She fed the cats then headed for Molly's, hoping to be the first one there and to help Molly greet the authors as they arrived. Sally-Jo came rushing in just a few minutes behind her.

"I looked for you at school today but you were a phantom. Plenty knew you were there but few had seen you."

"Locked away with parents and then reports, I'm afraid," Lizzie shrugged. "How was your day?"

"Oh, the usual third-grade kind of day. Let me rephrase, third grade on a Friday. It's like trying to keep the lid on a bubbling pot some days. Now, I brought some tchotchkes to put on the registration desk." She pulled four three-inch plastic skulls out of her cloth shopping bag. "What do you think of them? Don't they add a mysterious touch? Do you think Molly will like them?"

"Why wouldn't I?" Molly asked, joining the two in the foyer.

"Well, they're a bit kitschy. They're for the tables tomorrow. I happened to see them when I stopped in at the Piggly Wiggly for snacks. I think they'll be perfect."

"Skulls. How cute. They should add a touch of mysterious fun, I agree," Molly said. "Now, I'm glad you are both here. I wanted to talk to you about something before everyone arrives."

"What is it, Molly?" Lizzie asked. "Not a problem, I hope."

"Not really and I'm probably just being overly cautious, maybe even silly. Patsy called me this morning and told me how you had diverted a near-disaster last night, Lizzie. Do you want to tell us about it?"

"There's not much, really. It seems that when Lorelie Oliver arrived earlier than expected, like by half a day, she threw a snit about her room being smaller than that of Caroline Cummings. She just dug her heels in, even though Patsy went to great lengths to be courteous and explained that the Farrows got the only suite in the bed and breakfast. There are two of them, after all."

"Did she accept that?" Molly asked.

"After a few minutes thinking, and keeping us on tenterhooks, I might add, she did. It was very strange behavior."

"I've heard worse about that woman," Teensy Coldicutt said as she breezed into the kitchen. "I beg your pardon, Molly, but I heard y'all talking so I just walked right in." She set the large azalea plant she'd been holding on the counter and then gave them each a peck on the cheek.

Teensy, Molly's childhood friend, had moved back to

Ashton Corners after a decades-long absence as a newly published author and had quickly become embroiled in a plot to frame Bob Miller for murder. Not that she realized she was part of the plot. She floated around town in billowing dresses and tops, hiding her love of chocolates and bourbon, but announcing her arrival with the tap-tap of her signature stilettos. She'd quickly become an honorary member of the book club, though she didn't join them for their monthly meetings. Each of them counted Teensy as a valued friend, much to Molly's delight.

"That's quite the plant, Teensy," Lizzie said, admiring the red blossoms.

"Isn't it, sugar? I grew that plant from a baby bulb. Nursed it myself right in my back sunroom. I thought it would make an interesting centerpiece for tonight. Maybe not on the table where we'll be eating but out on the patio perhaps. Are we having drinkies out there?"

Molly nodded. "Why yes, it's such a glorious evening. And that will be perfect on the patio table. Thank you, Teensy. I'm so glad you were able to come over early. The caterers are arriving real soon so let's just gather all the beverages and move them out to the tables. What else do you know about Lorelie Oliver, Teensy?"

Teensy flicked her wrist and the sleeve of her purple blouse with yellow swirls floated around her face. She leaned forward, her face showing she was eager to pass on her information. "Well, I have heard that she and Caroline Cummings are most always vying with each other for the same awards and that often leads to some very catty remarks coming from both directions. Meow." She swatted playfully at the air. "And since Lorelie shed her latest husband, Caroline's been keeping close tabs on her own."

"Where do you pick up such things?" Molly asked,

stopping what she was doing, which was arranging pecan balls on a plate.

"Oh, here, there and the beauty parlor. Also, I follow this blog, *Cozy Comings and Goings*, real close, and the woman who writes it just can't wait to dish the dirt. My kind of gal. I'll send you the link, Molly, and you can enjoy it, too."

Molly shook her head. "Thanks, but I am not into blogs and all those other social-media things on the Internet. I'll just wait for you to fill me in," she added with a chuckle.

"So, do you think everything is really smoothed over at the B and B, Lizzie?"

Lizzie shrugged. "I think so. For now, anyway," she added with a grin.

"Hmm. Patsy had left me a message that there's someone from the publishing company coming, too. That's sort of last-minute. I hope we're not expected to do anything for this person, although I did extend an invitation for her to join us at dinner tonight."

Lizzie quickly shook away the moment of unease she felt.

"Now then," Molly continued, "on to what is happening tonight. I am so hoping you'll enjoy the authors, Teensy, because tomorrow morning is in your hands."

Teensy flapped her hand. "Tish, tosh . . . don't you worry, Molly. I'll have a grand old time, even if I have to behave. No gossip or innuendos, merely my thoughts on their books, which I've finished—their latest ones at least. They'll provide nice bits for my introductions."

Bob arrived as Lizzie picked up the tray of glasses and he quickly moved over to the door to hold it open for her. She took them out to the patio, followed by Sally-Jo with a couple of bottles of wine. "I think this could end up being a very entertaining weekend," Lizzie said with a laugh.

"All I'm hoping for is a big success for Molly," he said.

"Guess the weekend is about to begin," Lizzie said on hearing the doorbell ring. She arranged the glasses on the self-serve table as Molly and Teensy went back inside. She could hear the commotion indoors and decided to wait outside rather than enter into the fray. Within a few minutes, Teensy led Carter and Caroline out to the back patio.

Before Lizzie had a chance to welcome them, the back door opened again and A.J. Pruitt did a small bow from the waist to allow Lorelie Oliver to precede him outside.

Lorelie teetered down the two steps on her six-inch stilettos, air-kissed Caroline on both cheeks and did the same with Carter. Lizzie, standing a bit behind, noticed that Carter's hand slid down Lorelie's backside for a fraction of a second. She quickly looked away and straight at A.J., who gave her a wink and headed over to the table holding the drinks.

Teensy took the introductions in hand and waltzed up to A.J., intercepting him a couple of steps from the table. "May I introduce myself?" she asked with a coquettish smile. "I am Theodora Coldicutt, author, and more commonly known as Teensy."

A.J.'s eyes sparkled. He grabbed the hand that Teensy held out to him, bowed slightly and kissed the back of her hand. "And I am A.J. Pruitt, ordinarily known as Ambrose."

Teensy giggled and managed a slight curtsy. "So pleased to make your acquaintance, sir."

Lorelie had been watching from the bottom step and decided it was her turn. She said in a loud voice, "And I am Lorelie Oliver. Nice to meet you, Teensy." She'd chosen to do a dripping Southern accent.

Teensy turned to her and with a big smile on her face, and matching her accent, said, "Charmed, I'm sure."

Lizzie managed to suppress a smile, but when she looked

over at Bob, who had doubled over in laughter and was pretending to tie his shoelace, she lost it. She turned abruptly so as to not be seen by Lorelie and bumped into Mark Dreyfus, Ashton Corner's chief of police, whom she'd been dating for the past year.

She looked at him in surprise. "You got away early?"

He nodded and grinned, looking her up and down. "Good thing, too. I'm feeling hungry and you look like something I'd like for dessert."

Lizzie blushed in spite of herself. Really, they'd been intimate for many months now and yet she still couldn't help but feel herself right back in high school, watching Mark in his football uniform at an after-school game. He'd traded in his football gear for an army uniform and completed a college degree while serving. Then he'd been shipped off to Iraq, coming home eleven months later with an injured left knee. Soon after, he left the army and signed on with the Ashton Corners Police Department, eventually becoming its chief.

Although Lizzie had mooned over her football hero during senior year, she truly believed he never even knew she existed. She'd been happily surprised to learn otherwise when he'd investigated a body found outside Molly's house the night the book club held its first meeting. And she was happy to give up the infatuation for the real thing once she got to truly know the man. She gave his arm a squeeze.

"You know how to flatter a girl."

"Not just any girl," he whispered in her ear.

"Mark, I am so glad you were able to join us," Molly said, coming toward them holding a plate of deviled eggs.

"Here, let me take that for you, Molly," Lizzie said, grabbing the plate and setting it on one of the tables.

"I am not sure I should allow Teensy at the same table as Lorelie tonight," Molly said in a low voice.

"I think it might be quite entertaining," Mark suggested.

Molly let out an unladylike snort. "Nice to see you, Mark. Sort of quiet in the police station these days, I would imagine, without any murders," Molly said to Mark as Lizzie turned back to them.

"Shh, don't jinx him, Molly," she said with a small laugh.

The remaining book club members arrived, Jacob having picked up Stephanie and Andie. He looked around for Sally-Jo and made his way to her, giving her a quick kiss on the cheek. Lizzie wondered if they'd make an announcement about a wedding date soon. The way they looked at each other, it couldn't be far off.

Sally-Jo, a good foot shorter than Jacob and looking like a redheaded pixie next to his mild-mannered bear, looked like she was sparkling, Lizzie thought. The teal sheath dress she'd chosen set off her coloring perfectly. Jacob had shed his suit jacket and tie but still looked every bit the lawyer, or maybe that was just because Lizzie knew that's what he did for a living. She wished them well.

Molly grabbed Bob's arm and pulled him over to where A.J. was eyeing the table of hors d'oeuvres and introduced them. Bob pumped A.J.'s arm. "I'm rightly pleased to meet you. I hear you're a man after my own tastes."

When A.J. looked confused and didn't answer, Bob hurriedly went on, "I'm a police procedural reader. Can't get enough of them."

"That is probably because he is our former police chief," Molly added. "What do the initials stand for anyway?" A.J. took a bite of the cheese straw in his right hand and chewed it thoroughly, eyeing Bob. He finally swallowed and said, "Ambrose Jackson. I figured a gritty story by someone named Ambrose wouldn't do, and by the time I realized I wanted to write the lighter stuff, A.J. still seemed appropriate."

Bob looked befuddled. Molly chuckled and squeezed his arm. "I am sure you will find A.J.'s mysteries quite amusing, Bob."

Bob nodded at A.J. and made his escape to stand next to Lizzie. "I thought that guy wrote police procedurals," he said nodding his head in A.J.'s direction.

"He does, only not the kind you usually read. His protagonist is the sheriff of a small Southern town who keeps getting in over his head. They're really quite funny."

"Oh boy."

The back door swung open and all eyes turned to the two women who stepped outside, loudly chattering to each other.

"Oops, I'm so sorry," said the shorter of the two. "We didn't mean to make such a noisy entrance." Although the woman didn't sound too regretful at all, Lizzie didn't even notice her face. Her eyes were riveted on the second woman, who began speaking.

"We do apologize. You know what it's like when you get two women together." She smiled brightly and faltered only a second as she looked around the room, when she spotted Lizzie. "I'm Ashley Dixon, a publicist with Crawther Publishing and the go-to person for these amazing authors this weekend. And this is Gigi Briggs. We're so sorry for arriving late but the time just slipped away." She shrugged and winked.

Lizzie tried to smile but had to turn away to compose her face. Same Ashley. Same condescending tone. Causing the same ache, which felt physical to Lizzie.

"What's the matter?" Mark whispered. "Are you feeling all right?"

Lizzie took a deep breath and tried a small smile on for size. "I'll tell you all about it later."

Molly walked over to the two late arrivals. "I'm Molly Mathews and we are delighted you could come to our fair."

Molly turned to face the others. "I think we should get the formalities out of the way as I see our meal is ready. I would first of all like to say welcome to our visiting authors. We are just so delighted y'all agreed to attend our first mystery fair. I am sure you will get to know all of the members of the Ashton Corners Mystery Readers and Cheese Straws Society as the evening progresses. If there is anything any of us can do to make your stay that much more pleasant, please do not hesitate to ask. Now, shall we make our way into the dining room and we'll show you some Southern hospitality?"

Ashley ducked away from Molly and went over to Lizzie, giving her a hug. "OMG! I can't believe it's you. It really is Lizzie Turner, isn't it? Whatever are you doing here? Of course, Ashton Corners is your hometown, isn't it? I just never expected to run into you. And you're so involved in this whole book thing. Is it still Turner? I'll bet you haven't married yet. It's been a long time. It's so good to see you again." She turned to speak to the others. "Lizzie and I were roommates in college our first year at Auburn. We certainly had some good times. We have so much catching up to do. It makes this weekend even more promising." She winked, then hooked her arm through Lizzie's and ushered her around the others heading indoors.

Lizzie hadn't said a word yet. She couldn't think of a thing to say but Ashley didn't seem to notice. She'd launched into telling Lizzie about her job at Crawther Publishing and didn't ask any questions of Lizzie.

Molly gave Lizzie an inquiring look as the two women neared the table. Lizzie noted that Molly had place cards on the table and was relieved to notice she sat at the opposite end and side from Ashley. Mark held out her chair and then took his seat next to Lizzie.

"What's wrong?" he whispered, giving her hand a quick squeeze under the table.

Lizzie shook her head. This wasn't the place to go into it. She glanced over at Ashley. Not much had changed. Still the same straight shoulder-length blonde hair but now it looked more edgy, angled to frame her face and those pouty lips. Everyone's eyes were always drawn to them, and Ashley knew how to make the most of it. Lizzie quickly looked away before Ashley would notice her staring.

Molly waited until the wineglasses had been filled and then lifted her glass in a toast to the weekend. "I cannot tell y'all how thrilled I am, to have you all as my guests tonight. I wish all of our authors continued success with your various series and, of course, for us all, very good sales."

Everyone around the table clinked glasses with those closest to them and then eagerly started eating. Lizzie tried to concentrate on the lemon basil shrimp salad she'd lavished on her plate, obviously not paying much attention as she'd been helping herself to her food. It was tasty, which was not a surprise as it was known as the signature dish of Food Lovers' Delight. However, she was having a hard time finding her appetite and an equally hard time averting her eyes from the far end of the table, where Ashley held court. She could hear her voice clearly, though, and that was enough.

"I just love the publishing business," Ashley said in her sultry voice, her eyes riveted on someone at Lizzie's end of the table. Lizzie looked up abruptly and focused on the person drawing Ashley's attention. Mark. Lizzie gritted her teeth but then noticed that Mark didn't appear to be paying her any heed. Lizzie relaxed and tried to block out the rest of Ashley's words but didn't totally succeed.

"Get to meet such exciting people . . . don't usually send us on tours like this . . . value my opinion . . ."

Molly leaned over to Lizzie and placed a hand on hers. "What is wrong, honey? You look like you would much rather be someplace else."

Lizzie took a moment to take a deep breath in and drop her shoulders. She could feel the tension in them. "I'm sorry, Molly. I'm being a bad guest. I'll explain later." She gave Molly a reassuring smile and then turned to Gigi Briggs, who sat across the table from her, and asked, "Did you have a good flight?" Inwardly she cringed. Couldn't get much blander than that. She barely heard Gigi's answer.

Lizzie managed to eat her entire meal but had no idea what it tasted like. She was thankful when dessert was finished and they moved into the living room. Molly had recently redecorated the room that once graced the pages of *Ashton Corners Homes and Gardens*. The former elegant furniture and pale palette had given way to a fresher, updated look. The lush green walls were the perfect backdrop for the classicly styled love seats, three of them done in rich navy velvet. The occasional chairs were each outfitted in a different pattern or stripes in various shades of blue and green. The white trim and white accessories completed the picture.

Lizzie liked the new feel to the room, a welcoming vibe that helped lift her spirits. However, she intended to stay as far away from Ashley as possible, which turned out to be an easy task. Eventually, the authors decided to head back to their B and B en masse. As they were thanking Molly, Ashley sidled over to Lizzie and gave her a quick hug. She gave Mark a sidelong glance as she asked of Lizzie, "Are you two an item?"

Lizzie gave a small awkward laugh. "Mark and me? We're just friends."

Mark glanced sharply at Lizzie but didn't say anything.

Ashley's face broke into a devilish smile. "Why, that's nice for you, isn't it Lizzie? And extra good for me because I'm going to be spending time in your little town over the next while and it will be fun to have someone to play with."

Lizzie gritted her teeth. *Here we go again*.

Chapter Six

◇◇◇

I suddenly felt cold all over. I forced myself to take
a couple of deep breaths.

FILE M FOR MURDER—MIRANDA JAMES

Whenever Lizzie Turner thought about Picton Hall, her
memories went straight to a place that included her
daddy and her at a much younger age, maybe seven or so,
taking part in a square dance at the annual Pins and Cush-
ions Fair put on by the Ashton Corners Sewing Society. Her
mama had been a member, just as her mama beforehand,
and the dance remained a highlight of the Ashton Corners
social season for decades.

Lizzie could still hear the music, something she couldn't
name, but the beat allowed her to allemande left and back
around to the waiting arms of her daddy. She'd been so
proud, being part of that pattern usually done by the adults.
But her daddy had insisted she join in. That was just like
him. He had wanted Lizzie to be included, to learn new
things, to have fun.

She shook her head and guided her thoughts back to the

present, to present-day Picton Hall and what Sally-Jo was saying.

"Wasn't that a whole lot of fun last night?" Sally-Jo asked Lizzie.

They were putting the finishing touches on the registration table just inside the door to Picton Hall. Bob and Jacob had already been busy that morning setting up the chairs theater-style as Sally-Jo had requested, along with the casual seating for the panel members at the front of the stage. The bookselling tables were on the far side of the room, where Stephanie and Andie were busy laying out their displays.

"I noticed you seemed to have something on your mind, though," Sally-Jo continued. "You still don't seem your perky self this morning. What gives?"

"Perky? Since when am I the perky one? That's usually reserved for you."

"Uh, sorry. To rephrase, you're not your usual cheerful self but you are feisty."

"My turn to say sorry, Sally-Jo."

Lizzie sighed as she looked around the room, wondering if anything else needed to be done. "I'm probably being silly. Mark thinks I'm being silly." In fact, she'd had a devil of a time trying to explain to Mark why she'd chosen to describe their relationship as being "just friends." She'd played it down, feeling embarrassed to tell him she was worried Ashley would make a play for him. It would have sounded almost like she didn't trust Mark not to give in to Ashley's charms. She wasn't really sure if Mark bought her watered-down explanation. "But you know that publicist, Ashley Dixon?"

"Your former roommate?" Sally-Jo asked, shaking Lizzie out of her reverie.

"That's the one. There's a reason our arrangement lasted for only one semester."

Sally-Jo stopped her task of placing the name tags in alphabetical order on the table and gave Lizzie her full attention.

"She had to have it all, be the one getting all the attention all the time, which led to some tricky situations. Things were getting really awkward, so I asked to be moved for the winter semester but there was no one to switch with and no free rooms. And then she left Auburn, never came back from Christmas break. I was so relieved."

"And now she shows up here. Ouch. What did she do? Borrow your clothes, swipe your answers?"

"None of the above." Lizzie hesitated, wondering how much of the story she should share. She realized, even though she'd come to terms with what had happened, she hadn't totally forgotten nor forgiven. In fact, seeing Ashley had thrown Lizzie for a loop. Maybe the best way to get over old demons was to talk about them. "It started out real friendly and then this competitive streak took over. She didn't like it one bit that I got higher marks in the two classes we shared. And then one of her boyfriends, and she had lots of them, actually took a liking to me. He asked me out but I said no. I couldn't do that to a friend. But I guess I'd hurt his feelings, so he told her I'd come on to him and she made sure to make my life miserable whenever she got the chance. She started spreading ugly rumors and left nasty notes on my bed."

"Wow. Sounds like a psycho. How great that she left school."

"It was really a relief. I'd taken to sleeping on the floor of a friend's room during exams and I avoided seeing her before she left. I just made sure to keep my head down for the rest of that year, and by that time, I'd once again joined the anonymous masses. And I never gave her another thought. Anyway, I don't want to think about her now and

I'm sure she'll show up soon enough today so I won't be able to stop thinking about her."

"Maybe she's changed."

"I hope she has," Lizzie said, thinking back to how Ashley had eyed Mark the night before, "although I highly doubt it." Lizzie just hoped Ashley wouldn't consider this payback time with Mark as the prize.

Sally-Jo gave Lizzie a quick hug. "Just sic me on her if she's causing you any grief. Meanwhile, that coffee smells like it's ready. Let's grab a cup before we have to share it."

Molly joined them for a cup and drank hers leaning against the counter that served as a divider between the kitchen and the main hall. "I think it's looking good and I'm sure everyone will be pleased."

She didn't sound too sure, Lizzie thought. "It's going to be great, Molly. It's been the talk of the town all week and we're sold out."

"Oh, I know, honey. And the books are here ready to go. I'm just hoping all will go smoothly with the authors."

"Well, they seemed on their best behavior last night, except for that bit of cattiness over dessert."

Sally-Jo snorted. "You mean when Lorelie told Caroline that maybe her caterer character should take lessons from the people at Food Lovers' Delight? I thought that was hilarious. I had to duck out of the room so they wouldn't see me laughing."

Molly sniffed. "It was kind of funny but I do so want it to be a problem-free fair. And what about you, Lizzie? Will you be able to handle today?"

Oh boy. Everyone must have noticed my reaction last night. She put on a smile. "Of course, Molly. Everything's going to work out just fine." She gave Molly a quick hug and then grabbed their empty cups and refilled them at the coffee urn.

As she passed the cups back to the others, Bob was propping open the doors to the hall and they could hear the sounds of women making their way into the building.

"Showtime," Molly said and walked toward the doors.

Sally-Jo and Lizzie took their places at the registration desk, where their jobs were to hand out receipts if needed, make sure everyone filled out a name tag and check the attendance sheet. The noise and blur of forty-three women and seven men reached fever pitch by the time the authors began arriving. Lizzie sensed the electricity in the air the moment Lorelie and Margaret, or rather Caroline, sashayed into the room. She was sure Molly would be delighted.

They left the table set up with the remaining name tags in case the half-dozen latecomers were just that, arriving late, and went to join the throngs.

Lizzie heard Teensy's unmistakable laugh and zeroed in on her. It was up to Lizzie to make sure Teensy got onstage at the right moment and started her emcee duties on time. Lizzie was also on the lookout for Isabel Fox, head librarian at the public library, who would moderate the panel. As she formed the thought of her, Isabel appeared in her sight line. Lizzie went over before anyone could corner Isabel in a conversation. Since Isabel hadn't been able to make the dinner last night, Lizzie wanted to introduce her to the authors before the program started.

"Hi, Isabel. Are you all set to take on these criminal minds?"

Isabel laughed. Her eyes crinkled in an already lined face, one that matched perfectly with her salt-and-pepper hair, worn in a pixie cut. A pale blue pantsuit and burgundy blouse suited her trim five-foot-three stature. "I'm really quite excited, Lizzie. Most librarians are author groupies at heart, you know, and it's such a pleasure to meet them. I see Caroline Cummings over there. I recognize her from her jacket cover. May I get a cup of coffee first and then on to the introductions?"

"Of course. I'll just grab a refill at the same time." Lizzie walked with her to the counter, filled their cups and then they headed toward Caroline.

"Caroline, I'd like to introduce Isabel Fox, our librarian, and your moderator," Lizzie said.

Caroline held out her hand and smiled sweetly, only to have Lorelie Oliver shimmy in between the two of them.

"Is this our moderator, Lizzie?" she asked, grabbing Isabel's outstretched hand. "I'm Lorelie Oliver, author of the Southern Fashionista series. It's such a pleasure to meet you."

Caroline moved to Lorelie's side and inconspicuously shoved her aside. "For me also," she told Isabel. She took Isabel's arm and steered her away from Lorelie. "Why don't we go find the others and I'll do the introductions, while I tell you all about my Southern Caterer series." She looked over at Lizzie. "I know you're probably swamped with things to do here."

Lizzie nodded but didn't get a chance to say anything before they'd moved away. Oh well, there was a lot that needed doing. Isabel would have to fend for herself, as Lizzie knew she could.

"Lizzie." Lizzie knew that voice. She turned around to give her best friend, Paige Raleigh, a big hug.

"I'm so glad you were able to get here," Lizzie said with a grin.

"Are you kidding? Brad had no choice but to babysit the girls today. It's mama's day off and I expect to thoroughly enjoy myself. So, what's the scoop?"

Lizzie sighed. "I think we're all set. Molly's been working so hard to make this run smoothly, we all have, so I hope there are no hitches."

"Well, I think it's pretty exciting. There hasn't been

anything like this in Ashton Corners for a long time, if ever. Oh sure, Jensey Pollard used to host the odd signing at the Book Bin but she never put on a full-day event. And I'm pretty certain the library hasn't done anything like this, either. You guys are to be congratulated for sure."

"It's been pretty exciting except for the fly in the proverbial ointment."

Paige raised her eyebrows in question.

"I'll explain later," Lizzie said, lowering her voice. "I shouldn't have mentioned it now, not when there's so much to concentrate on and so many people around."

"Well, then you'd better get your butt over to my place for dinner sometime soon. Like one night this week," Paige said with a laugh. "I don't like to be on the outside of a good story."

Lizzie was spared having to answer when Molly breezed up to them, gave Paige a hug and spirited Lizzie off to help put some floral arrangements out on the dining tables.

What seemed like a short while later, Lizzie was surprised to see it was almost ten when she looked at the clock that hung above the kitchen pass-through. Time to round up everyone and get them onstage. She looked over at the bookselling table to see a short lineup keeping Stephanie and Andie busy. Sally-Jo caught her eye, pointed to the clock and started shooing people away from the eats.

Teensy had a rapt audience of attendees around her when Lizzie approached. "I'm sorry but I'm going to have to ask you all to take your seats. We're about to begin. And Teensy, you're needed on the stage."

"Oh my, yes, sugar. It's been so nice talking to y'all," she said to the women who had started to disperse. To Lizzie, she said, "I just want to run to the little girls' room and powder my nose. Won't be but two shakes of a rat's tale." She scurried off at a faster pace than Lizzie had seen her move before.

By the time Lizzie had rounded up the authors and seated them, Teensy sashayed through the door and climbed the three stairs leading up to the stage with a flourish. She added an extra swirl to the movement of her full-length peach-colored crinkle skirt. She'd chosen a navy scoop-necked top with flowing sleeves and hemline to complete the look.

"Why, y'all look so readerly and a bit mysterious at the same time," she told the audience, much to its delight. For the next five minutes, Teensy entertained them all with tales of her writing experiences and a welcome from the Ashton Corners Mystery Readers and Cheese Straws Society.

"And as a special treat," she continued, "the names of the attendees had been put into a box and a draw for the winner of a grand prize will be held at the end of the question period." Teensy pointed to a large gift basket encased in multicolored clear wrap and everyone started clapping. Then she introduced the authors, using the notes they'd prepared about themselves. After introducing Isabel Fox, she turned it over to her and the conversation began.

They'd decided, in consultation with Isabel earlier on, that rather than have a formal panel, the five would sit in a semicircle and treat it more like an afternoon chat. The format seemed to go over well with the audience members, who were invited to interrupt with questions whenever they felt like it and, indeed, did so.

Isabel had managed to dig deep into their biographies and sprinkled some personal questions about them throughout the ones focusing on the craft of writing. Lizzie sat back and began to enjoy the morning. Isabel had indeed been the right choice. The audience obviously agreed. As Lizzie looked around she was pleased to see that most people appeared interested and hanging on every word.

An hour and a half later, Teensy walked back onstage. "I want to thank all our fascinating authors for agreeing to be here, and for being so loquacious. Don't y'all think they're so interesting you just want to read everything they've ever written?"

The audience started clapping and the authors beamed.

"Well, here's your chance. There are tables set up by A Novel Plot over to my left, along the wall there, in case you hadn't noticed. So shop your hearts out, ladies and gentlemen, and help to keep these writers writing and our wonderful local bookstore in business. The authors will be signing at various points in the afternoon at that other little table over there. Thank you, also, to our wonderful moderator and ever-efficient librarian, Isabel Fox. We have a small thank-you gift for you." She pulled a brightly colored gift bag from the shopping bag she was holding and crooked her finger at Isabel. After embracing, Isabel returned to her chair with her bag.

"And now, as my daddy used to say, it's chow time. The tables have been set up and the lovely ladies of St. John's Evangelical Church have prepared a delicious array of foods, so y'all know it's mouthwatering good. It's all set out buffet-style on the tables at the back of the hall, next to the kitchen. We'll reconvene right back here for the author readings in two hours. Y'all enjoy."

Although the authors had been asked to mingle with the audience and sit one to a table during the meal, Lizzie noticed that Caroline and Lorelie had chosen the same table, different sides, different ends. Lizzie shook her head, taking an empty seat at a table next to the counter, and after some small talk, quickly ate her food.

"This is certainly delicious," said a pleasant-looking woman sitting across from Lizzie, having just finished her dessert, a piece of homemade pie. "Of course, St. John's ladies are known for their cooking."

The woman next to her, possibly a few years older and

certainly a few pounds heavier, huffed a bit and said, "I don't know. I think my own caramel apple pie is much tastier. I tend to add a touch of bourbon, you know. Don't raise your eyebrows at me, Dora Wilkins. This is good. Mine is better. Case closed."

Lizzie took a drink of her coffee in order to hide a smile. Eunice Strange and her neighbor, Dora, had been bossing each other around for as long as Lizzie could remember. They seemed to thrive on it and everyone who knew them enjoyed the banter. The minute Lizzie tasted the pie, all thoughts of conflict flew out of her mind. She spent the remainder of the lunch break enjoying her food and chatting with the readers around her.

Teensy summoned everyone back at the appointed time. A few stragglers who had gone for a walk outside for some fresh air tiptoed to their seats as Teensy explained the format for the readings. Each author would have fifteen minutes, followed by a ten-minute question period. It would be done alphabetically; therefore, Gigi Briggs would lead off, followed by Caroline Cummings. A half-hour tea break would follow and then Lorelie Oliver and A.J. Pruitt would round off the afternoon.

Lizzie noticed Ashley enter the room just as they were getting started. She'd thought it odd that the publicist hadn't been around to hear her authors onstage, but at the same time, she'd been thankful. Now, Lizzie focused quickly on the stage before Ashley could notice her.

A hush fell over the audience as Teensy introduced Gigi once again. She stood and removed the light overcoat she'd been wearing. Lizzie had thought it odd since the outdoors temperature hovered in the mid-seventies, but she realized its purpose now. The audience gasped as Gigi moved over to the podium wearing what was obviously a ringmaster's outfit. The black minidress with black tights and a dark red jacket with black fringed shoulders and purple cuffs, gold trim and polished gold buttons made it look like she'd stepped right out of one of her books. The top hat and tall boots added a nice touch. In spite of the bold getup, Lizzie thought she looked a bit hesitant.

"Before I begin my reading, I'd like to assure you, this isn't my typical attire." Everyone laughed. "I think it helps if the author doing a reading feels in character, wouldn't you agree? So, my heroine is an aerialist who hires on with various visiting circuses and the like. She's also available to perform at birthday parties, if that's of interest to anyone here." Another laugh. Lizzie looked around the room. Gigi certainly knew how to entertain.

Gigi cleared her throat, signaling a change in demeanor, and gave a brief overview of her book, *High-Wire Hijinks*, and then started reading from the first chapter. She had chosen to skip throughout the first half of the book, weaving together an outline of the plot. By the end of her fifteen minutes, all eyes were on her as she asked for questions from the floor.

Teensy cut off the questions at the ten-minute mark, assuring everyone there would be plenty of time after the readings to talk personally to the authors. Next up was Caroline Cummings. She repeated the intro Isabel had given, expanding a bit on the awards she'd won, and then, when Teensy started clearing her throat, began to read from her latest novel, *Catered to Death*. Lizzie hadn't heard Caroline do a reading before and was impressed by the feeling she put into it.

By the time the question period had ended, Teensy announced that since everyone was now primed for food, having heard about recipes and murder for the past while, tea and sweets had been set up on the tables. The audience laughed and applauded.

"And I'd like to thank so much the Bethany Church ladies

for putting out such a fine spread. I have my eye on a plate of sugar cookies. I can see it right from here. I can. I have superpowers when it comes to cookies of any persuasion. Now, enjoy. We'll regroup in thirty minutes to hear from A. J. Pruitt and Lorelie Oliver."

The audience happily followed Teensy's orders. They chose seats and kept up the chatter while passing the serving plates between themselves.

Lizzie mingled with everyone while at the same time keeping an eye on the plates of sweets at each table, ready to replenish as needed. She heard snippets of conversation around her.

"I think that Caroline Cummings is just so sweet and ever so clever with words," one elderly woman was saying to her companion.

A younger woman, closer to Lizzie's age, snorted and said under her breath, "Looks can be deceiving."

Lizzie was pleased to see that Gigi Briggs circulated from table to table, stopping to have a cookie at one, a tart at another, all the time carrying her teacup and a handful of bookmarks that she gave out as she chattered away.

When Teensy called for everyone's attention, the plates that were once piled high with treats were almost bare. Lizzie was tempted to help clear the tables but moved out of the way as the Baptist ladies took over.

As Lizzie slid into her seat next to Sally-Jo in the back row, Lorelie Oliver jumped right into her reading. She'd chosen to save her comments for the end, and when she closed the book, she explained how she'd come to write the Southern Fashionista series.

"My dear mama was a seamstress, as were many of the young ladies of her position in the mid–nineteen hundreds. She instilled in me a love of beautiful clothing." She paused to casually glance down at the bronze two-piece silky outfit she wore. "I thought it only fitting that I write about something I love and know so well."

Sally-Jo leaned over and whispered, "Oops, great outfit but her ego is showing." Lizzie nudged her with her elbow and bit back her own smile.

A.J. turned out to be quite the charmer, having both young and old hanging on to his every word. He had the endearing habit of pushing back a large patch of hair that kept falling forward each time he bent his head to read from his book. Lizzie felt sure he would have the longest lineup for autographs at the end of the afternoon.

The next hour and a half went quickly, and after the final question period, Teensy wrapped up the event with a thank-you to the authors and the readers who had supported this first book fair. Then, with much ado, Teensy made the draw for the gift basket. While the excited winner went up to the front to collect her prize, some of the audience left, although many headed to the bookselling tables to make final purchases and then move over to where the four authors had taken their seats, pens in hand.

Lizzie helped Sally-Jo clear the registration table and then walked over to talk to Isabel Fox. "I didn't get a chance to tell you earlier, but you did a really fine job as moderator."

"Thank you, Lizzie. It seemed like a challenge at times. I know everything was peaches and cream on the surface, but I was sensing some really strained vibes onstage, between Caroline Cummings and Lorelie Oliver."

"Really? Like what? Any ideas?"

"Oh, I'll bet it's just good old-fashioned rivalry. Or jealousy. They're both powerful personalities, they write in the same genre and are sure to go head-to-head with some of the awards."

"Hmm. I've seen snatches of what that can lead to. I don't

think I'd like to be caught in between if something erupts," Lizzie admitted.

"Pity the poor publicity gal, Ashley," Isabel suggested. "She's got to keep them both happy."

Lizzie didn't want to get into a discussion about Ashley. "Well, thanks again, Isabel. I hope you had fun."

"Absolutely, and I'd happily do it again. Now, if you'll excuse me, I must run off and pick up some wine for tonight. See you soon." She gave Lizzie a quick hug before leaving.

Lizzie moved over to the book table and started helping the girls pack away the remaining stock. She turned abruptly as Ashley walked over to talk to her.

"So, where's your hunky guy today, Lizzie? Lovers' spat?" Ashley laughed, the same old condescending laugh that Lizzie knew so well. "Don't think I believe for a minute that line about being friends. I saw how you were looking at him. You're still not any good at lying."

Ashley took a break to wave at a couple of women close by who appeared to be very interested in what was being said.

"Now, I think Mark's your beau and wouldn't it just break your lil' old Southern heart if he fell for someone more glamorous?"

Lizzie could feel her anger increasing. She took a deep breath, meaning to turn away and get back to packing books but Ashley grabbed her arm.

"I know just the type he would go for, too," she taunted.

"All right, Ashley. If it's the truth you want, yes, we are a couple and Mark would never fall for someone like you. He's a cop and that means he can read people well enough to know your sweet exterior hides a venomous soul. Why don't you just go back to New York and leave us all alone?" She tried staring down Ashley but didn't get very far.

"Aw, Lizzie. Don't you think a bit of tit-for-tat is fair play?" Ashley said with a menacing laugh, gripping Lizzie's arm even tighter. "You do like to sound so righteous and all."

"Don't you think you've already done enough damage? You've spread lies about me. You've stolen every guy I was interested in back then. I've had enough of you. Just back off, or else." Lizzie snatched her arm away, taking Ashley by surprise. She tottered a second before gaining her balance.

Lizzie looked around herself in horror as she realized how quiet it had gotten in the room and how loud her voice had grown.

Ashley's smile was cruel. "Why, Lizzie, you never could control yourself, could you?"

Chapter Seven

◇◇◇

You know what they say about misery loving company.

BEELINE TO TROUBLE—HANNAH REED

Lizzie slipped out of bed the next morning, careful not to wake Mark. She had still been seething when she'd arrived home from the book fair the night before.

Mark had been waiting, a home-cooked meal of grilled chicken and grits ready to be served. He'd taken one look at Lizzie's face, steered her over to the love seat and poured her a glass of wine. Then he'd demanded she talk. The food had chilled by the time Lizzie was all talked out and they were ready to eat. It took some more talk before she finally calmed down enough to get some sleep.

The cats were not happy to have Lizzie move. They'd hovered on the edge on her side of the bed, their usual spot when having to share it with one more body. They hung back when she headed downstairs, knowing Mark's year-old hound, Patchett, was curled up in the kitchen on his bed away from home.

Lizzie shook some dry food into their bowls, leaving them on the counter out of Patchett's greedy reach, gave him a couple of treats and headed out the door for a short run. She needed to clear her head, that much she knew.

She felt depressed about having seen Ashley and realized there was still a lot unfinished business between them. She'd never told Ashley just how badly she'd been made to feel, choosing to turn tail and hide instead. And seeing her again had brought back all those feelings of being powerless and unhappy. But whether or not she had any more nerve these days, she wasn't quite sure. No, that wasn't right. She had stood up to Ashley, in a manner of speaking, although losing her temper and making a spectacle of them both had not been very clever.

Lizzie sighed. She'd certainly made a fool of herself, and she knew that before long, the entire town would be talking about it. And how could she face the book club knowing she'd ruined the event they'd been planning for so long. At least the fair had ended and she had no reason to see the authors again, even though they were staying on for a couple of days.

Lizzie shook her head and tried to focus on her surroundings. It was too beautiful a morning to waste being stuck in her head. She concentrated instead on the sights of an Ashton Corners morning. She headed straight to the river path and allowed the morning mist rising from the river to shroud her in a cloak of anonymity and serenity. The early morning path was hers alone and she tried to keep her mind on the number of steps she was taking, rather than letting it dwell on what had happened the day before. She stopped rather suddenly at the sight of a deer that had wandered down the bank on the opposite side of the river for a drink. Lizzie looked around, hoping there wouldn't be a jogger with a dog running along the other side or, worse yet, a hunter.

After a few minutes, the deer raised its head and looked around before scrambling back up the bank and leaping away into the woods. Lizzie remained standing in the same spot for a few more minutes, drawing in the beauty of the morning. She finally started moving at a slower pace, building back up to full speed by the time she reached Glendale Park. Thirty minutes more and she turned onto her street.

By the time she opened the kitchen door, she felt ready to face the day, Sunday anyway. Mark sat at the kitchen table reading the copy of the *Birmingham News* that had been delivered. He had a cup of coffee in front of him and Patchett at his feet. *Domestic bliss.*

Lizzie gave him a quick kiss on the top of his head as she headed for a glass of cool water. After drinking two, she sat down across from him.

"Man and dog. Right off a calendar page."

Mark grinned. "Did you have a good run?"

"I did. In fact, I'm so energized, I may even make you breakfast," she said.

"Now, I hate to pass that up but I thought I'd take you out to Oscar's for breakfast." He looked hopefully at her. Oscar's was his favorite breakfast spot.

"Sounds like a plan," Lizzie said, standing. "I'll shower and get ready. What about Patchett? When will you walk him?"

"I'll do that while you're getting ready. Just a short walk and then a longer one later." He reached out for her hand and pulled her over. "How are you feeling today?"

"Like I said, energized."

"I mean about the Ashley Dixon thing. No lingering upset or dwelling on bad memories?"

"No. I'm good," she said and meant it, as long as she didn't give Ashley a thought.

He gave her a quick kiss on the back of her neck as she tamped some freshly ground coffee into the holder for her espresso machine.

She drank her espresso slowly, as she did each time, trying to get the most enjoyment before it was finished. All too soon. She rinsed her cup out then ran upstairs to her bedroom. Both cats sat on the bed and gave her an apprehensive look as she entered.

"Just me, darlings. The other two have gone for a walk, so you're free to roam. Then we'll all be out of here and the house will once again be yours."

Mark had made the bed. Housebroken, she thought with a smile. She laid out her black jeans and long-sleeved yellow-striped blouse on the pillow shams so the cats wouldn't curl up on them, then headed for the bathroom.

By the time Mark got back, Lizzie had showered, dressed and treated herself to another espresso.

"I'm assuming we're dropping Patchett off at your place first?" she asked.

Mark glanced at the cats, both sitting on the backrest of the love seat. "I think that's advisable. Are you ready?"

She grabbed her small clutch bag and followed him out the door, Patchett leading the way. By the time they arrived at Oscar's, the place was packed. Mark had thought to phone ahead and reserve them a table by the side window, overlooking a small courtyard that was also full. Lizzie sat back and relaxed, enjoying the din of happy customers and busy servers. Cheerful red-and-white-checkered tablecloths and seat covers complemented the casual look of pine walls and tables.

Lizzie looked around the room and spotted one of the teachers and her family at a table close to the back. She hadn't been noticed, so she didn't wave. She was surprised to see A.J. Pruitt, sitting alone at a small table on the other side of the room. The breakfasts at Oscar's were always a favorite part of anyone's visit to Ashton Corners, so she guessed perhaps he needed some space from the dueling divas. She'd stop by his table and say hi as they were leaving, if he were still there and if she could get up the nerve. She realized that she might indeed run into the authors in a town the size of Ashton Corners. Oh well, she'd just have to make the best of it.

Mark ordered his usual—three eggs sunny-side up, bacon, sausages, grits and coffee. Lizzie decided on a vegetarian omelet. After their coffee mugs had been filled, Mark sat back in his chair.

"So are things looking a bit brighter today?" he asked.

She sighed. "I guess I can get pretty wound up about something that's really minor in the whole scheme of things. College was a long time ago and what happened is ancient history. And I suspect I won't see Ashley Dixon again, despite her warnings of hanging around town more often, whatever that means. So yes . . . much brighter. And I'm off to see my mama this afternoon, so it's all good. Do you want to come along?"

Mark gave it a moment's thought. "I'd be happy to but you know how she sometimes gets agitated by a stranger."

Lizzie nodded. "That's odd, isn't it? Usually she doesn't recognize me, and yet on some level, she does, because it's only people she rarely sees who have that effect on her. It would be nice if she grew into a level of comfort with you, though." She smiled knowing he understood her meaning.

He leaned forward and covered her hand. "I agree. So it's your decision. I'll come anytime you want me to."

Lizzie looked out the window, at the sun reflecting off the windows of the décor shop on the other side of the courtyard; at the patio umbrellas tilted to keep the patrons in the shade; at the red maple trees and Mexican sage that bordered the patio. Life was good. "Yes, please come with me today."

"You've got it."

Their meals arrived and they ate in companionable silence. When they'd finished, Lizzie enjoyed a third cup of coffee. "Let's give Patchett that longer walk right now," she suggested. "Mama will probably just about be heading into lunch. We can go over after."

Mark grinned. "You will so be at the top of Patchett's list. Mine, too, I might add."

She glanced at A.J. as they walked to the door but he was immersed in reading the newspaper and she was happy to have a reason not to say hi. Mark grabbed her hand as they walked back to where he'd parked his Jeep.

Lizzie approached her mama's room feeling happy. Gone was the anxiety of the past few days. She marveled at how spending time with Mark could set all right in her world. As if he sensed her thoughts, Mark slid his arm around her waist and gave her a squeeze. She opened the door and first thing she saw was her mama, sitting in her favorite chair staring out the window. Lizzie walked over, being sure to make a lot of noise so she wouldn't startle her.

"I'm here, Mama," she said, bending down to give her a hug. Evelyn Turner shifted in her chair and turned to face Lizzie although she didn't speak. She glanced at Mark, who stood just behind Lizzie, but didn't acknowledge him, either. A coughing spell overtook her and Lizzie passed her the glass of water that sat on the nearby table. Evelyn finished it off and then turned to face the window again.

Lizzie was quite used to this welcome. There'd be many

days when Evelyn didn't even acknowledge her presence. Today could be counted as a good day. Although Lizzie never expected to be recognized, she hadn't totally given up hope and launched into a monologue about the week's events.

Mark had pulled up a chair beside Lizzie and talked about the repairs being made to the Civil War monument in the center of town. He then leaned across Lizzie and showed Evelyn a picture of Patchett on his smartphone. He often kept her apprised of the dog's progress at each visit. Evelyn glanced at the photo with little interest.

Lizzie found the box of chocolate from the Chocolate Gallery in Huntsville that Molly had brought in, and they each had one. She followed her mama's gaze and although there was no activity in the yard, the hedges of soft touch holly and occasional colorful burning bush made an inviting scene.

"I never thought about it before," Lizzie said, "but this looks a lot like Molly's backyard, doesn't it, Mama?" She glanced over and saw a small smile tug at the sides of Evelyn's mouth. *Yes!* Lizzie launched into a description of that yard and her many memories walking the large maze that Molly's husband had commissioned for it. She held on to her mama's hand and from time to time felt a small returning squeeze.

They joined the other residents in the grand room for afternoon tea and cookies. Lizzie knew many of the people from being such a regular visitor over the years, and she exchanged greetings with a lot of them. Mark was a great hit with the older women. Several hobbled over to the grouping of love seats and chairs where they were sitting to say a few words to him. Lizzie glanced at Mark and was pleased he seemed to be enjoying the attention.

After they'd finished their tea, Lizzie led her mama back

to her room and helped her settle on her bed for a short nap. Routine. It was all that was left to Evelyn. Mark had headed home to work in his yard and also do some prep work for a trial he'd be testifying at the next afternoon.

Later that evening, Lizzie had just finished a quick supper of pasta and chicken strips, and had settled down on the love seat to read. She'd picked up what had been on top of her TBR pile, *The Sayers Swindle* by Victoria Abbott. This was the second in the Book Collector series and Lizzie was really looking forward to it. Brie had commandeered her lap immediately, leaving Edam to stretch his long body out across the top of the love seat. Neither cat was pleased with the interruption of the telephone ringing.

Lizzie managed to extricate herself and grabbed it on the final ring before the answering service clicked in. She was shocked when she recognized Ashley Dixon's voice.

"Now, please don't go hanging up on me, Lizzie. I know you want to and I really wouldn't blame you. Just hear me out. Please?"

Lizzie took a few moments before answering. *What was Ashley's game?* She could at least listen. "Fine."

She heard an audible sigh. Of relief?

"I wasn't very nice to you yesterday, or back in college. We don't need to discuss it. I just wanted to tell you I know what a wretch I was and I want to apologize."

Lizzie took another moment. "Why?"

"As I said, I may be spending more time in Ashton Corners, and although I know we'll never be friends, it would at least be nice not to have to avoid each other. I don't know what got into me yesterday but I am trying to change. Really."

"Why will you be around here more?"

"Things are happening." Lizzie could almost hear the

shrug at the other end of the line. Still not able to give a straight answer.

"I'd like to give you the benefit of the doubt, Ashley, but I was the one you were talking to on Saturday and I was in the room on Friday night when you flirted outrageously with my boyfriend." *Boyfriend?* She felt like she was right back in college when Ashley had tried to get even by stealing the next guy Lizzie went out with.

"You're right and I guess I'm not totally reformed. I'm attracted to cute guys and your guy certainly is that. I didn't mean anything by it, as I'm sure he knew. I don't know if I can totally change that flirting thing but that's all that it is. Really."

"So, why are you calling, Ashley? What do you expect me to say?"

"That you'll meet me for coffee tomorrow morning."

"What?" Lizzie couldn't believe her ears.

"It's just a coffee, Lizzie. I don't expect us to become buddy-buddy but it will make things less awkward in the future. What do you say? I'll even buy."

A part of Lizzie longed to say no. She still wasn't sure if she trusted Ashley but she realized she needed to face her. And, if there was the possibility of them running into each other in the future, then it needed to be settled right now. Besides, she had to admit, she was curious about what there was in Ashton Corners that would keep Ashley hanging around.

"All right. Coffee tomorrow. Do you know the Cup 'n Choc on Main Street? It's right across from the police station."

"I'll find it."

"Okay. I have to be at school at nine, so how about eight?" Lizzie suggested.

"You've got it. See you then."

Lizzie felt too unsettled by the call to finish reading. She decided to make some tea and ended up cleaning out the upper kitchen cupboards. At eleven she glanced at the clock and gasped. Time for bed if she planned to handle Ashley tomorrow.

Chapter Eight

◇◇◇

If you thought about the unthinkable long enough
it became quite reasonable.

—JOSEPHINE TEY

Lizzie slept poorly. She kept waking every few hours and had a hard time stopping the thoughts from whirling through her head. She knew it was all because of her coffee date with Ashley. Such was the power of dread.

She finally dragged herself out of bed at six and donned her running outfit. After feeding the cats, she took the long route along the river and through town, hoping to strike some sort of equilibrium before eight o'clock.

A quick shower when she arrived home did little to help. She opted for a protein smoothie for breakfast, wanting something fast and energizing. She took more care than usual in getting ready for school, applying her favorite eye shadow and lipstick colors as a shield against the disquieting effect of Ashley. She chose her outfit with equal care and decided on a gray pencil skirt, white sleeveless cotton blouse with a shirred bodice and black linen jacket. She pushed the sleeves up to just below her elbows and looked in the mirror. It would have to do.

She made sure she had everything she needed for her morning at school. She had one meeting with parents and a staff meeting at lunch. The rest of the time she had papers to mark from the previous week's evening literacy class. What with all the preparations for the book fair, she hadn't found time to do her own homework and needed to have the papers ready to hand back to class on Tuesday night.

She went to check her cell phone to make sure it didn't need recharging, something she realized she should have done the night before. It wasn't in her handbag or on the table in the hallway, where she usually stashed it overnight. She tried to think when she'd last used it but couldn't remember. Certainly not on Sunday. Had she even had it with her? She glanced at the clock on the bookshelf. No time to search for it.

She arrived at the Cup 'n Choc a few minutes early and staked out a small bistro table at the front window. She ordered herself a double espresso, thinking she needed it and would allow Ashley to buy her a refill.

Sitting at the table, watching the customers come in to grab their mug of brew on the way to work, Lizzie tried to create a positive frame of mind. It wouldn't do any good being antagonistic, especially if Ashley were sincere about her apology. But as she well knew, Ashley Dixon could be very two-faced. She just hoped this wasn't one of those times. She hated being so uptight about something that was out of her control.

At eight fifteen, she started wondering if Ashley had once again played her. Or, thinking with the more generous part of her brain, had something come up and Ashley wasn't able to make it? Maybe Ashley had left her a phone message at home. She realized she hadn't given Ashley her cell phone number, not that it would have done her any good right now, but she had written down Ashley's when she'd called the day before. She went over to the pay phone hanging next to the restroom door and tried calling it now.

After five rings it went to message. Lizzie said she would wait at the coffee shop another ten minutes and then head to school. She asked Ashley to please call and left the number of the pay phone.

By eight thirty with still no Ashley, nor a call from her, Lizzie shook her head, chiding herself for being so gullible. Ashley was playing games again. Well, she wouldn't cave this time. She returned her cup and saucer to the counter and left for school.

L izzie was called to the office just as she was heading to the noon staff meeting. The secretary handed her the phone when she asked what was up. She answered, curious who would be phoning her on the school line.

"Lizzie, you're not answering your cell," Mark said.

"Hi, Mark. Actually, I may have lost it. I couldn't find it this morning but I wasn't able to spend too much time searching for it. What's up?"

"I'm not quite sure how to tell you this," he started. She immediately tensed, wondering what was coming.

"I'm at the White Haven Funeral Home . . ."

"Not Mama," Lizzie cried out.

"No," Mark almost shouted. "No, nothing like that. I'm sorry, I'm not doing this very well. I should have thought about that. No, it's Ashley Dixon. Her body was found this morning."

"What? We were supposed to meet for coffee this morning. She didn't show. Was she already dead? How did it happen? Where was she found?"

"I can't give you any details right now but I wanted to phone to tell you that Officer Craig is on her way over to the school. She'll escort you to the station to answer some questions."

"Why? What's going on?"

"Lizzie, listen to me. I wish I could be the one to interview you but I can't be seen to be any part of this, not with our relationship. There's a message from you on her cell phone and several people are aware of your feelings about her, especially after that argument on Saturday. So I have to play this by the book and have you answer some questions. It's all routine. It will be fine. You know Craig, she'll get you back to school in no time at all."

"But why are you so cautious about all this? Sure, I didn't really like her and we did have a few words but that was it. Should I be worried?"

Mark was silent for several seconds. "Lizzie, I know where your cell phone is. It was found near the body."

Lizzie realized she was shaking. She couldn't think of anything to say. She had no answer to that. She closed her eyes, hoping to calm her heartbeat.

Finally, she took a deep breath and said, "Mark, Amber Craig doesn't have to come and get me. I can drive over on my own after school or right now if you want."

"Trust me, Lizzie. Like I said, it's better if we do this totally by the book. Trust me, baby . . . okay?" He was pleading. Which frightened Lizzie even more than the thought that just struck her. She was the main suspect.

"I'm recording this interview, Lizzie," Officer Amber Craig said as she switched on the tape machine. She then ran through the standard questions of name, address and occupation.

She gave Lizzie a quick, reassuring smile before continuing. "You knew the deceased, Ashley Dixon?"

"Yes."

"Tell me about your relationship."

Lizzie explained having her assigned as a roommate that first year at Auburn University, but by the second year, she roomed with someone new, and she hadn't seen Ashley since then.

"Why did you get a new roommate?"

Lizzie hesitated then cleared her throat. "I asked for one."

"And why did you do that?"

"Because we weren't compatible. We parted ways after the first semester." Lizzie didn't want to make Craig's job any tougher than it was but she knew from watching TV cop shows that it's best to give the minimal amount of information.

Craig had obviously watched the same shows. She shook her head and leaned back in her chair. "And how did this manifest itself?"

"Ashley liked to be top dog and she didn't like the fact that I got better grades in the two classes we shared."

"That was the big issue?"

Lizzie paused, wondering how to phrase her answer. "It started out with that but then progressed."

Craig's right eyebrow shot up. Lizzie wondered just what she'd been expecting her to say. "Tell me about it," Craig said.

Lizzie sat back also. She knew she had to cooperate and not hold anything back. "Ashley liked the attention of guys and she had lots of boyfriends. She never dated the same guy more than a few times. But there was one who decided he wanted to take me out. I said no but he told Ashley I'd come on to him. She started paying me back right away."

"How?"

"If she knew I was interested in a guy, especially if I'd

had a date with him, she would flirt like crazy and usually ended up dating him herself. Then, and I'm assuming this is the reason, when she figured I'd lost interest, so did she."

"Did that make you angry?"

"Sometimes, depending on the guy. But that was a long time ago." Lizzie laced her fingers together and then quickly undid them, wondering if that was a sign of someone with something to hide.

"And yet, as I understand it, you weren't too happy to hear that Ashley Dixon was in town. Is that right?"

"Yes," Lizzie answered softly.

Craig sat quietly. Eventually, Lizzie gave in and started talking.

"It went beyond the guys. She accused me of stealing some of her things. And then she started spreading rumors about me."

"That must be hard to get over," Craig said, her tone matching Lizzie's.

"Things got better once she moved away and I got on with my life. I hadn't thought about her since then."

"And when you saw her here?" Craig prompted.

"I was shocked."

"Did you talk to her?"

"Yes."

Craig remained silent again. Eventually Lizzie continued.

"She intimated that she might make a play for Mark." Lizzie swallowed hard. She knew others had heard and the argument could get back to Officer Craig one way or the other.

"When did you last see her?"

"At the book fair on Saturday."

"You talk then?" Craig asked.

Lizzie assumed she'd already heard. "We had a discussion, in fact. Raised our voices a bit."

"About Chief Dreyfus?"

"Basically."

"Tell me about the book fair."

"Well, Molly Mathews came up with the idea and the book club helped with the planning and the event. Four authors were invited and the public bought tickets to the daylong fair. That got them lunch, tea and two sessions with the authors as panelists, doing readings, book sales and signings. That's about it."

"How did you decide on the authors?"

Lizzie thought a moment. "Molly had a promotional flyer she'd received at the bookstore about these three authors who were on tour. It seems they do this a lot, so Molly contacted the publisher and the arrangements were made."

Craig looked at her notes. "There were four authors, though, weren't there?"

"That's right. The publisher suggested adding Gigi Briggs to the list. She's someone they're really pushing."

"And Ashley Dixon? How did she happen to be included?"

"I understand that the authors invited her. She just appeared on Friday, although she'd phoned the Quilt Patch to confirm a room beforehand. You'll have to ask Patsy Kindall about that."

"I plan to," Craig said, a touch of sarcasm in her voice. "How did they all get along?"

Lizzie shrugged. "I think there are some egos involved, but other than that, they seem to be friends."

Craig nodded. "Did you have any other contact with Ashley Dixon?"

Lizzie realized that Mark must have told her about the phone call. She hadn't mentioned it to anyone else.

"Yes, she phoned me on Sunday night and asked to meet for coffee the next morning."

"Why would she do that?"

Lizzie searched Craig's face, hoping to see some sign of how the interview was going but realized Craig's "police face" would give nothing away. In her mid-twenties, Officer Amber Craig wore her long blonde hair pulled back in a bun. Her clear skin and angular features attracted second looks from most men, but the icy blue eyes usually made them have second thoughts.

Lizzie cleared her throat. "She apologized and said we should clear things up since she would probably be spending a lot of time in Ashton Corners in the future."

"What did she mean by that?"

"I have no idea. She didn't explain." Lizzie shifted in her chair, realizing that Craig had sat perfectly still throughout the interview.

"How did the fact that you'd be seeing a lot more of her make you feel?"

"She'd alluded to that earlier in the weekend, so I was ready for it. In fact, I knew what she suggested was right. We needed to set things straight."

Craig's eyebrows shot up. "What do you mean by 'set things straight'?"

Lizzie looked horrified. "I only meant we needed to talk things out."

"Is that what she said at your coffee date?"

"No. She didn't show up. I waited for half an hour but then I had to get to school."

"Where were you meeting?"

"At the Cup 'n Choc."

"What did you think when she didn't show up?"

Lizzie shrugged. "I thought either she'd forgotten, slept in or something else had come up." She just about added that it would be like Ashley not to let her know if that's what had happened.

"How did your cell phone end up at the scene?"

Lizzie gulped. "I have no idea. I noticed this morning it was missing but I can't remember when I last used it."

Craig looked skeptical. Even Lizzie thought her answer sounded made up. Wasn't that what they said in the movies? My car was stolen this morning? Somebody must have taken my purse? I haven't seen it in days? But she wasn't lying. Something had happened to her cell phone. Or someone. She actually flinched at her next thought.

"You don't think someone is trying to frame me?" Lizzie asked, feeling a bit sick to her stomach.

Craig had been watching her closely. She now lifted her shoulders slightly. "It's possible. Anything is possible at the start of an investigation. Do you have any ideas who might try something like that?"

Lizzie sank back in her seat and gave that some thought. Ashley came to mind, but of course, she was dead. She finally shook her head. Being framed was an equally upsetting proposition. Well, maybe not quite as bad as being accused of murder.

"Look, I didn't like her but I didn't kill her." She took a deep breath. "Can I ask you something?" Lizzie asked, trying to cover her growing fear.

"Okay, but I may not be able to answer."

Lizzie nodded. "What about her family? I think her folks passed some time ago."

"The local police are tracking them down."

"Where was she found and how did she die? Was it suicide? Was she murdered? Obviously, or you wouldn't be questioning me."

Craig thought for a moment. "I can tell you that her body was found at the White Haven Funeral Home this morning around nine thirty."

"I knew that. What would she be doing in the funeral home?"

"She wasn't in the funeral home," Craig said. "You know that coffin they have affixed outside under their sign? She was found in it."

Chapter Nine

◇◇◇

A pessimist gets nothing but pleasant surprises, an optimist nothing but unpleasant.

FER-DE-LANCE—REX STOUT

Lizzie couldn't stop shaking as she walked back into the school. She glanced at the main office, wondering if anyone had noticed her being dropped off by a police car, although they might not question it, knowing of her relationship with the chief of police.

She was back in time for her appointment with a single parent of a boy in fourth grade. He wouldn't read. Absolutely refused to, no matter what cajoling or coaxing or threats took place. Lizzie had already met with the anxious mama once before and, having determined she wasn't against his reading, had suggested some ways to entice him. The homeroom teacher had reported he was less belligerent and would on occasion attempt to read, so something was working.

Lizzie had a hard time focusing on her meeting, and after giving the mama some reassurances and more exercises to try with her son, was relieved to finally be alone. She stayed in her chair in the vice principal's office, trying to figure out what was going on and just how badly she was involved.

She hadn't heard from Mark, although she hadn't really thought she would. She longed to talk to him, though, to have him tell her again that the questioning was strictly a formality, but she had a nagging feeling that it was so much more. She finally picked up the phone and called Molly.

"Will you be home for a while?" she asked. "I really need to talk to you and I can come over now. I don't have anything scheduled until two."

"That would be lovely," Molly said, "although you're sounding like this isn't strictly a social visit. Have you eaten? I'll make up some wraps for lunch for us. You come as soon as you're able."

Lizzie avoided anything more than quick greetings to anyone she passed in the hall and made it over to Molly's house in record time. She walked around to the back, thinking with such a warm fall day they might be eating outside. The patio table was set with plates and glasses on a colorful floral tablecloth. She could hear Molly singing inside and smiled as she opened the back door.

"Can I help you, Molly?" she asked.

"Yes, you can grab the pitcher of iced tea, please, and then hold the door for me." Molly made her way carefully to the door with her tray of wraps, a plate of raw vegetables and what Lizzie hoped was her famous avocado dip.

Once they had taken their seats and each put food on their plates, Molly asked, "What's on your mind, honey? I can tell something's bothering you."

"Oh boy, Molly. That's an understatement. Ashley Dixon has been murdered and right now I'm the prime suspect. Officer Craig took me in for questioning this morning."

"What?" Molly almost dropped her fork. She placed it

carefully on the table, then turned to face Lizzie. "I don't know what shocks me more, Ashley being dead or you being a suspect. But I've certainly had experience with that, when Frank Telford's body was found outside our meeting and my dear departed Claydon's gun was the weapon. I wouldn't worry too much about it. We all know how early in a murder investigation almost everyone is suspect."

Lizzie busied herself pouring their tea and choosing a wrap. She sure didn't have an appetite but she didn't want a lecture from Molly about her eating habits. She took a couple of bites while thinking through what she wanted to say.

"I know you're probably right," she began, "but no one else in town knew her and it seems like a lot of people knew I disliked her. I made that fairly obvious, unfortunately. In fact, we did have that argument in front of several people on Saturday after the book fair wrapped up."

Molly nodded.

"You heard it?" Lizzie knew the answer already. "And the others? They heard, too?"

Molly reached over and touched Lizzie's arm. "It was hard not to, honey."

"I'm so embarrassed. And so awfully sorry for ruining the book fair."

Molly shook her head. "You didn't ruin it, Lizzie. In fact, I've heard nothing but good things. Everyone is raving about it and no one is talking about your argument, at least not in front of me. Now, just put it out of your mind."

"That's hard to do when the police are investigating me."

"Hmm. But that's hardly a motive for murder, honey. And there's opportunity. When did she die?"

"I'm not sure but her body was found at the White Haven Funeral Home this morning. You know that coffin they have outside? She was in it apparently. Very ghoulish. The incriminating part is we were supposed to meet for coffee this morning but she never showed."

Lizzie bit into her wrap but realized she had no appetite. Chewing seemed to take forever. Finally she swallowed and said, "And then there's my cell phone. It was found at the scene."

"Your cell phone? You're kidding. Are they sure it's yours?"

"Yes, Molly, and mine is missing. I noticed this morning that it wasn't in my handbag or anywhere in the house, although that's always what the suspect says, isn't it?"

"Perhaps, and I'm certain it's true in many cases. Like now. So tell me, why were you meeting her anyway?"

Lizzie told Molly about the phone call and waiting at the Cup 'n Choc until she had to leave for school.

"But that's great, lots of folks must have seen you at the shop. It's usually so busy, especially in the morning."

Lizzie shrugged. "I don't know what they've found out or if they've even questioned anyone at the coffee shop yet. I also don't know what time she died, so they could say I murdered her, stashed the body and then pretended to wait."

It was easy to say the words but Lizzie couldn't control her body shaking at the thought of what she'd just described. She couldn't picture Ashley dead, no matter how much she disliked her.

Molly stood quickly and rushed around to put her arms around Lizzie. "It's okay, honey. It'll all be okay," she said soothingly. "You know, you've got the police chief on your side," she said with an attempt at a chuckle.

"Not really. Mark was the one who let me know what had happened but said he had to keep at arm's length from that part of the investigation so that it wouldn't seem like he was playing favorites. I know he's right but I feel so alone without his support."

Molly gave her a final hug and sat back down. "Now stop that, Elizabeth Eveline Turner. You are not alone. You have me and the entire book club and we're not going to let anything bad happen to you. You have my word on that."

Lizzie finally smiled. She knew Molly was good at keeping her word. She just hoped it was possible this time.

Lizzie headed back to school and after her meeting, decided to finish several reports she'd put off doing. She chose the far corner of the library office, knowing she wouldn't be disturbed. The reports didn't want to be done. She found her thoughts wandering to the more gruesome scene of Ashley's body being found. Although she hadn't been there, Lizzie's imagination could work in overdrive, filling in more details than she ought to know. Eventually, she sat back with a sigh, the list of reports checked off and those needing to be sent elsewhere by email on their way. A few minutes after the final school bell rang, Sally-Jo came rushing in.

"Lizzie, I cannot believe what Molly just told me." She sat down across the desk from Lizzie and reached across to touch her hands. "Ashley is dead and you're a suspect? Are you all right?"

"Molly called you?"

"You bet and she's calling everyone together for an emergency book club meeting tonight at her house. I'm to tell you about it." Sally-Jo paused and peered closely at Lizzie. "Is there anything I can do? How are you feeling about it all?"

"I truly don't know. I feel like I'm sort of in a fog at the moment."

Sally-Jo nodded. "I know what that's like. Remember when Derek Alton was murdered?" She shuddered as she thought about it. "I couldn't believe I was a suspect. But y'all came through for me and I was soon off the hook. The same thing will happen here, believe me."

Lizzie thought about it a moment. They'd encountered real murders, not just the ones found between the book covers, on three separate occasions and each time, the book club had worked together to find the real culprit. She felt a bit better. This time it would be the same.

"Do you want to grab a coffee and talk?" Sally-Jo asked.

"No, thanks anyway."

Sally-Jo stared at her a few seconds. "All right. I'll see you tonight." She stood up. "If you need to talk or anything, just give me a call."

Lizzie nodded and focused again on the computer. She didn't notice Sally-Jo pausing at the door, a worried look on her face.

Chapter Ten

◇◇◇

There are two actions that are almost equally reprehensible to me. One is the act of beginning a sentence and then refusing to finish it. The other is murder.

THE TANGLEWOOD MURDER—LUCILLE KALLEN

"I think that's the most danged foolish thing I've ever heard in my life," Bob Miller ranted between bites of the cheese straws in his hand. "Lizzie here could no more take a life than . . . than Molly could."

Andie jumped out of her chair. "You're so right. It's wrong that they're even thinking you're a suspect," she said as she started pacing the length of the room.

Lizzie held up her hand, willing Andie to stop. "Thank you for your faith in me but it's going to take a bit more than that, I think."

"I know," Andie said. "We've got to do something. What can I do?" She stopped abruptly and stood with her hands wringing the tail end of her cover-up, a purple cotton T-shirt with short sleeves and an even shorter hemline, falling off one shoulder. There were letters printed across the front but they were totally unreadable. Lizzie wondered if she needed to be standing in front of a mirror in order to be read.

"For starters, you can sit down and relax, young lady," Molly said. "Of course, we're going to do something about it. Now, we all know the facts, let's figure out who's on the suspect list."

Andie flopped onto the vacant stool beside her and looked expectantly from Molly to Lizzie.

Sally-Jo and Stephanie started speaking at the same time. Stephanie blushed and nodded to Sally-Jo to go ahead. "The four authors have got to be at the top. They're the only ones here who knew her."

"But do we know that for a fact?" Bob asked. "Didn't you say that Ashley mentioned being around here for some time to come?"

"She did but she didn't say why or if she knew anyone," Lizzie said.

"Well, let's just assume she might have. What other reason would she have for moving to Ashton Corners?" Molly asked.

"She didn't say she was moving here, though."

"Well, it's certainly not a vacationer's paradise," Bob said sarcastically.

Lizzie shrugged. Maybe not, she thought, but it sure appealed to all the anglers in the area, like Bob. Even sitting all dressed up, which for Bob meant a clean plaid shirt overtop a plain white T-shirt and freshly washed blue jeans, he still looked like he'd rather be fishing.

"Well, I still say we should ask around and see what she'd been up to," Molly said.

Bob nodded. "I'll do that. Now, what about these authors? Do they have any reason for doing her in?"

"I'll talk to them," Lizzie volunteered. "Tomorrow after school."

"I think it would be a good idea if someone did that with you," Bob suggested. "We want someone who can corroborate anything you say you're told."

Lizzie looked skeptical. "Okay."

"I'll go with her," Molly said.

Bob gave a quick nod. "Try to find out where they were at the time of death. Do we even know the time of death?"

"Not that I've been told. But I spoke to her on the phone at about ten last night, so it was after that," Lizzie said. "And she was found sometime early this morning, I'm thinking."

Jacob piped up. "Lizzie, what evidence do the police have against you?"

Lizzie shifted on her chair. "Well, I told Mark and several other people about my history with Ashley and that I really disliked her. We had that argument at the book fair, and it wasn't in private. Unfortunately." She felt her cheeks getting hot as she looked around the room. "I'm sure y'all heard it. Not one of my finer moments and I want to apologize to everyone for putting a damper on what should have been a wonderful day."

Molly held up her hand. "I've already said it, Lizzie. The book fair was great and we all know you must have had a very good reason to get into such a tizzy. We all agree, don't we?" She looked around the room and everyone nodded. "All right then, no more talk like that. What happened next?"

Lizzie sighed. "I'd agreed to meet her Monday morning at the Choc 'n Cup, but as Mark pointed out, I could have shown up there knowing she was dead, just to look like I didn't know."

"He didn't say that?" Molly sounded exasperated.

"He was playing devil's advocate, Molly. And then, the most incriminating thing is my cell phone was found with the body."

Andie gasped. "Whoa. Somebody stole your phone and tried to frame you?"

Lizzie gave her a small smile. "Thanks for thinking that, Andie. And that's exactly what happened. I can't remember using or looking for my phone after Saturday."

"That's not good," Jacob said. "But it's not conclusive, either. You need to put some thought into it, Lizzie, and see if you can figure out if someone is deliberately trying to frame you. And we need to concentrate on Ashley. It would help to know about her role with the authors. I'll give her employer a call and try to get the details as to what she was expected to do here. And also, any other information that might be helpful."

"Good idea," said Bob. "Oh, and Lizzie, while you're at it, you'd better ask Patsy Kindall about her weekend guests. She just might have some interesting tidbits to throw in the fray."

"What about if the authors have already left town?" Stephanie asked.

Bob shook his head. "Remember, they're here until tomorrow and then I'm thinking they'll be invited to extend their stay a few more days, at least until they can be totally eliminated as suspects."

They tossed around some possible theories until no one had any new ideas. "I think it's time for those of us with school tomorrow to head home," Lizzie finally said, looking directly at Andie.

"I was just thinking," Andie said, ignoring the suggestion, "that I could do some computer searches on the authors. See if I can dig up any things on their websites or Facebook that may be a clue."

"I hardly think they'll give advance warning of any intention to commit murder," Jacob said with a smile to soften the comment.

Andie looked perplexed. "No, of course not. But one of them might have said something trashy about Ms. Dixon or that they weren't happy with the publicity, or something."

"That's possible," Lizzie jumped in. "Thanks for think-ing of that, Andie."

Andie grinned. She grabbed her backpack and stood, then looked over at Jacob. "And you know, there have been cases of murderers announcing their intent to kill in the past. Look at the mass shootings and things."

Jacob looked startled then nodded.

As they were leaving, Lizzie arranged to meet Molly the next day at the B and B over her lunch break.

Andie had asked for a ride home and as Lizzie turned onto her street, Andie asked again about her cell phone. "So, you need to get a new one, right?"

"I hadn't really thought about it."

"Well, you do use it every day, don't you?"

"Obviously not or I would have noticed it was missing."

"But that was the weekend. Different happenings and all. I really think you should get yourself a new phone."

"Hmm. You're probably right. Who knows when the police will return mine, although I could ask."

"Seriously. Get a new phone. Now's the time to get with it and upgrade."

"Upgrade? What are you suggesting, Andie?"

"An iPhone. You love your iPad, don't you? This would be just as great. I'll even help you choose one."

Lizzie pulled up in front of her house. "An iPhone. That's a bit costly."

"It's an investment and someone who's involved in so many things really needs the latest technology."

"Are you on commission or something?" Lizzie asked with a smile.

"Mine's so cool. And you can get some really awesome

covers and keep changing up the look. You'll thank me. Trust me."

L izzie was just about to crawl into bed, ready for what she was sure would be yet another sleepless night, when the phone rang. She felt cheered when Paige Raleigh's name showed on caller ID.

"I'm sorry to call so late," Paige said, a little out of breath.

"Not a problem. I'm not in bed yet and from the sounds of it neither are you. What did you just do, run the marathon?"

Paige giggled. "Umm, no, just escaping from a frisky husband. I didn't get a chance to call you earlier because we had a business dinner to attend but I need to know how you are. I heard about Ashley Dixon on the news today. Um, is everything okay?"

"Not really." Lizzie settled on the bed and got ready to bring Paige up to speed. When she'd finished the update Paige gasped.

"I can't believe you're a real suspect. Mark knows you'd never hurt a fly. Okay, well maybe a spider but not a fly. Honey, everyone in town knows you'd never do something so terrible."

"Thanks, Paige. You're good for the soul, as usual. However, as you well know, Ashley and I did have an argument at the book fair and several others heard it, too. So I'm sure the story has done the rounds by now. And then there's our history."

"What did Mark say when you told him?"

"He didn't jump up and down and call her a witch, if that's what you mean, but I think he could understand my feelings."

"He'd better or I'll go down there and lock him in his own jail cell."

"Oh, that'll be a big help." Lizzie laughed.

"Good to hear you laughing, girl."

Lizzie sobered right away. "And then there's the fact that my cell phone was found there."

Paige gasped. "Well, it was an obvious plant. But who would want to do that to you?"

"Good question and when we answer it, we'll have the murderer."

Neither said anything for a few moments, then Paige asked, "How about meeting for lunch tomorrow? Can you get away from school?"

"That sounds like a great idea. Noon at Barney's Bistro?"

"You're on."

Chapter Eleven

◇◇◇

When nothing is as it seems, then what? Take
another look from another angle. Stand on your
head if you have to.

DEATH AL DENTE—LESLIE BUDEWITZ

After glancing at the clock radio by her bed for about the
fifth time, finding she'd been in bed for only one hour,
Lizzie sat up and turned on the lamp. She looked at her short
version of a TBR pile and chose the third one down. She'd
always found Krista Davis's Domestic Diva series to be
soothing, even with the liberal dose of murder and sleuthing.
After an hour she decided to try for some sleep. This time
she dozed on and off, her mind playing with the murder, her
past dealings with Ashley and the fact that Mark hadn't even
called to say good night.

She dragged herself out of bed, knowing the best thing
in the world for her at this moment was a run. She changed
into shorts and a tee, then fell forward on the bed for a final
snuggle with Brie and Edam, both still luxuriating in a few
more minutes of relaxation.

"Sorry if I kept you both awake," she said, stroking two

backs and desperately wanting to close her eyes. That would not be good.

She pushed herself off the bed and by the time she'd reached the bottom of the stairs, Edam sat at his cat dish, awaiting breakfast. She spooned out the canned food, rattled some dry kernels into the other side of the divided dishes and replenished the water. Brie obviously preferred some more beauty sleep to being fed.

Lizzie took her favorite route: the one along the river, through Glendale Park and back through town, hoping the scenery would lift her mood. The reality of Ashley's death had sunk in somewhere in the overnight hours. Here was someone with whom she'd shared the rituals of sleeping, studying, getting ready for dates, all the minutia of college life for several months. Sure, she'd ended up really disliking Ashley, or maybe that was partly mixed with a dollop of envy. Ashley got what, and whoever, she wanted. But at the beginning they'd been friends, and now she was dead.

Lizzie was so deep in thought it took until she turned into her driveway to realize Mark's Jeep was parked there. She took a deep breath before opening the back door.

He sat at the table, in uniform, a mug of coffee in his hand, an equally haggard look on his face. Lizzie closed the door behind her and stood for a moment, suddenly a bit unclear about what to do.

Mark rose quickly and pulled her into his arms. "I know this is awfully hard on you," he whispered, "but I want you to know I believe in you."

Lizzie pulled back. "Thanks, Mark. I needed to hear you say that. It's just that your actions say something entirely different."

Mark led her over to the table and sat her down across from him. "Listen to me, Lizzie. I know you're not capable of murder and we're busy interviewing the authors but it's a slow process. It's also all circumstantial evidence leading to you, although your cell at the scene is the most damning piece, but we've got to treat it all seriously and follow through."

He ran his hand across the stubble on his right cheek. Lizzie could see how tired he looked. Either he hadn't had time to shave or he hadn't been home, changing into the spare uniform he kept at the office.

"The entire town knows about our relationship," he continued. "That's why I'm stepping back from any bits that have to do with you. If it takes a while to sort things through and find the murderer, I don't want it said that I bent the rules for you or anything like that. Think of what it would do to your reputation if there were any hint that I covered up something. The murderer needs to be found, which is what I'm concentrating on, and your name needs to be cleared, which is what Officer Craig is trying to do."

Lizzie's eyebrows shot up.

Mark nodded. "Believe me, she doesn't think you're a murderer, either, and while following through on the questioning, is looking for ways your answers clear you."

Lizzie relaxed a little. "That's good to know. Does this mean you'll be keeping your distance? I know you're here now, but it's early in the morning."

"I'm not abandoning you, Lizzie."

Lizzie let out the breath she'd been holding. She got up and poured herself a glass of water. "Can I ask you a few questions?"

Mark leaned back in his chair. "Only if you'll make me some more coffee."

Lizzie smiled. For a few minutes anyway, things felt back to normal. She glanced at the clock. Just enough time to make another brew and she needed some answers. She put another disc in the single-cup coffeemaker and ground some espresso for herself. When they both had coffee in hand, she asked, "Do you have a time of death?"

"Probably after midnight, in the early hours of the morning."

Lizzie shuddered. "So she was already dead while I was waiting for her at the coffee shop."

Mark nodded. "That's why, although we're checking to see if you were seen waiting, it isn't going to do a lot of good. You could, arguably, have stopped in to wait even though you knew she was dead, hoping to show you didn't know she was already dead."

Lizzie opened her mouth to argue. Mark held up his hand. "I said 'arguably.'"

Lizzie grimaced. "You are trying to cover all the bases."

Mark sighed. "Lizzie, I'm thinking about this from every angle. I don't want to be blindsided by anything later on."

"I can't begin to imagine how my cell phone ended up there." As she said the words, the panic she'd been trying to squelch inside started pushing upward.

Mark shook his head. "I don't get it, either, unless someone was trying to frame you. Can you pin down exactly when you last used it?"

"I got a text message from George Havers saying the *Colonist* reporter would be arriving a bit late. That was probably around nine forty-five A.M. on Saturday, just before the doors to the book fair opened. Then, I can't remember if I stuck it in my handbag or just what? I'm pretty sure I didn't use it after that."

"We've checked it out and that jibes with its use. Wherever it was after you sent the reply to Havers, it wasn't used."

"I can't imagine anyone wanting to frame me, though. Are there any fingerprints on the phone?"

"We're checking that out. When we find the murderer, we'll have our answer to who put it there." He paused a moment. "Can you think of anyone who might try to frame you?"

"Amber Craig asked me the same thing and I can't think of anyone."

He shook his head. "I didn't think so. I can't imagine who'd want to do that, either." He gently rubbed her arm. "Don't get too overwrought about it, but if someone comes to mind, call me right away."

Lizzie nodded. "Any idea when I can get my cell back?"

Mark shrugged. "Not in the immediate future, I'm afraid."

"Okay. Andie said I should get another one. An iPhone was her suggestion. Guess I'll give it a try. Another question. How was she killed?"

"By a blow to the back of her head. She died from massive internal bleeding around the brain. The object used must have been quite heavy."

"Yikes. That sounds premeditated, doesn't it?"

"Absolutely, since she was hit from behind. Or else she fell but we haven't found any evidence of that as yet. And, somebody did put her body in the coffin."

"Wow . . . that's an awful lot of unknowns." She was back to dejected. "How was her body discovered if it was in that coffin?"

"One of the hinges needed repairing for some time now apparently, and it worked loose. The cover slid partially off and an arm had fallen out."

Lizzie made a gagging sound and took a quick sip of water.

Mark squeezed her hand. His expression made her even more anxious. "I've had some experience lately with solving murders, if you'll recall. I don't intend to let this one get away from me."

Lizzie tried to smile. "I know," she said softly. "What about the authors?"

"None of them has a solid alibi except for possibly Margaret Farrow, or Caroline Cummings as she wants to be called. She took a sleeping pill and her husband verifies that she was out for the count. Of course, he could be saying that to give himself an alibi."

"But he's not really connected to this. He's not even an author."

Mark gave her a pained look. "We are checking out everyone, Lizzie. That should be a relief to you."

She nodded in agreement.

"They've been requested to stay put until we can determine, without a doubt, that none of them had any involvement in this. I was happy to hear they were all planning on staying until today anyway, and after a bit of grumbling, they've agreed to a few more days. But I can't officially hold them in town unless I have something to go on." He paused. "It would help if you and Molly could come up with some event or something to distract them. That way, they won't get too antsy about sticking around, and maybe they'll be in a bit more cooperative mood when I question them again."

"That's a good idea. I'm sure we can put together some signings and things."

"Good. I'm also following up on what you mentioned, that Ashley Dixon planned to spend time in town. I want to know why and if she knew anyone."

Lizzie visibly relaxed. "I do trust you, Mark. I know you'll solve this, and in the meantime, I'm going to stop feeling sorry for myself."

Mark stood and pulled Lizzie up at the same time. He kissed her and held her a few extra moments.

"It will turn out okay. I promise."

That was two promises she had. Lizzie intended to hold Mark to it as well.

Chapter Twelve

◇◇◇

I felt the room give a lurch as my reality had its feet
kicked out from under it.

CLOCHE AND DAGGER—JENN MCKINLAY

A police cruiser sat parked in the circular drive in front
of the Ashton Corners Elementary School when Lizzie
arrived at work the next day. As she passed the principal's
office, the secretary called out to her.

"Lizzie, Mr. Benton wants to see you." She grimaced and
inclined her head toward his office. "He's waiting."

Uh-oh. The new principal was not a favorite with any of
the staff. Although an efficient administrator, he lacked the
people skills so necessary in a small community. Rumor
had it, he'd moved to Ashton Corners in the late spring from
Birmingham. Speculation as to why he'd undergone such a
drastic change of location ran rampant. The consensus held
that there must be hidden secrets or else this was penance.
Neither a good option. Lizzie had heard that he'd chosen
Ashton Corners because of cousins or something in the area.
That sounded much more realistic.

Lizzie knocked on his door, wondering what he wanted. So far their only contact had been a brief "get to know you" meeting at the beginning of the term. She waited for him to call out and then entered. "You wanted to see me, Mr. Benton?"

"I do. I'll get right to the point. I understand the police are here interviewing various teachers about your habits."

"My habits?"

"Yes. You're a suspect in a murder case and they're checking your movements, if I have that correct. I want you to know that this is very disturbing to me and to the school board. I've been in touch with the superintendent." He shuffled through some papers on his desk while Lizzie stood in shocked silence.

He eventually placed the papers on a pile to the side and folded his hands on the desktop. "It's disturbing the routine and upsetting the children to see the police in the school."

Lizzie couldn't stand it. "I'm sorry, Mr. Benton, if you find it disturbing but they are here before school hours and the children have seen the police often and, for the most part, are very comfortable around them." *Unless their parents are criminals.*

Benton looked surprised. Lizzie wondered if he was unused to being challenged.

"Yes, well the fact that a staff member is a suspect in a murder investigation won't sit well with the board. Parents will also object. I want to nip this in the bud before it gets out of hand. I have enough on my plate to deal with without this."

Lizzie braced herself for what was to come.

"I'd like you to take a leave of absence until this matter is cleared up."

She hadn't expected this. She couldn't believe it. "But I

have appointments lined up with parents, and sessions with students already scheduled."

"You are not the only person in the entire school district who is capable of doing your job, Ms. Turner. Now, you will remain on the payroll. I will make an announcement at a staff meeting at noon. If and when this is all cleared up, get in touch, and we'll see about getting things back to normal." His tone was dismissive.

Lizzie could not think of anything to say. Her hand was on the doorknob when Benton spoke again. "Good luck, Ms. Turner."

Lizzie sat at the banquette in Molly's kitchen and went through the story while Molly sat slack-jawed in surprise. When Lizzie had finished her account, Molly sputtered, "Why, I cannot believe that man. That makes no sense at all. Why, I'm going to get on the phone to the school board chairperson right this minute."

Lizzie put out a hand to restrain her. "No, Molly. Please don't. That won't do any good and will just draw more attention to the matter. He is new to the school and the community and doesn't know me. I guess he's just being overprotective. Who knows what he's had to deal with in the past?"

"He's being biggity if you ask me. And, you're being way too understanding, honey. It just makes me mad as a wet hen."

Lizzie chuckled. "Me, too. But at least it allows me time to do some sleuthing." She tried to sound perkier than she felt. She tried not to dwell on the fact that she might need a lawyer real soon and that would cost big bucks, not readily available on a school employee's salary.

"That's right." Molly visibly brightened. "In fact, why

don't we just head on over to the Quilt Patch right now. We're bound to catch some authors at breakfast and I've always believed that mealtime is a good time to get people talking. Their guards are down then."

"Sounds like a plan," Lizzie said, standing and clearing their coffee cups off the table. "By the way, Mark asked me if we could set up some signings to help keep the authors occupied over the next few days."

Molly chuckled. "I'll bet he wants us to butter them up for him so they'll spill all. Well, let's get to it as soon as we get back."

"Great."

The phone rang and after a few comments, Molly handed the receiver to Lizzie.

"Lizzie, it's Mark. I thought you might be at Molly's when you didn't answer at home. Amber Craig just told me what happened at the school. She was totally outraged and so am I."

Lizzie sighed. "I'm not too happy about it, either."

"I'm really sorry, babe. I had no idea my sending Craig over there would lead to this." He sounded so sincere, Lizzie almost burst into tears.

"It's not your fault, Mark. You have a job to do and, I guess, so does he. At least I'm giving him the benefit of the doubt. For now."

There was a moment of silence. "What are you planning for the rest of the day?"

"I'm going to hang out with Molly for a while, then I've got a lunch date with Paige and I'll run some errands after that."

"I hope by 'hanging out' you don't mean you'll start doing some investigating about this case." He sounded stern.

"I'm just going to do some things that will help take my mind off all this."

"Good. I've gotta go but I'll call you later."

He rang off and Lizzie faced Molly's questioning expression.

"Well, I am. If we can figure out who the murderer is, I won't have to dwell on it and be depressed."

"That's my girl."

Chapter Thirteen

◇◇◇

There's no point in mourning mistakes when you can fix them.

THE TOADHOUSE TRILOGY:
BOOK ONE—JESS LOUREY

Patsy Kindall greeted them at the door of the Quilt Patch. "Why, it's so nice to see you this morning. Do come in. How about some coffee?" Patsy held up the coffee carafe in her hand. "I just gave Mr. Farrow a refill. If you want to join him in the breakfast room, I'll bring you some cups."

"That's thoughtful of you, Patsy. We'd be happy to."

"Isn't that just the most terrible thing to happen?" Patsy continued before they had a chance to move off. "That poor young girl. I mean who would do such a dreadful deed?"

Molly patted Patsy's arm. "It is terrible and I'll bet you're feeling shaken by it, too."

Patsy nodded. She sniffed and looked like she might burst into tears. "Now, you go on and sit and I'll bring that coffee."

Molly led the way to a small sunny room off the dining room, facing the backyard.

"What if they all know I'm a prime suspect?" Lizzie whispered.

"If they ask, just acknowledge the fact and give no details. We won't offer the information." Molly took a second to squeeze Lizzie's hand before continuing on.

"Good morning, Mr. Farrow," Molly said as she swept into the room. "I hope you don't mind if Lizzie and I join you?"

Carter Farrow tried to stand but got caught up in the tablecloth.

"Don't stand," Molly said. "We're not that formal around here, especially in the mornings."

Lizzie smiled at him as she sat down. "You're on your own for breakfast this morning?"

Carter sat back and sighed. "The gals like to sleep in. It's really my only quiet time of the day," he said with a chuckle. "But I am happy to have the company of two such charming ladies. I didn't think we'd be seeing any more of one another, though. It's such a shame about the circumstances."

Lizzie felt a moment's unease but she was pleased that he presented the opening. "Yes, it's such a horrible thing. I can imagine all of you were shocked by the news of Ashley's murder."

Carter nodded. "You cannot begin to imagine the histrionics that accompanied that news. Even A.J. was beside himself."

"Did you know her very well?" Molly asked.

"Not really." Carter shook his head. "I'd met her at the odd event where Margaret's publisher had a presence but this is the first time she'd spent so much time with us."

"I wonder why that was?" Lizzie murmured.

Carter looked at her sharply. "What do you mean by that?"

"Oh, just that why would she come to Ashton Corners

rather than a big book conference? Did she say anything about her reasons for that?"

"I really didn't spend much time talking to the young lady. I think the girls were planning on another book tour or some such, and wanted to go over the details with her. I get filled in at the last minute, since I'm often the driver." He chuckled.

"What about A.J. Pruitt? Was he involved in that?" Lizzie asked.

"I'm not certain. You'll have to ask him. He was out and about again real early this morning, though."

Lizzie made a mental note to find out where A.J. Pruitt had been and just how early. "Did Gigi Briggs go along on any of their tours?"

"Nope. This is the first I've seen of that young gal."

"I suppose the chief has asked y'all to stay in town awhile longer," Molly said casually.

"He has and I don't know what good that will do him," Farrow said, his voice filled with anger. "The girls certainly had nothing to do with it. And it's a great inconvenience for us. Margaret wants to get home and get back to writing. She has a deadline approaching and it's so hard for her to write while on the road, you know."

"I'd imagine it is," Molly replied.

"And I'm sure it's the same for Lorelie. The gals' books always seem to have much the same timing." He finished off the last of his coffee. "I should think we could be on our way, especially when it appears the murderer may be someone local." He glanced at Lizzie but looked embarrassed to be doing so.

Lizzie was at a loss for words but Molly came to the rescue. "That's total nonsense. However, the chief does have to cover all bases."

Farrow made a big show of looking at his watch. "I guess

I should take a cup of coffee up to Margaret. She likes to start her day that way. Ladies," he said as he stood and dropped his napkin on the table. At the door, he turned and said, "I think Ashley said there was someone in town she wanted to see." He shrugged. "I could be mistaken. I wasn't really paying much attention to her."

He wandered into the adjoining kitchen as Molly poured them both another coffee from the carafe Patsy had left on the table.

"Yikes. Just as I thought. Word gets around," Lizzie said. "Do you think I was supposed to look guilty or something?"

"Don't let that bother you, honey. Keep focused on what we're here to accomplish." She patted Lizzie's hand.

"What now?" Lizzie asked. "Should we wait and see who next appears?" Lizzie chose a pecan swirl from the plate on the table. She did love Patsy's baking.

"Let's wait until Mr. Farrow departs upstairs and then have a chat with Patsy. If we hang around long enough, we may get a chance to talk to one of the divas before we leave." Molly made a face and Lizzie started laughing. It felt good. She knew she was under some strain but this showed just how much.

They sat in silence, enjoying the warmth of the sun shining through the large picture windows, and watching the colorful flower garden that festooned the backyard. To the left of the back door, stretching from the sidewalk to the back fence, was the equivalent of an English country garden. Too many varieties of flowers, all sizes and colors, vied for attention, giving the impression of organized chaos. To the right, an old-fashioned wooden two-seater swing with seats facing each other had been surrounded by smaller shrubs and a border of annuals.

After several minutes they were joined by Patsy carrying

a plate of sour cream twists. "May I interest you ladies in a freshly baked twist?"

Molly answered for them both, "That would be lovely, Patsy. Your sour cream twists are to die for."

Patsy laughed. "You are my best promoter, Molly. Truly. Here you go and arrange for the inn to be full this weekend, usually a slow time of year, and you're always recommending my baking. You're such a good friend."

Molly beamed, looking pleased at the compliment.

"Can you take a few minutes to sit with us?" Lizzie asked.

Patsy glanced into the kitchen. "I never know when those two women will be up but they've convinced me to do up a late breakfast if need be. I do probably have time for a cup of coffee myself." She cleared away Farrow's dishes and then sat in his chair.

"Are you able to take on having them all here for several more days?" Molly asked.

Patsy sighed. "Oh yes. I've hired that cute little Missy Townsend from the Koffee Klutch to help with the cleaning. She'd asked me a while ago if I needed some help. She's trying to earn some more money so she can go traipsing around the world. Imagine. Well, she's young enough to do it. She'll travel until she needs more money, then get a job and so on. Oh, to be young."

Molly chuckled. "I often think the very same thing."

"But isn't this just the most awful way to end the weekend?" Patsy asked, suddenly serious. "I cannot believe that young woman was staying in this house and now she's dead."

"Have the police said anything to you about it?" Molly asked.

Patsy shook her head. "No, they haven't but they've been through her room and asked me to hang on to all her stuff for the moment."

"Who will take it?" Lizzie asked, curious.

"Oh, I think someone from her office is coming down later today. And then there's that young man."

"What young man?" Molly asked sharply.

"Quite a good-looking fellow. From New York, he said. He came around here Sunday afternoon asking for Ashley. He'd asked me to tell her Nick was staying at the Ashton Inn. She was out but came back just as he was leaving. She didn't look any too pleased to see him, let me tell you."

"Did you tell the police about him?"

"Of course."

"Did Ashley say anything about him after they'd spoken?" Lizzie wanted to know.

Patsy gave it some thought. "I didn't speak to her. I watched them a few minutes and then went into the kitchen. I heard her come back in but she went straight to her room. In fact, I didn't talk to her again after that. So sad."

"Did you hear her go out again that night?" Molly asked.

"I heard people going and coming a few times that evening, but I was so tired I just stayed put in my sitting room and watched some TV. I'm not sure who was doing what." She glanced at the large round clock hanging beside the window and gathered their mugs.

"I'm sorry but I should check on my baking. I'm now doing up a fresh batch of shortbread for sherry hour today."

"That's quite all right. I guess we should just be on our way," Molly said, with a glance at the hallway. "Thank you for the coffee."

Lizzie took her own mug into the kitchen and said good-bye, joining Molly at the front door. As they were about to leave, Lorelie Oliver called out as she descended the stairs.

"Oh my, you are early birds around here, aren't y'all?"

Molly took a deep breath and turned to face her. "We

just thought we'd stop by to see how you're doing. It must be so upsetting with what's happened to Ms. Dixon."

"Oh, Ashley. Hmm. Yes, it's very upsetting. We were all just so distraught when we heard about it. She was such a dynamic child and brimming with excellent marketing ideas. It's a loss to us all." She paused on the bottom step, tying the sash of her silk Chinese kimono more tightly around her waist.

Lizzie noticed the time for histrionics had obviously passed. In fact, Lorelie seemed quite dispassionate about it all.

"And what are your plans now that you're required to stay extra time in our fair town?" Molly asked.

"Oh my, I hadn't given it much thought really. I suppose there's not much to do around here, though." She sniffed. "It's really most inconvenient. I had to cancel plans for several appointments. And I had to make sure my dog sitter could continue taking care of my dear little Blossom for a few more days. It will be only a few days, won't it? Oh, it better be. I don't know what I'll do otherwise. Of course, I should be doing my writing. There's another deadline looming. There always is."

"Well," Molly ventured, "you could always look at it as a chance to do some research on small-town living. It might come in handy for a future book."

Lorelie gave it a moment's thought. "You might just have a point there." She smiled. "On the other hand, I am always working flat out, so I'm trying to look upon this as a gift of time. Time to relax and play."

Molly inhaled deeply. "Well, Lizzie and I are going to put our heads together and line up some events for y'all, to help make it worth your while. But for now, I thought you and Caroline might enjoy a tour of our town this afternoon.

We could stop at Designs by Dora, which has a wonderful array of gifts and clothing, and then have tea at the Jefferson Hotel. They do a proper English tea there."

Lorelie's eyes had lighted up at the mention of clothing. She answered without much thought, "That would be delightful. And we'd all love to do some more events. It's always so much fun to meet our adoring fans. Thank you so much for suggesting it all, Molly."

"That's good then. Would you be so kind as to invite Caroline to join us? And we'll come by for you at around two," Molly added.

"Of course." Lorelie stepped back to allow Patsy entry to the breakfast room, her tray laden with a coffee carafe and covered basket of sweet breads.

Molly and Lizzie left as Lorelie settled herself at the table.

Chapter Fourteen

◇◇◇

A perfect opportunity, I thought with a grin. For
what, I didn't know. But at least it was a start.

YOU CANNOLI DIE ONCE—SHELLEY COSTA

"That was brilliant, Molly," Lizzie said as they got into
the car.

"It just struck me while talking to Lorelie, shopping and
tea with the divas would be a good way of extracting information from them. You'll come, of course?"

"Wouldn't miss it."

"Good. Now, we have just enough time to plot some dis-
tractions over lunch at my place. I have some butternut squash
soup I made yesterday."

"My favorite."

"They're all your favorite," Molly said with a chuckle.

Lizzie grinned. "But I was supposed to have lunch with
Paige today. I hate to cancel this late but maybe I can change
it to tomorrow."

"Why don't you invite her over? I haven't seen Paige in
a long time."

"That's nice of you, Molly. I'll give her a call when we get back to your place. Do you mind if we take a small detour on the way?"

Molly raised her eyebrows.

"I'd just like to run by the White Haven Funeral Home and have a look at where they found the body."

"Certainly. But what if the police are still there?"

"We won't stop. We're just two women out for a leisurely drive."

Lizzie noticed two white compacts parked in the lot at White Haven Funeral Home when they cruised past. They certainly didn't look like police cars, so she turned her car around and went back, parking just to the right of the entrance where the funeral home sign was on full display.

The name was spelled out in large letters, about two feet high, black and cut out; suspended from the letters was a green sign with black lettering, about four by six feet, the top of it at least ten feet off the ground, stating this was a funeral home, established 1986, proprietors Ivan and Francis Abernathy, along with a telephone number. The space underneath it was empty at the moment but Lizzie could picture the very plain wooden black coffin, about six feet long, tipped on its side, hanging by two large hooks. She imagined it was at the police station being processed or something. Maybe it was being held as evidence since it was the final resting place of the body.

Lizzie stared at the space for the longest time. "You know, Molly, someone would have had to remove the top, heft the body inside while preventing it from tumbling out since it was hanging on its side, and replace the cover, making sure it stayed put."

"Just how did the body get discovered?" Molly asked.

"Mark said that the cover had come loose and an arm had slipped out." She shuddered as she visualized it.

Molly didn't seem to be too bothered by the image. "I doubt a woman could manage that."

"Ashley must have weighed about 120 pounds. The upper edge of the coffin hung about four feet off the ground. It would be a tricky maneuver but easy for a woman if there were an accomplice." She wondered if Mark had come to the same conclusion. Two murderers? Cohorts? Why not?

"That makes sense logistically, but doesn't it become even more difficult to discover a motive? Unless all the authors had ganged up on Ashley. But why would they?"

Molly was silent for a few moments. "Huh. It could be just like *Murder on the Orient Express* by Agatha Christie."

It seemed ridiculous to be even thinking it, but these people were all accomplished at plotting murders. Now Lizzie was really looking forward to the afternoon shopping excursion.

Molly had gone upstairs to refresh herself before they left to pick up the divas. Paige had begged off the lunch, agreeing to meet Lizzie the next day instead. She'd been shocked at the news of Lizzie's enforced holiday but agreed it was a good time to do some snooping, as long as Lizzie stayed safe.

Lizzie sat sipping her iced tea out on the patio when the phone rang. Lizzie waited to see if Molly would pick up, and after another two rings, went inside. Mark's number showed.

"I'm so pleased to hear from you," Lizzie said when she answered. "But, is this a business call?"

Mark laughed. "No. This is very personal. I've been thinking about you since we last spoke and want to hear you say you're all right. I figured, once again, that no answer at home meant you were at Molly's."

"Hm. What does that say about me?" She gave a small laugh. "Actually, I'm looking at this as a mini-holiday with time to get caught up on some things. Besides, I still have my literacy class that meets tonight. I'll have to prep for that later."

"That's good to hear. But I'm also a little worried that this extra time will go into your doing some sleuthing into this case. I won't even ask you to tell me that's not so."

"Very wise. I do want to ask you something, now that I have you on the phone. Who is this Nick person who visited Ashley?"

"Where did you hear about him? Never mind. Patsy Kindall is good friends with Molly, isn't she?" He sighed. "I guess I can tell you that he and Ashley were engaged for a few months until she broke it off, just before she came down here. He followed her to try to patch things up."

"Is he a suspect? A broken heart is a good motive."

"It is and he's on the list. It seems they also worked together at the publishing house. I'm going to send Officer Yost up to New York with some questions for the staff. I want to make sure this isn't an internal work problem that followed her to Ashton Corners."

"Sounds like a good idea."

"Glad you approve. Now, since I've told you all that, there's no need for you to try to figure it out. In fact, I'd really be happy if you told me you're going straight home and staying there for the afternoon and preparing for your class tonight."

"Really. Well, Molly and I are taking the divas on a little fashion tour of town this afternoon. Molly thought they might be getting a bit antsy and there's no better soother than some shopportunities."

Mark laughed, although it sounded a bit strained. "I sense

an ulterior motive here. Have fun but be sure to let me know if you learn something about the case."

"The case? I'm sure I don't know what you're talking about, Chief."

That sigh again. "All right, we'll let it go for now. But one day, Lizzie, we're going to have a serious talk about boundaries, as in who is the cop around here."

Chapter Fifteen

◇◇◇

My eyes locked with hers. "Good question."

ROSEMARY AND CRIME—GAIL OUST

Lizzie didn't have time to think about Mark's statement, although she realized he'd been very serious about it. Molly joined her outside a few minutes later. "Let's take my Audi. It's more spacious."

"Good thinking."

On the drive over to the Quilt Patch, they plotted methods to get the divas talking about their relationships with Ashley, deciding that they'd just play it by ear. The way those two talked, surely someone would introduce an opening. As soon as Molly pulled into the driveway, the two women appeared on the porch and made their way to the car. Caroline wore a green knit dress with short sleeves, while Lorelie had on cream pants with a multicolored flowing top. Lorelie grabbed the handle of the passenger front door.

"I do hope you don't mind, Lizzie, but I find it so difficult sitting in the backseat of a car."

"Of course not," Lizzie said as she leapt out.

Lizzie settled in the backseat along with Caroline, who started talking the minute the door closed. Molly waited until she took a break and then said, "I can see you're both up for having a good time of shopping. I thought we'd head straight over to the one really chic shopping area we have in town. It's just a block long but I know you will just love the shops."

"Well, I can hardly wait," said Lorelie. "I need something to raise my spirits and shopping always does the trick. What about you, Caroline? You were much closer to Ashley than I."

Lizzie breathed a sigh of relief that the topic had been broached. Now, she wouldn't have to think of how to draw the two into a conversation about their publicity person.

"Why yes, she was a sweet girl and certainly did her best at getting me signings and the like. But I'll just bet you were cooking something up with her, Lorelie. You two were huddled in the corner more times than not this weekend."

Molly pulled into a parking spot on Yancy Street before Lorelie had a chance to respond. Lizzie was determined to get them back on track as soon as possible.

"Oh my, just take a look at that absolutely breathtaking negligee over there in that store window," Lorelie squealed as she closed the car door behind her.

Caroline looked uncertain. "And why would you need something like that? Rather racy, isn't it? For someone your age, I mean."

Lorelie sniffed. "You're only as old as you believe yourself to be, Caroline, and I am still in my twenties."

Molly laughed good-naturedly. "I wish that worked. I'd like to shave a few years off, for sure."

Lorelie walked over to the window and stared at the sexy black outfit. "I've been divorced four times. Never could find a man I wanted to keep seeing year after year. But I'm still young enough to enjoy myself. Why do you think my readers always just love all the romance I infuse into each of my mysteries?"

Lizzie heard Caroline mutter under her breath, "Just because you don't have enough meat for a full-blown mystery."

Molly grabbed Lorelie's arm and pointed her toward the Designs by Dora shop. "I'd like to suggest we start shopping at this here quaint little store run by the daughter of an old friend. I'm sure you two will be more than delighted by what you find in here."

They walked without comment the few steps to the shop but once indoors, Lorelie said in a loud voice, "Oh my saints, you are so right Molly Mathews. This shop is just heavenly. It was practically put together just for me."

Caroline looked around at the designer sportswear. "I think it will suit me just fine also."

They drifted in different directions while Molly went over to speak to the owner. Lizzie wasn't in the market for any new outfits, nor could she afford the prices in the shop, so she wandered over to the array of scarves and sorted through them, while watching the two authors.

They'd often make eye contact and nod a tacit approval or the opposite when the other held up an item. Lizzie found that very odd for two women who were reportedly trying to outdo each other at every opportunity.

By the time Molly suggested trying out other stores, both authors agreed they were shopped out and looking forward to the high tea Molly had promised.

"I do believe you've bought the shop out, Lorelie," Molly said, laughing as she held the door open for them.

"I did try my best. Caroline did very well also."

Caroline laughed. "It's so liberating some days to just

spend money. Now, I'll have to sneak these into the room. Carter does have a fit when he sees shopping bags galore. He's such a grump sometimes."

Lorelie replied, "You're just not treating him right, sweetie."

Caroline shot her an icy glare.

"We could walk to the hotel," Lizzie suggested quickly. "It's just a couple of blocks along."

"That's a fine idea," Lorelie answered. "It's a perfect day to be outside in the glorious fresh air. Just a perfect temperature, too. I'm sure fall is my favorite time of year."

"You say that every spring, too," Caroline pointed out.

Lorelie just smiled and sped up a bit to walk beside Molly. Lizzie and Caroline brought up the rear.

After a few minutes of quiet, Lizzie said, "I find it very interesting that you two seem friendlier this afternoon."

Caroline shrugged. "You noticed. Well, Lorelie is very mercurial, to say the very least. I never know what or who to expect. It all depends on what review or bestseller list she's just read. And, just between you and me, she had quite the spat with Ashley on Saturday night after the fair. Lorelie told Ashley she wasn't putting enough time in promoting 'an author of her stature.'" Caroline snorted in disgust. Lizzie could almost see the quotation marks.

They'd arrived at the restaurant and Lizzie watched carefully as the two made their way into the Echo Lounge. *Two times in one month.* The birthday lunch for Stephanie was the first time in years that Lizzie had been there and now here she was again just two weeks later.

After they'd filled their plates, Molly asked Caroline if she had anything she'd like to specifically do while they were still in town.

"It's really such an inconvenience having to stay on longer. On the other hand, it's high time I took a little break.

I've had such a rugged writing schedule for the past year. A few more days off are most welcome," she said, nodding as if agreeing with herself.

"Well, you are right about that, Caroline," Lorelie jumped in. "We've both been slaving away without much playtime. I think I, too, am ready to just relax for a few days."

"I hope you won't mind, in that case, but as I mentioned earlier to Lorelie, we were thinking of setting up a couple more events while you're here. Maybe something at the library for starters," Molly suggested.

"Oh, that would be delightful," Caroline gushed while Lorelie nodded happily.

"We're always ready to do a reading," Lorelie added.

Molly smiled. "Well, I'm so glad you agree. Lizzie and I will get right on it and see what we can get going."

Lizzie nodded, took a bite of her watercress sandwich and asked, "What do you know about Ashley's job?"

"What do you mean, dear?" Caroline asked.

"I'm just wondering if she mentioned how she liked the job or if there were any problems either with her coworkers or any authors in particular."

"You mean, aside from us?" Lorelie asked with a laugh. "Don't look so surprised. We can be exasperating now and then. Ashley had traveled with us a couple of times early on in our careers with Crawther but she said she wasn't meant to be a mediator, so she left us to our own wiles."

Caroline took up the thread. "She was good at lining up events for us and media opportunities but I always got the impression she had bigger fish to fry, so to speak."

"Like anyone or anything specific?" Molly asked.

"Oh, not that I could say for sure. She didn't get to work with their top mainstream authors, I know that. So that was probably her goal. Although those *authors* are highly over-rated. I truly believe that those of us who write genre are just as capable and creative as the rest of them. And, we're so much nicer to our fans," Caroline said. "I did think that Ashley had a lot of drive and wanted to get ahead."

"But she joined you down here," Lizzie stated.

"Yes, that was a surprise. It could have been because of Gigi. I think they've got big plans for her. She's already been nominated for a couple of awards this year." Lizzie was surprised at the hint of maliciousness in Lorelie's voice. "Of course, if Gigi wins, that's good for the company and I'm just so certain that Ashley would have made it all about herself. You know, how she's managed to boost sales, get more readers, la-dee-dah."

"I think she was making a play for Carter," Caroline said after finishing a mini watercress sandwich.

"What?" Lorelie sounded shrill. "That's the most foolish thing I've ever heard you say."

"What makes you think that?" Lizzie asked Caroline.

"Because I've seen her approach him a couple of times, even grab him by the arm. And I think she looks the part of the innocent-looking but scheming young businesswoman who'd do anything to get ahead."

"You're starting to believe your own mysteries," Lorelie snapped. "You know that Carter would never look at another woman and besides, Ashley was young enough to be his daughter. And furthermore, what could he do to further her career? You're the one in power in that marriage."

Caroline turned beet red but kept her voice deceptively calm. "Nicely done, Lorelie. Two jibes in one sentence."

Lizzie finished the small sandwiches in silence, wondering why Lorelie was defending Ashley in the first place, as Molly and Lorelie discussed the décor in the room. Caroline had turned her full attention to the two-tiered dessert dish.

"Lizzie?" Lorelie was talking to her.

"Oh, I'm sorry. What did you say, Lorelie?"

"I just wondered if you knew Ashley's fiancé, seeing as you and she went back so far."

Lizzie cleared her throat. "Uh, no. We hadn't been in touch for many years so I have no idea what's been going on in her life. Did either of you know him?"

"Only that he's an editor at Crawther," Caroline answered, almost back to her old self. "I've never met him."

Lizzie nodded.

"I wonder if anyone has told the poor man?" Lorelie asked.

"Oh, he knows," Caroline answered. "In fact, he's in town."

"How do you know that?"

"Well, I happened to see him Sunday afternoon. He was just leaving the bed and breakfast when I came back from my afternoon walk."

"Well, why didn't you tell me?" Lorelie sounded almost angry.

"Why should I do that? I just saw him, that's all." Caroline glared at her.

Lizzie wondered what that was all about.

"Maybe you should offer to console him, dear," Caroline said.

That sounded a tad catty to Lizzie.

"One at a time, darling," Lorelie said, with her Cheshire smile.

Chapter Sixteen

◇◇◇

"I know," Molly said, "but everything's out of whack."

A RARE MURDER IN PRINCETON—ANN WALDRON

Lizzie thought about the afternoon's conversation as she was getting ready for the literacy class she was teaching that night. She was having a tough time figuring those two out. What had all that interchange been about? She had the feeling there was a lot more going on just below the surface. She doubted it had anything to do with Ashley's death but her curiosity was piqued.

Maybe A.J. Pruitt would know. She'd try to have a talk with him tomorrow.

In the meantime, she had some essays to hand back tonight to her class of four students. All were in the twelfth grade and all were in serious risk of failing their GEDs.

The weekly classes were held in Molly's house. Lizzie taught a class of four and Sally-Jo had five in her group this year. The literacy program, Words for Change, had been using Molly's mansion for five years now since she was on its board of directors and very committed to helping the young adults in their quest for a higher degree of literacy or that evasive GED. It was just one of the many philanthropic interests that Molly was involved in. Her house, given its size, turned out to be ideal for many ventures and events.

Lizzie mentally ran through a list of possible assignments for tonight's class. She'd decided to wait until the discussion was in full swing before choosing which of the three possible tasks she had prepared. The assigned reading was an essay on writing short stories and Lizzie had hoped it would inspire some of them to suggest their own topic for a very short story based on their own interest. The students were unpredictable, though, and often didn't flow the way she envisioned.

First thing Lizzie noticed when she arrived in the library, now her classroom, was that Tyler Edwards had skipped the class. She hoped the reason was a valid one because she'd been working hard to spark some interest there. Tyler had his own agenda, though, and often surprised Lizzie either by being totally engaged or else spending the evening texting.

"Are we going to do a Rapid Read anytime soon?" asked eighteen-year-old Priscilla Ingersoll. Her dark brown hair was streaked with an almost fluorescent purple, reminding Lizzie of Andie's former look.

"We can," Lizzie answered, grateful for the show of interest.

"Can I ask a question about the book thingy on the weekend?" Noelle Ward asked. Her straight blonde hair had been fastened to one side with a blingy black clip and cascaded over her right shoulder. Long, thick bangs draped over one eye. They reminded Lizzie of the photos of the 1940s starlet Veronica Lake, one of many whose photo her mama had cut out of the movie star magazines she brought home from the five-and-dime. *Silver Screen* had been her favorite. Lizzie used to look forward to the quiet times she'd spend with her mama looking through her scrapbook.

"Sure." Lizzie was surprised but pleased.

"My mama made me go with her. She thinks I tell such great stories I should know something about writing them down and one of her favorite writers was there. That Lorelie Oliver. Huh. I didn't really think she was so hot but I gotta admit, I don't read what she writes. But my mama thought she was awesome. Now that Gigi chick looked more my style, especially in that getup. So, I heard that one of them had been murdered."

Lizzie heard a gasp from the others. Obviously not up on local news.

"That's right," Lizzie answered hesitantly, wondering where this was leading.

"Do you think it's one of them? The murderer, I mean. Do you think one of the writers killed her?"

Lizzie wondered if it was ghoulish interest that made Noelle ask the question. She thought about her answer before speaking. "It's possible but then there are lots of other possibilities, too. It's a long, involved process for the police and they're busy investigating it all right now."

Priscilla's hand shot up. "That's right, there was a murder last year, too, and you caught the killer, didn't you?"

Lizzie had everyone's attention now.

"The police caught the murderer but I was involved, a bit."

"Do you think you can catch the killer this time?" Noelle asked.

Oh boy. "I think we're getting a little bit sidetracked here. What about the essay?"

"What about if that was our research topic? We could talk to the police and witnesses and everyone and do our papers." Priscilla paused to look around at the others. "It would be way more interesting than anything that's in the book."

Lizzie was tempted for a nanosecond. Great to have more minds working on it and good for building research skills but not practical or safe. "That's not a good idea. The police are way too busy to be interviewed right now and they wouldn't want anyone else talking to witnesses until they've completed their investigation."

"Huh," Priscilla said and folded her arms across her chest. Her face managed to look disappointed and defiant at the same time.

Lizzie did some quick thinking. "Maybe we could visit the idea again after the case has been solved. It would be just as interesting to track the process at that point."

Priscilla brightened somewhat and Lizzie managed to divert them back on topic. After everyone left, Lizzie sat in Molly's kitchen with Sally-Jo and Molly, sipping tea.

"You know, the kids were really hoping to get involved with the murder case," Sally-Jo said.

"You're kidding," Lizzie exclaimed. "My class, too."

"Too bad we can't harness some of that energy and inquisitiveness and actually use it to figure this out."

"No way," Lizzie said. "Mark would have a fit, for starters. And secondly, it could be way too dangerous for them to even be thinking that way. Who knows who might want to carry it further and then we'd really have trouble."

"You are so right, honey," Molly agreed.

"I haven't had a chance to tell you what Caroline said to me as we were walking over to the Jefferson Hotel. She said that Lorelie had an argument with Ashley after the fair, accusing her of not working hard enough on her promotion."

Sally-Jo raised her eyebrows. "Yikes. I sure wouldn't have wanted Ashley's job, not for any amount of money."

Lizzie had to agree.

"That certainly keeps Lorelie on the suspect list but not really a good motive for murder, I'd say."

"You're right again, but Ashley didn't control the publicity machine and with her gone, there'll be someone new who may or may not be what Lorelie considers better for her career."

"For now, on to other matters. I think it would be good to get Sally-Jo's input into the readings we're planning," Molly said and explained their task of organizing some events for the authors. "And I think that the library is a natural for a reading if they have an opening one evening or even an afternoon."

"Okay, I'll call Isabel first thing in the morning." Lizzie pulled her iPad and started writing.

"How about something outdoors?" Sally-Jo suggested. "The long-range weather forecast is good. What about a reading at the band gazebo in the town square on Sunday afternoon? Of course it depends on how long Mark wants them kept here."

Molly thought it over. "I'm hoping we won't need to look that far ahead because the murderer will be behind bars but I think it's a grand idea even if Mark doesn't need them kept in town. I think we should plan on it anyway. October is usually a lackluster month in town." She nodded. "Yes, it's a great idea."

Lizzie grinned, also pleased with the idea. "We'd be able to get something about it in the *Colonist* this Thursday. And put up some posters around town. Do we need to have food or anything?"

"I don't think so," Molly said after some thought. "I'll be sure to have books set up for sale, though. Now, just let me call to Annie at the parks department tomorrow and make sure that it's free, and if so, I'll book it."

* * *

Lizzie's phone rang as she turned out the downstairs lights before heading to bed. It was Lorelie.

"I just thought, in all good conscience, that I should tell you about an argument Caroline had with Ashley on Sunday morning after breakfast. The boys had gone off to do their own things and it was just Caroline and myself finishing off a leisurely cup of coffee. Then Ashley waltzed in looking for her breakfast."

"All right." Lizzie couldn't help but wonder why Lorelie had decided to spill the goods.

"Well, you know that it's been many books since Caroline was on any bestseller list, whereas I might point out that I was in the top twenty of the Barnes & Noble list just last spring with my latest Fashionista book."

Lizzie wasn't sure if this required an answer. However, as she hadn't known that fact, she decided to remain silent.

Lorelie continued as if Lizzie had acknowledged the fact. "And it just frosts her, partly because she so hates to be outdone by me. So she was on Ashley's case, accusing her of not giving her enough attention and saying had she been doing her job properly, and helping to get the word out about Caroline's book, she'd probably have made it to the top ten this time." Lorelie snorted. "As if that's going to happen. But that's not the point of this story."

"What is?"

"Well, you see, I think Ashley was mighty stressed out about something because she usually just takes that uppity tactic with us and makes it sound like it's our own darned fault. Well this time she actually admitted Caroline was right. Imagine that."

"That doesn't sound like an argument to me," Lizzie suggested.

"No? Well, Caroline kept on going, not knowing when she'd won, as she's wont to do, and suddenly Ashley turns on her heels and stalks out of the room, throwing over her shoulder a comment about Caroline doing her own you-know-what promotion from now on and that she, meaning Ashley, soon wouldn't have to worry anymore about such unimportant things. Imagine that!"

"What did Caroline do?"

"She said that the uppity Ashley would get hers."

Chapter Seventeen

✧✧✧

It was all the encouragement we needed to make up our own minds.

MAYHEM AT THE ORIENT EXPRESS—KYLIE LOGAN

Lizzie had a plan by the time she got back home from her morning run and it included a morning coffee with Ashley's ex-fiancé. She fixed herself an espresso and ate a banana with some spoonfuls of almond butter, brushed both cats, who were following her around ready to trip her whenever she turned around, had a shower and quickly dressed.

She phoned Isabel Fox first and was pleased to be able to arrange a reading for the authors. Fortunately, there was an opening on the library schedule for Saturday afternoon and Isabel was delighted to pen them in. They'd have the large activity room from three to five P.M., plenty of time for four readings with signings to follow. And Isabel would have the library email the information to its patrons later in the day. Hopefully, Molly would have some luck with her pursuit of the band gazebo in the town square. That would keep the authors happy, for the weekend at least. But what about next week, if the investigation stretched out that long?

Lizzie planned to stop at the bed and breakfast later and fill the authors in on the new agenda. She was also hoping to corner Caroline for a little question-and-answer session about what Lorelie had said. It was definitely time to talk to A.J. Pruitt and Gigi Briggs. They'd been scarcely seen since the murder. For that she'd need Molly, of course. She gave Molly a quick call to fill her in on the library event and to ask if she was free to go to the B and B later in the morning.

With that done, she drove to the new Target on Cole Street in search of a new cell phone. By the time she'd decided on a model and gotten it all set up, it was later than she thought but there was still enough time to drive over to the Ashton Inn. She hoped to catch Nick Jennings in the restaurant having breakfast, or if not, she planned to call his room and invite him to meet her for a coffee.

She wasn't sure what to expect—a grieving lover, an angry, rejected and scorned guy or a man in complete control of his feelings and not willing to give anything away. Her questions were pretty basic and would do for whatever mixture of feelings she encountered.

Fortunately, Jennings sat at a corner booth in the hotel's restaurant, as pointed out to her by the young, giggling server. "Oh, that's him all right, ma'am. He's such a good tipper and always takes the time for a nice chat."

So, maybe not too grief-stricken, Lizzie thought, walking over and introducing herself.

Jennings looked surprised but quickly recovered and invited her to join him. She ordered a coffee and made the usual comments about the nice surroundings until she'd had her first sip. It also gave her the opportunity to size him up.

He looked to be about six feet tall with brown wavy hair cut in a corporate style. She guessed him to be in his forties, not too much older than Ashley. His Michael Kors striped shirt spoke of good taste and a healthy shopping budget.

"I'm real sorry to intrude on your privacy at a time like this," Lizzie said, "but I was Ashley's roommate in college and I'm just so shocked at what's happened. I felt I should make contact with you and see how you're doing. I understand you two were engaged?"

Jennings cleared his throat. "At one time, yes. In fact, Ashley had just broken it off before leaving on this trip." His finger tapped the side of his cup. "It wasn't the first time. I don't know how well you knew her but Ashley could be quite flighty at times. The last time she walked out on me, it was because I refused to take her with me on a business trip to Las Vegas. Anyway, I relented that time and we made up. I figured this was much the same thing, so I followed her down here."

"And what would the reason have been this time?"

"Pardon?" He looked surprised.

"The thing she wanted to change your mind about, if that's why she broke it off?"

"That's just it. I didn't know."

"You met with her down here?" Lizzie asked, knowing the answer.

"Just briefly at the bed and breakfast. She said she didn't want to talk about it while here and I should go home."

"But you didn't."

"Of course not. I figured it was all part of the game. She was playing hard-to-get. Again."

Lizzie could picture Ashley acting exactly like this. "Hmm. And you really have no idea why she wanted to break it off?"

"I'm telling you, I thought it wasn't for real. She could

be flighty and was forever changing her mind about things, so I fully expected her to tell me all about it when she got back to New York."

"But you didn't leave?" she pressed.

Jennings looked around the room and leaned toward her. He spoke in a soft voice. "I thought she might want time off for a little fling here in town, so I thought I'd stick around and see who the guy was."

"What made you think that?"

"She did say something earlier about wanting to see somebody here. I knew it wasn't on book business. So, knowing Ashley, I put two and two together."

Lizzie wondered if that had been what Ashley had meant when she said she'd be spending more time in Ashton Corners. If so, who could it be?

"Do you have an alibi for the time of her murder?" Lizzie wondered if he would answer her.

"That's what the police wanted to know. And no, I don't. I was in my hotel room all evening and morning. Alone." He glared at Lizzie but after a few moments his look softened. "Look, I don't know how close you were to her but I'd like to give you my condolences, too. It's hard when someone so young and so vital dies in such a senseless manner."

Lizzie started to say they weren't close but closed her mouth quickly. Jennings was right. It was a shame when such a thing happened and everyone, no matter how far removed from Ashley, was affected.

She thought about that on her drive to Molly's. When she looked closely, she was sad that Ashley had been murdered. They would never have become friends again, she was sure about that, but they had been at one time, even if for a brief period, and that mattered. Putting things into perspective, it was no longer just a quest to prove her innocence by finding the murderer. It was also something she owed Ashley. Her killer would be found.

Lizzie found Molly out in the garden putting some of her summer flowers to bed, although there weren't many as the fall foliage had already filled in most spots, and eventually the next cycle of plants would do so also. Colorful sage in a variety of hues, coleus and gomphrena abounded everywhere with a lot of varieties Lizzie had never heard of. The backdrop was the amazing acre of property, most of which was filled with an actual walk-through maze with hedges of holly, originally laid out by Claydon Mathews, now reaching ten feet tall. Molly had a yard maintenance company that took care of the larger areas, including keeping the maze trimmed back and the pathways easily navigated.

Lizzie looked longingly at the maze, wanting to wander through and lose herself to the magic of it all, as she'd done so many times over the years. However, she felt they were running out of time to find out what had happened to Ashley. And there were two more authors who needed to be questioned.

"Hey, Molly. That's a never-ending job."

"Lizzie. You startled me. Yes it is, dear, but I get so much satisfaction out of doing it I always reserve this task for myself." She glanced at her watch. "Oops, it seems I've lost track of time. I thought I'd just do a little pruning. How did the fiancé seem?"

"Ex-fiancé, actually. I've just had a coffee with Nick Jennings."

Molly sat back on her heels. Her eyebrows rose, questioning. "Ex? Hmm. And was it useful?"

"Not so much. He says Ashley broke it off just as she was leaving, so he followed her to get some answers."

"And did he?"

"Not in so many words. She did mention to him that there was someone she wanted to see down here. And I'm sure she wasn't meaning me. It sounds like she was just being Ashley, tired and wanting to move on."

"But what were his thoughts on that? If he wasn't ready to let go . . ."

"He sounds sincere. I think he's truly upset that she's dead but he doesn't have an alibi." She paused to give Molly a hand in standing up. "Do you think we could go to the Quilt Patch now?"

Molly took a quick look down at her clothes. "Why don't you help yourself to some coffee from the carafe—it's fairly fresh—and I'll just get myself ready."

Lizzie had just finished her second cup when Molly appeared wearing a denim shirt and a pale red cashmere sweater.

"I feel more like talking to those two now," Molly said, grabbing her handbag off the counter. "By the way, we're all set to use the band gazebo for a reading on Sunday afternoon. I thought maybe two to four would be good."

"Great news. I sent George Havers an email last night and asked if we could get a short announcement in Thursday's paper, maybe at the last minute. I called him with the news about the library event earlier this morning and once we're parked I'll send him this added information. Do you have any ideas for next week, in case we need them?"

Molly nodded. "What do you think about the big talent night that the Ashton Corners Service Club is putting on? It's a major fund-raiser for them and I don't see why authors can't be involved, doing readings. That's a talent."

"I think that's a great idea. I've only been to one of them and it was heavily into music, but I agree, writing is a talent and these authors are all performers. We've seen that."

"Good. I'll check with the club and see if the authors do indeed qualify. If so, we can talk to them about it."

Lizzie found a parking spot right in front of the Quilt

Patch. She took a few minutes to send George a message on her new iPhone. As they made their way inside, she wondered about a plan B in case their luck ran out.

She needn't have worried as they found Gigi alone in the dining room eating a late breakfast. Gigi looked pleased to see them and asked if they'd like some coffee. Lizzie momentarily thought about giving the coffee a pass but changed her mind when she smelled the fresh brew.

Gigi looked pert, her long blonde hair pulled back in a ponytail, wearing a black T-shirt with Italian cities written in bling and skinny jeans. Lizzie wondered how it would feel to be that thin.

"Do you mind if we ask you a few questions about Ashley?" Molly asked after they'd exchanged comments about activities around town.

"Not at all. It's sure sad, isn't it? I can't believe it's happened. I mean, it's one thing to write about murders but quite another to have someone you actually knew and had been talking to found murdered." Gigi punctuated her sentence with a shudder. "I also heard that, like, you're the main suspect." She stared straight at Lizzie, obviously wanting a response. Lizzie decided not to give her one.

"Did you know her well?" Lizzie asked, thinking back to their arrival at Molly's dinner on Friday. Lizzie hoped that meant Gigi knew something about Ashley's plans. Although Lizzie couldn't discount the fact that Gigi could have had plans of her own, namely to murder Ashley. The question was why.

"As well as you can with a basically email relationship. I'd met her at a couple of conferences but she's always too busy at those, what with all the authors and even some editors in town, and they're all wanting to see her. We did manage to mark out some time for a coffee at the Readers and Riters Festival last weekend. She was really nice to talk to."

"Hmm. Do you know anything about how she got along with the other authors?"

"I think they liked what she could do for them. She was like a cheerleader, you know, always up and always ready to support us and our books." Her look darkened. She opened her mouth to say something but then closed it again.

Lizzie jumped in, wondering what that look was about. "I bet her job was a bit trying at times, especially with four authors to attend to. I get the impression that Caroline and Lorelie can be very demanding at times."

Gigi stared at her for a moment before answering. "You've got that right. They each want all the attention because they've won some awards. Well, I'm up for two this year and although I didn't win last weekend, I've got a good chance at the other one. So Ashley and I spent a lot of time discussing promotional strategies. I think the others were miffed. At least Lorelie was downright catty about it." She sat back, a satisfied smile on her face.

Lizzie wondered if she felt like she'd put one over on the divas.

"You know," Gigi continued, "she did go over and above for me. I'm planning on a new series, which has been accepted by my editor, and the main characters are a family that runs a funeral home. Don't look so surprised," she said with a laugh. "My best friend's parents ran a funeral home and I spent a lot of time at her place. They lived above the funeral parlor and I guess I was being real ghoulish. Maybe that's how I got my interest in writing mysteries."

"Anyway, I thought I might combine this trip to Ashton Corners with some research. My setting is a small Southern town and this sounds about the right size, so I asked Ashley if she could set me up with an appointment at the White Haven Funeral Home." She glanced down at her hands, a dark expression on her face. When she looked back up, it had passed. "I wanted to talk to them and maybe spend a couple of days shadowing them."

Lizzie shuddered. Not her idea of a pleasant time. "And, did they agree?"

"Oh yes. They were quite thrilled, apparently. I was to have gone there on Monday, but having Ashley's body found there, that sort of put the kibosh on it. Oh my gosh, I wonder if she'd gone over there because of my story? Do you think that's it? I sure hate to think that. The owners are still pretty upset. I did stop by yesterday, though, and they answered a lot of my questions but I didn't really feel all that welcome. I hope to spend some more time before I leave town. I've taken ten days off from work to do some writing. I'd planned to go on to Mobile, maybe rent a room by the water, but I can write just as well here and I'll be close to the funeral home, too."

"When did Ashley set up this meeting?"

"Several weeks ago," Gigi said. "I googled Ashton Corners after getting the invitation to the book fair and I got all the details about the White Haven Funeral Home, then emailed Ashley to see if she could set something up. I thought it might sound more impressive if a publicist approached them first. Ashley said she'd be happy to help me in any way she could."

Lizzie gave it some thought. Ashley had contact with the funeral home and then her body was found there. Either there had to be a connection or else it was a very freaky coincidence. But did that mean Gigi was the killer? Nothing seemed amiss in their relationship. So far, anyway.

Lizzie realized that Molly was speaking.

"I hope that works out for you, dear." Molly finished off her coffee. "You don't happen to know if any of the other authors are around, do you? We wanted to let y'all know that we've arranged a reading event at the public library this Saturday from three to five, and on Sunday, another reading at the band gazebo in the town square from two to four, followed by dinner at my place."

Lizzie raised her eyebrows at the additional news about dinner but was pleased Molly had thought of it. More author time meant more question time.

"Gosh that's great. I'm really excited to hear that and I know the others will be, too. Caroline and Lorelie are off in their rooms writing and you know that's a no-go zone, if you want to keep all your limbs intact." She laughed as she said this. "I'm happy to fill them in on everything, though."

Lizzie asked, "You don't happen to know where A.J. is, do you?"

"No. I don't see much of him. I don't even know if he eats breakfast here. I do know he's out in his car most of the day, doing his own touring. I did ask if I could tag along but he refused; said it would interfere with his plans, whatever they are. I thought that was very rude of him actually."

They stood to leave. Lizzie asked, "One last thing. Did Ashley ever mention to you that she knew someone here in town?"

"Only you, and that was after dinner on Friday night. She was sure surprised to see you."

Lizzie cleared her throat. "So, she didn't say anything about planning to spend more time in Ashton Corners?"

"No. Wait a minute, she did say something when we went out for a bite on Sunday night." Gigi's face twisted into a look Lizzie couldn't quite peg. "What was it? Oh yes, how one person's secret can be another's pot of gold."

Paige Raleigh was already seated in their usual booth at Barney's when Lizzie arrived a bit after twelve thirty. A half-empty wineglass sat on the table but Lizzie knew it held tonic water. Paige just liked to have her sodas in wineglasses.

Lizzie pointed at it as she sat down. "Oops, I'm late, am I?"

"Not very. Only six minutes by my watch." She held up her glass. "But I was thirsty. Would you like some wine?" She waved the server over.

"I'll have the same as she's having," Lizzie said to the young girl dressed in black pants and a tailored pink shirt, with her hair in a ponytail. "Do you think she's playing hooky?" Lizzie asked Paige in a soft voice after the girl had wound her way through the tables toward the back.

Paige snickered. "I'll bet she's not a day under twenty-four. I, too, looked that young and innocent at one time, you may remember."

"Oh yeah. That was you." Lizzie sank back against the cushioned seat. It felt good to be spending time with Paige, her childhood friend and confidant. They'd been through a lot together over the years. In fact, it was Paige who helped Lizzie cope with her mama's illness when it first started creeping into their lives. Paige and Molly, of course. Lizzie counted herself truly blessed to have such close and caring friends.

"Now, tell me all about all this horrid stuff that's been happening," Paige said, tapping her fingers on Lizzie's hand.

"Well, you know the most of it. In a nutshell, Ashley is dead and I'm a primary suspect because of the argument that you saw and heard. Of course, the fact that I couldn't stand her counts, too."

"I cannot imagine how you kept it to only one argument after all that woman had put you through in college."

Lizzie smiled, grateful for the support. "Spoken like a true friend. And you know, I might have been able to hold myself in check if she hadn't mentioned Mark."

"What? She didn't!"

"Oh yes. She said words to the effect that he was good-looking and she was looking."

"I know you didn't do it, but if you had, it would have

been ruled justifiable homicide," Paige said, keeping her voice low.

Lizzie grimaced. "You do my spirits good, Paige Raleigh. We shouldn't be making light of such a horrific occurrence but I think I'll just start screaming if I don't keep it light."

Lizzie's drink arrived and after the server left with their orders, Paige said, "I know, sugar. *She who laughs, lasts . . .* right? So she was here because of the authors?"

"That's right but Ashley did say she might be spending more time in Ashton Corners but I don't know why. No one here seems to know her, so what could be her interest in the town?"

Paige was thoughtful a few seconds. "Does Mark have any other suspects lined up?"

"He's being very careful of appearances. He doesn't want anyone pointing a finger later and saying I got special treatment. So, he's not really sharing too much information, either. Except to say none of the authors have solid alibis."

"Well, that's something, isn't it?" Paige paused again when their orders arrived.

She had a taste of her veggie chili while Lizzie tried to decide where to start with her roasted sweet potato salad.

"Oh, this is divine. I so love the food here," Paige finally said after several mouthfuls. "Look, Lizzie, is there anything I can do? I mean, I'm not much of a sleuth and you've got the book club doing that part, if I'm guessing right. But you know you can count on me for anything. Just ask."

"Thanks, Paige. I know and, believe me, I will if there's something I think you can help with." She tasted the arugula on her plate. "This lime vinaigrette is so yummy. Let's not ruin the meal with more talk of murder. Tell me about my two favorite munchkins."

"Well, Jenna is playing the role of big sister to the hilt, being in kindergarten and all. And Cate demanded her own school pack and supplies. She pulls them out and sorts through the paper, crayons and colored pencils while Jenna does her 'homework.' "

"I love it."

"Why don't you come over for dinner sometime on the weekend? Maybe you could help them both with their homework."

Lizzie laughed. "I'd love to but we've got some events lined up for the authors to keep them from getting too antsy and wanting to leave town. Once this all settles down, it's a date." *If it does settle down.*

Paige kicked her under the table. "I can read your thoughts you know. Stop it right now. It's going to turn out just fine. I truly believe that Mark will not let anything bad happen to you."

Lizzie sighed. She really did believe that, too. But was it enough?

Chapter Eighteen

◇◇◇

Waking is like rising from the dead. The slow climb
out of sleep, shapes appearing out of blackness, the
alarm clock ringing like the last trumpet.

THE CROSSING PLACES—ELLY GRIFFITHS

Lizzie woke with a headache the next morning. She knew
immediately what had caused it. The late-night phone
call from Caroline Cummings. She thought back through
what Caroline had said, wondering if it would be useful.
She could hear Caroline's sugary voice telling her about yet
another argument she'd overheard between Lorelie and Ashley. One that had happened this past weekend.

"That Lorelie likes to appear all sweet and sugary but,
you know, deep down she has a mean streak," Caroline had
said. "Why, she tore a strip off Ashley for one tiny little
mistake she'd made and not only that, she threatened her."

"Exactly when did this happen?"

"Why, it was Sunday just after supper. Carter and I had
just gotten back to the Quilt Patch and came upon Lorelie
and Ashley out on the front porch. Lorelie had worked herself into a good one. I think the entire neighborhood heard

her. After which, her royal highness stomped off down the street and Ashley went up to her room."

"What was the mistake?" Lizzie asked.

"Ashley, who really was overworked taking care of so many of us, forgot to send in copies of Lorelie's book to the Cozy Lovers awards this year. You'd think that Lorelie had missed trying on the glass slipper or something, the way she carried on."

"What did Ashley say?"

"Well, I must admit, she added fuel to the fire with her attitude, but that's what Lorelie does, she brings out the stubbornness in people."

"But what words did Ashley use?" Lizzie was starting to get annoyed and she was so tired on top of it. She had little patience for another diva episode.

"Well," Lizzie could tell Caroline would be enjoying repeating the next part, "she said she had more important things on her plate than pandering to a diva's ego. She actually called her a diva." Caroline snorted. "Lorelie looked like she'd split her corset. She sputtered and told Ashley in no uncertain terms that she'd regret what she'd just said and what she hadn't done."

Lizzie had found it hard to fall asleep after the call. She'd wondered if this was tit for tat. Maybe Caroline had learned about the earlier call outing her own argument with Ashley. Lizzie finally fell asleep wondering just what made the divas tick.

She willed herself to get out of bed and she headed straight for the shower. No run this morning although it would do her a world of good. She knew she needed to make a list. It's what would save her sanity and stop her from thinking about not having a job and not hearing from Mark. In fact, she'd make two lists: one with suspects, motives and opportunities; the other, a to-do list for the day.

As she dressed she thought about the evening ahead, looking forward to the monthly meeting of the Ashton Corners Mystery Readers and Cheese Straws Society. Tonight they'd be discussing Bob's choice, *Shoot the Dog* by Brad Smith. She'd finished reading it a couple of weeks ago and was extremely relieved that it didn't live up to its title. She wanted to give it a quick perusal at some point during the day.

After fixing her first espresso of the morning, she grabbed the new issue of the *Ashton Corners Colonist* out of her mailbox and spread it open on the table. Just as promised, George had put in a short note about the authors remaining in town a little while longer and the two events that had been planned.

Lizzie felt like she was on a Ferris wheel, unable to get off. Had one of the authors indeed murdered Ashley? It was apparent nobody was likely to confess. She wondered if they could trick the murderer into it, but first, they'd have to know just who it was. It had to be one of the authors. Who else knew Ashley? Maybe that elusive person that Ashley had known in town. But what if they never found out that person's name?

She needed to talk to Mark, to see him face-to-face, to help settle the panic that lay just below the surface. Maybe she could use Patchett as bait. Offer to walk him and suggest Mark join them, for a short while anyway.

The phone rang as she eyed the espresso maker. It sure felt like a three-cup day. Sally-Jo's excited voice greeted her when she answered.

"You'll never guess what the staff is doing," Sally-Jo jumped right in without a greeting.

"Probably not, but by the sound of your voice, it should be good."

"It is. They're passing around a petition to get you back on the job. Most of the staff members have signed and now they're inviting your students' parents to join in. Isn't that just great? Benton can't possibly keep you out of the school when he sees how in demand your skills are. They've already sent a copy to the superintendent and to the entire school board."

"I'm speechless," Lizzie said, feeling deeply moved. "Who thought this up? Wait, it was you, wasn't it?"

"Of course. Benton is being such a turkey and there's absolutely no reason you should be treated this way. We need you back here and I think you need to get back to work, too. Or are you having too good a time sleuthing? What's the latest, by the way?"

"Molly and I will tell you all about it tonight at book club. Back to the petition, dare I ask who didn't sign? No, don't tell me. I think I can guess the woman, teaches fifth grade, very opinionated and doesn't take kindly to advice."

"You got it. I think she doesn't want you back because she's gotten you out of her hair and can just do dipsy-doodle about the reading schedule you set up. Or maybe, she's in cahoots with Benton and they're trying to take command of the system."

"Umm, conspiracy theory. Maybe not so. But I do really appreciate it."

"Well, let me know when the old goat calls you and make sure he goes down on bended knee."

Lizzie laughed. "He's not proposing. I hope. Well, just in case this works, I'd better get going on a few of these things on my to-do list." She glanced at it and shook her head. Pitiful as it was.

"Great. I'll see you tonight but I'm hoping to hear from you sooner."

The call spurred Lizzie into action. She'd head on over to Mark's house to rescue Patchett from a day spent indoors.

In the meantime, she'd let her subconscious play around with the suspects list. She knew she was being too emotional about this, since she was at the top of the list, so maybe a little distance would help put things into perspective. She didn't expect the murderer's name to suddenly start flashing but a little illumination would help.

Mark wasn't in his office, so Lizzie sent him a text once she'd arrived at his house. She heard Patchett's plaintive yowl as she inserted the key into the back door. He came waddling over to her but stopped at her command and stared at her, large dark eyes pleading, large pink tongue hanging out of his mouth.

"You are so pathetic looking, Patchett," Lizzie said. "No wonder you wrap us all around your big paw."

She snapped his lead on and had just locked the door behind them when Mark pulled into the driveway. He parked behind Lizzie and sat looking at them a couple of seconds before getting out.

Lizzie wished she'd taken time to get a bit more presentable. She wondered how she looked. That part she hadn't thought through. Just see Mark, talk to him and find out what's what.

He reached them and first of all patted Patchett behind the ears, then gave Lizzie a big hug followed by an equally deep kiss. Her toes did the tingly thing and she felt her world click back into place.

"It's good to see my gal with my best pal," he whispered in her ear.

She pulled back, a mock look of hurt on her face. "And here I thought I was your best pal."

He laughed. "Always. But a guy's got to have the four-legged kind, too. Thanks for thinking of him. I'm afraid his walks have been infrequent these past few days."

"It's not entirely altruistic," Lizzie admitted. "I miss seeing you and, just as important, I need to know what's going on. I feel like I'm going to burst at times."

Mark sighed. "Let's start walking and we'll talk."

They followed the street to the end and turned toward the high school. They were well along the path that worked its way to the river by the time Mark spoke.

"I sent Yost up to Crawther Publishing in New York to talk to some of Ashley Dixon's coworkers and her boss. Nobody pointed the finger at anyone else. She seemed to have a good working relationship with everyone, even with Nick Jennings, her ex-fiancé. Her boss was surprised that she wanted to join these authors here in Ashton Corners and at first said no. But she did tell him she had some business from the past to settle, so would take it as holiday time and still help out the authors while here."

Lizzie looked at Mark. His face had clouded over as he said the last bit. "You think she meant me? That business about the past?"

He shrugged. "I don't know, Lizzie. I haven't been able to find any other connections here in town."

"Even if that's true, 'settling' things doesn't have to be a negative thing. I mean, she wanted to be friendly but I doubt she'd come here just to do that. Besides, she was as surprised to see me as I was her. She may, as she told me, have wanted to patch things up, at least to the point where we could coexist with a certain amount of civility. And if that were so, why? I'm not the reason she'd be spending time in Ashton Corners." Lizzie shook off memories of Ashley's interest in Mark. "Remember, she said that's what she'd be doing in the future."

"I'm not forgetting, Lizzie." Mark sounded exasperated. "But it's just that I'm not coming up with a reason for her being here, other than the book event."

"What about her car? She had a rental, a bright orange convertible."

"We've taken a look through the car, which was parked in the lot at the funeral home, and there's nothing suspicious in it."

"So, do you think she went there intentionally to meet her killer?"

"That could be. Or else she was followed, but if that's the case, we still don't know why she went there."

"You know, Ashley had arranged for Gigi Briggs to spend some time at White Haven Funeral Home doing research."

"I do know that, Lizzie. It's part of Ms. Briggs's statement. Where are you going with this?" Mark stopped to watch Patchett suddenly chase a squirrel.

Lizzie stopped beside him. "Well, don't you think it's odd that Ashley set that up and then her body is found out there?"

"You know I don't believe in coincidences. We are checking out all possible angles."

Lizzie nodded. "But what if something went wrong with it all? Maybe the funeral home backed out at the last minute or something and Gigi got all angry, killing Ashley in a fit of rage? And what better place to leave her body than at the funeral home?"

"I have talked to the owners and they said Ms. Dixon stopped by to see them over a month ago and made the arrangements. Gigi Briggs confirmed an appointment with them by email a couple of weeks ago and they hadn't heard from or seen either of them until the body was found. But even if the deal had gone south, I think Briggs would be smart enough to realize Dixon might be able to set up something elsewhere, so why kill her? Seems to me it wasn't a once-in-a-lifetime opportunity."

Mark put his hand on Lizzie's elbow and gently steered her toward home.

"Hmm. I guess not," Lizzie agreed. "But that means Ashley had already spent time in town. I wonder who all she saw? Any indications?"

"Not aside from her visit to the funeral home."

"Hmm. Can't you tell from the GPS in her rental car or something just where she traveled in it? That might give you an idea as to what her other reason was."

"You've been watching too much TV. We've got the mileage and she obviously put some miles on it, but there's no way to know where she went. Look, try not to worry about it. I'll keep looking, you know that."

Lizzie sighed but not too loudly. "By the way, we've arranged two events for the authors," she said and explained the details.

"Glad to hear that. I'm sure they won't keep asking me when they can leave, until next week anyway."

They walked in silence for a few minutes. Lizzie felt both hope and despair at the same time. Mark wouldn't give up on her but the future did look bleak. If she couldn't find the murderer, at least she could try to find out Ashley's connection to the town.

That gave her a bit of a lift as she and Mark parted ways back at his house.

At the meeting on Thursday night, Bob kept trying to get them all settled and talking about the book he'd chosen, rather than socializing around the food.

"I'd say the sooner we settle down and talk about this here book, which I might remind you is what we do as the Ashton Corners Mystery Readers and Cheese Straws Society, the sooner we can get onto the important part of the meeting and try to solve Lizzie's problem," he finally said, exasperation making his voice much higher pitched than usual.

"Just calm yourself down, Bob," Molly said, thrusting a plate of cheese straws at him, "or you'll soon be asked to join Lizzie's choir, as a soprano."

The others laughed and Bob soon joined in. "All right, you've got yourself a point there, Molly. But so do I. Now then, I call this here book club meeting to order." He looked over at Molly. "I can do that, can't I?"

She nodded and sipped her tea. Everyone took their seats and waited for him to continue.

Lizzie let her gaze wander around the library, one of her favorite rooms in Molly's house. She didn't let her attention wander during her literacy classes held in the same room. But for now, she could enjoy the feel of old-world charm afforded by the three walls covered with dark oak bookcases. Two settees faced each other across an Oriental carpet, and three club chairs upholstered in burgundy velvet had been pulled up to either end. The elegance of the room was highlighted by brocade beige drapes, which were still open despite the fading light outside, and the sprawling lawn at the side of the house was visible through the large picture window.

"I first of all want to thank Stephanie for putting me onto this here book. I'd been looking for a new police procedural and she pulled this one off the shelves and said I oughta give it a try even though it wasn't exactly what I had in mind. So, I did and I'm here to say, I'm going to read everything else the boy has put out. Okay, so what did y'all think about it?" Bob wanted to know. He eagerly searched the faces of everyone in the room.

Stephanie checked to make sure no one else was starting to speak, then said, "I know it isn't a police procedural." She smiled at Bob, looking apologetic. "But we do see the investigation through the eyes of the female police officer, Claire, at least part of the time. And what I like most about it is the details. I grew up in farming country and Brad Smith has sure got it right. I also really, really like Virgil Cain."

Lizzie agreed. "There's something really appealing about Virgil Cain, which is what we want in a main protagonist. He's his own man, knows what's important in his life and isn't about to let his head get turned around by what's going on in the movie world."

"He also sounds really, really sexy in a quiet way," Stephanie jumped in.

Lizzie laughed. "I do agree. It's also a good mystery. I didn't figure out who the killer was, although I'm not surprised by the ending."

"Oh yeah. No way I got it," Andie agreed. "But I think it was, like, way too slow moving." She shrugged and looked around at the others.

After another twenty minutes of lively talk, Molly finally entered the conversation. "I'd like to thank you, Bob, for suggesting a book that brought about so much discussion. That's what this group is about, that's for sure."

Bob beamed. "Well, you're most welcome. Now come on, Molly, tell us what you thought about it?"

She took a moment before answering, as if carefully choosing her words. "I must say, Agatha Christie it is not, but I did enjoy reading it. Maybe a tad too much language for my tastes but even those parts did belong in the book, I have to admit. And I, too"—she looked over at Stephanie then Lizzie—"thought Mr. Virgil Cain to be most intriguing. Now, next month belongs to Jacob. Do you have a title chosen already?"

"I sure do. It's *Junkyard Dogs* by Craig Johnson. I thought it was time to introduce everyone to a Western style of police procedural."

"I look forward to it, Jacob." She smiled, although it looked a bit strained. "Now, may I refresh anyone's tea before we get on to the business of the murder?"

Andie jumped up and grabbed the pitcher of tea and started pouring before Molly had a chance. Molly passed along the plates of cheese straws and pecan squares.

"Can I just mention the book I'm picking for December?" Lizzie asked. "Just in case any of you want to get a jump on reading."

"Go for it," Jacob said, taking a bite of a cheese straw.

"It's *Scandal in Skibbereen* by Sheila Connolly. And before you start groaning, Bob, it is a cozy but it has a bit of an edge to it. And besides, we'll have just finished two somewhat gritty books in a row."

Bob nodded. "Wasn't going to say a word, Lizzie. Except if maybe you'd said it was by Agatha Christie." He glanced at Molly and winked.

"Huh," was all Molly said. She glanced around the room. "By the way, Lizzie and I wanted to share with you what we've been doing."

"You've been detecting?" Andie asked, sounded excited.

"What I meant was that Chief Dreyfus asked if we could arrange some events to keep the authors busy and maybe they wouldn't be so anxious to leave town. So we did. Lizzie, do you want to talk about it?"

Lizzie nodded. "Happy to. We've got a reading and signing event at the library on Saturday afternoon, three to five, and I'll be in charge of the book table since Stephanie will be in the store. Andie, do you think you could give me a hand? Or do you have plans?"

Andie had just taken a bite of a cheese straw and chewed quickly before answering. "I can do that. It'll be fun."

"Good. Now, the next event will be on Sunday afternoon at the band gazebo in the town square from two to four.

Molly was able to clear it with the city and the weather report sounds good, so it should be a good opportunity to sell books, too."

"I can sell at that, for sure," Stephanie said.

"Me, too," Andie agreed.

"How will we get the word out?" Jacob asked.

"I gather you didn't read your *Colonist* this morning," Molly said with a stern shake of her head, all the while trying to suppress a smile. "We managed to get George Havers to put a small item in about them both."

"And the library is sending out the word on its own system. I've also submitted a public service announcement to the radio station."

"You ladies are marketing dynamos," Jacob said, approval in his voice.

"And, there's more," Molly added. "Just in case we need to keep them here awhile longer, Lizzie and I talked it over and I looked into entering them in the talent show the Ashton Corners Service Club is holding on the following Wednesday. I haven't mentioned it to the authors yet. What do y'all think?"

"You think they'd fit in?" Bob asked. "Last year there were singers and piano players, even old Mort Hanson on his accordion."

"You're right about last year," Molly agreed, "but I saw that this year somebody from the community center drama club is doing a recitation and there's even a potter who'll demonstrate and talk about making pottery. I think some readings sprinkled throughout would work just fine. The lineup seems a bit short this year. And we can really push the publicity angle when telling the authors about it." She looked expectantly from one to the other. "I did check with the service club and they were quite pleased with the suggestion. Something new, they said."

"I think it's a great idea," Lizzie agreed. "We can at least give it a try."

They all looked at Bob who finally nodded.

"That's all well and good," he said, "and I do mean that but it seems to me our most pressing question is who or what was the reason Ashley Dixon was planning to spend more time in town? I think it's great that you've come up with all this, but the authors will start getting antsy at some point and if Dreyfus hasn't found anything incriminating about any of them, they'll be out of here. It still seems to me that one of them is the best bet for being the killer since they're the only ones who really knew her. So we need to get serious about this. Time's a-wasting. Now, I've been asking around and no one seems to have known her, or will admit to it."

Molly agreed. "I, too, have been asking and no one knows her name or has even met her. Seems she didn't talk to many townspeople, just those involved with the fair."

"But there's got to be something more," Lizzie said, exasperated. "Was she buying some property?"

"I thought of that," said Jacob, "and couldn't come up with anything in the land registry. I even made some calls to local real estate agents and nobody had spoken to her."

"Somewhere, someone knows something," Sally-Jo said. "We just have to find that missing link."

"Well, I checked for anything to do with Ashley Dixon on the Internet and there was a lot of business connections, like LinkedIn and such. She's on Twitter and Facebook, too. But I couldn't find anything to do with Ashton Corners." Andie pulled a notebook out of her backpack. "But I gotta tell ya, these authors really know how to use social media. Except for maybe A.J. Pruitt. He's got a Facebook page but he doesn't do much with it, same with his website. Gigi Briggs is on everything imaginable. You should see what she's doing on Pinterest. And the other two are pretty good also. Lots of stuff the fans eat up on anything they're on."

"Sounds nice for them but you haven't said anything about anything incriminating," Bob said kindly.

Andie pouted. "That's because I couldn't find anything. You were right, Jacob. No messages about planning a murder or even anything mean, although Lorelie Oliver did say at one point"—Andie looked down at her iPad and read from the page—"*I've been at the writing business for a long time now and while I love my publisher I have to say, this social media is really important and plays the biggest role in getting out to all you fans. I don't think their publicity department can touch it. Or maybe it's just the current personnel.*"

Andie stopped reading. "In other words, she wasn't a happy camper."

Chapter Nineteen

◈◈◈

"I'll make us some coffee." she said. "It will keep us
alert. We need a plan of action."

WARNING AT ONE—ANN PURSER

Lizzie tried to get on with her to-do list the next morning
but she kept an ear peeled for the phone, hoping the
principal would be calling to invite her back to work. By
noon she'd given up hope that would happen. Maybe
Sally-Jo's confidence was misplaced. Lizzie almost wished
she hadn't known about the petition. At least she wouldn't
be obsessing about it all day.

She was just about to sit down to a lunch of granola and
sliced peaches when the front doorbell rang. Lizzie looked
through the peephole and saw Lavenia Ellis, the lady friend
of her landlord, Nathaniel Creely, looking upset.

"Lavenia, please come in," Lizzie said as she pulled the
door open.

"I'm so sorry to just drop in like this, Lizzie, but I need
to talk to you and it really isn't something to discuss over
the phone." Lavenia had shoulder-length gray hair and gentle

curves from her face to her feet. She wore a long-sleeved pullover in muted rose and pink tones with tailored denim pants. *Yet another elegant aging Southern lady.*

"It's not a problem. Come in and have a seat. May I get you some tea—hot or iced?"

Lavenia took a deep breath. "Yes, some hot tea might be calming. I could use that right now."

Lizzie was back in a flash with a cup for them each. Lavenia took milk but passed on the sugar. She picked up her cup but put it back down immediately and sat wringing her hands.

"I can see you're upset," Lizzie finally said when it looked like Lavenia was having trouble getting started. "What can I do to help you?"

Lavenia sighed. "It's Nathaniel." She put out her hand to reassure Lizzie. "No, he's not ill or anything. It's just that I've been receiving some phone calls."

Uh-oh. Not more phone calls. Lizzie flashed back quickly to the late-night calls she'd received about her daddy not too long ago, calls that had put her on a trail of a killer, and then more recently, querying calls from the women of Ashton Corners about visiting and newly deceased author Derek Alton's phantom new book.

"What are these calls about?" Lizzie asked.

"Well, it really started with an email a few weeks ago. It said that Nathaniel had murdered his first wife."

"What?" Lizzie couldn't have been more stunned if she'd been told that Nathaniel was a serial killer. "That's utter nonsense. Nathaniel wouldn't hurt a fly."

"I know. And," Lavenia said quickly, "I don't believe it, not for one minute. But if someone's telling me this, I'm worried she'll soon pass it around. I mean, why else start that rumor if not to get Nathaniel in trouble? I'm so worried about what it will do to him when he hears."

"You haven't told him."

"I daren't."

"Good idea." Lizzie thought a moment. "Did you keep the email?"

"Yes. I really wanted to destroy it but I thought I should hang on to it, just in case." She shrugged. "I don't really know why."

"That's good, though. Will you forward it to me?"

"All right."

"And there were calls, too? Can you tell me anything about the voice?"

"It's a woman with a very high-pitched voice but I'd say she was doing that to disguise it. I don't recognize it at all."

"How many calls and what exactly did she say?"

"First time she said she was calling with some friendly advice and that I'd better watch myself if I didn't want to end up like Nathaniel's first wife. That was all. It was a couple of weeks ago. Then about three nights later, she called and said he'd murdered his wife and I was being foolish not breaking up with him."

"Any other calls?"

"Yes, last night. She said since I wasn't taking it to heart and obviously not concerned about my well-being, she'd be forced to tell the town and make sure he hurt no one else. I'd tried to put it down as a crank caller, for whatever reason. But last night, I got scared. If that story gets out, it will crush Nathaniel. I know it's not true but you know how rumors linger on and there's always a taint on the person."

Lizzie nodded, feeling miserable. Who would do such a thing to Nathaniel? He was the kindest, most gentle man she knew, truly a Southern gentleman. She knew he'd never do anything to hurt anyone, so why would anyone want to hurt him?

"What do you want me to do, Lavenia? Tell Nathaniel about it?"

"No . . . no. I'm hoping we can resolve this without his knowing. Can you talk to your friend, the police chief, and see what he says?"

"Of course," Lizzie agreed, knowing there wouldn't be much Mark could do at this point. "Do you have caller ID?"

She nodded. "The identity was blocked."

"What about the email? There must have been an address in the from-box."

"It looked like any other spam email I get."

"I wonder why this is all happening at this time? Is there anything that's different lately?" She wanted to ask if they'd made any announcement, say, an engagement or something that would have triggered the viperous tongue. "Something that's drawn attention to you two?" A better way of putting it.

Lavenia took another sip of tea and thought for a few minutes before answering. "Not that I can think of."

"Think back. Where had you two been just before you received the email?"

"I'd have to look at my diary to be certain but I think it's probably the Ashton Corners Garden Club meeting at the public library. That's the first Monday of every month." She nodded. "Yes, that was probably around about then because I was checking for the minutes from the meeting. I was supposed to do something and I'd forgotten what it was." She shook her head. "It happens far too often as you get older, Lizzie. But I didn't want to have to ask anyone, so I checked every day for the minutes." She stared at her teacup for a few moments. "Do you think that's significant? We go to the same meeting every month, though. So why now?"

But does everyone else? Lizzie wondered. She didn't want to pursue that line with Lavenia and make her suspicious of her cohorts, especially if it turned into a dead end.

"Who runs the group?"

"Oh, there's a proper executive. Ethel Lee, the assistant librarian, is the president this year. Why do you ask? Do you think there's a connection?"

Lizzie shook her head sort of noncommittally. "Just grasping at straws. Has anything unusual happened in Nathaniel's life lately?" As she asked, Lizzie realized just how little she'd spoken to her friend in the past few months. She'd been so busy with back to school, and since Lavenia had entered his life, Nathaniel had little time to spare. Lizzie regretted it but she was also happy he had found someone so warm and obviously caring.

"Not really," Lavenia said, giving the question some thought. "We seem to be quite busy but there hasn't been anything unusual. And he hasn't mentioned anything, either." She glanced at her watch. "Oh dear. I should be going. Nathaniel is at a doctor's appointment and I thought it would be a good time to pop by. I don't want him to know I've been here, all right?"

"Sure. I won't mention anything about all this to him. I'll get back to you if I find out anything."

"Thank you so much, Lizzie." Lavenia's eyes glistened with tears. "I just can't believe anyone would be so cruel to Nathaniel."

Lizzie couldn't believe it, either. She thought through their conversation but wasn't sure what her next move should be. She debated about telling Mark but felt there wasn't much he could do at this stage. Also, she didn't want to even hint at the possibility that Nathaniel had committed such a deed. She knew it wasn't true but she also knew that Mark was a cop. What she didn't know was whether he'd feel he had to look into the matter of Mrs. Creely's death. No, she'd hold off telling Mark, for now, until it escalated, which she hoped with all her heart it wouldn't. A better alternative was to contact Ethel Lee and see if there had been any change in dynamics at the Ashton Corners Garden Club. Silly to believe there was a connection but you never knew.

Lizzie glanced at the phone. No, she couldn't stay in and just wait for her own phone call that would never come. She grabbed her bag and headed for the library. She would check with Ethel and at the same time, return a book on literacy that a colleague had suggested she read.

L izzie stuck the key in the car ignition and glanced to her right.

"Yikes."

She sat back in her seat and just stared, not actually computing what she was looking at. Finally, she reached over to clear away the broken glass on the front passenger seat. And stopped. Someone had broken her car window. Probably overnight. She glanced around inside the car. The radio hadn't been touched. That was the most valuable item. She didn't think there was anything worth stealing. She stopped herself from opening the glove compartment. Fingerprints. Cops.

She shakily pulled her new iPhone out of her purse and punched in the police station number, asking for Mark when the desk constable answered. While waiting for him to pick up, she got out of the car and walked around to the side. Only a few chunks of glass lay on the ground but nothing incriminating, like a hammer or a wallet that had fallen out of the person's pocket. *As if.* When Mark came on the line she quickly filled him in on what had happened.

"If a murder hadn't just happened that ties in to you, I'd probably assume it was vandals and tell you to just go ahead and get it fixed after checking with your insurer. The deductible will probably be higher than the replacement cost, though.

But because of all that's been happening, I think we'll check this out. I'm coming over. Don't touch anything."

She continued inspecting the outside of the car while she waited for him to arrive. By the time his Jeep pulled up out front, she'd taken to sitting on the front porch, trying to relax.

He leaned over and gave her a quick kiss on the forehead. "Did you notice if anything's missing?"

"The radio's still there and I can't think of anything else anyone would want to take. I didn't open the glove compartment."

Mark nodded and walked over to the car. He took a quick look at the outside, pulled on gloves and slid into the driver's seat as a police cruiser pulled up behind his Jeep. Lizzie nodded at Officer Yost as he walked up the driveway.

She stood and stretched, then eased over to the car, trying to hear their conversation. Mark looked at her as he slowly emptied the glove compartment. "Everything here that should be?"

Lizzie looked over the small pile of articles on the dashboard. City map. Mazda manual. Hand wipes. Flashlight. Tire gauge. It was all there.

Next he did the same routine with the compartment between the two seats.

"Coins," Lizzie said. "I keep a bit of loose change in a small change purse. It's just a cheap cloth thing I bought at the Alexander Craft Fair and I only keep a couple of dollars in it. That's missing. It's not much of a take for doing so much damage. Oh boy, what a mess."

Mark stood and watched as Yost finished putting his fingerprinting kit away. Yost then bent over again and started picking up the larger pieces of glass, dropping them in a plastic bag he'd pulled out of his pocket.

"Evidence?" Lizzie asked.

"Tidiness," Yost answered with a quick smile.

His hand moved from the floor mats to under the passenger seat. He glanced quickly at Lizzie before pulling out a cell phone. "Found this, boss."

Mark looked at Lizzie. "It's not yours, I assume?"

She shook her head. "I've never seen it before. Do you think the thief dropped it by accident?"

"It was under the seat," Yost answered. "It wouldn't have just fallen there."

"Do you think someone planted it there? But why? Does it have anything to do with my cell phone? Who does it belong to?"

Mark nodded at Yost, who slipped the phone into a plastic bag.

"We'll check it out, Lizzie. I'd bet it's tied in some way to the murder. Now, I suggest you drive on over to Quick Fix Glass Shop on Highway 2 and they'll replace the window right quick. Remember to check with your insurer first, though."

Lizzie nodded, still a bit stunned. He gave her a quick hug and left with Yost pulling out behind him.

Lizzie pulled into the parking lot at the public library a little after noon. The new window sparkled as Lizzie walked around the car, yet again, checking it out. She was pleased it looked just like new, like nothing had happened. *If only.* She gave Mark a quick call to let him know.

She was smiling as she climbed the stairs to the front door of the library. She spotted Ethel Lee in the far corner, right in the middle of the travel section, talking to a couple of high school girls. Fortunately, Isabel Fox sat behind the librarian's desk. Lizzie slipped her book into the returns slot on the way over. She still felt a bit rattled after her morning adventure with the smashed window but she tried to concentrate on her reason for being at the library.

"It's so nice to see you, Lizzie. How did the rest of the weekend go?" Isabel asked.

"The weekend itself was a success but the day after, a disaster. Did you hear about Ashley Dixon, the publicist, being murdered?"

Isabel nodded. "I did. That's so sad. She was such a pretty young thing. Do the police know what happened?"

"The police are still investigating." Lizzie didn't want to share the fact that she was at the top of the suspect list in case Isabel hadn't heard. Better to change the topic. "I wanted to talk to Ethel Lee but it looks like she's busy."

"She's just filling our new pages in on their duties. It's part of their community volunteer credits. She shouldn't be much longer. What's your book club reading next?"

"We just had a meeting last night and Bob Miller's choice was *Shoot the Dog* by Brad Smith. I think it's one of the first meetings we've had a general agreement about the book. Usually Bob's reading taste is strictly for police procedurals while Molly is an Agatha Christie fan."

Isabel chuckled. "More like fanatic . . . but don't tell her I said that."

Lizzie smiled conspiratorially. "Next month we're reading *Junkyard Dogs* by Craig Johnson. Seems like we're going with a theme these days."

"I've read that. In fact, I've read all ten books in the series. This one's about halfway along. I'll just bet you haven't read any, though, so this will give you a good taste of Johnson's writing style. He manages to mix humor with crime and some very poignant moments. Have you watched the TV series based on the books?"

Lizzie shook her head.

"Good. Be sure to read the books first."

"I may just use your description at book club if I can't think of anything on my own to say. If you don't mind, of course."

Isabel laughed, a soft chuckle that Lizzie remembered so well from her early teen years spent in the library, cozying up with a good book while her mama's friends were at the house helping to put things in order. After a moment Isabel said, "Looks like Ms. Lee is finished." She waved to get her attention.

Ethel joined them and switched places with Isabel, who gave Lizzie a quick hug and went into a back room. She looked pleased to see Lizzie. "Someone was in and mentioned you several weeks ago. I don't usually remember these things but when I saw her picture yesterday, it came back. Such a horrible thing, to be killed and stuffed into a coffin." She shook her head and rested her arms on the desktop.

"Ashley Dixon was in here?" Lizzie asked in surprise.

"Why yes. It was early last month. A Friday. I remember because it was a really busy day here. We had a school group in and an inspection by the fire department. Everything happening at once. Ms. Dixon said she was down here setting up a meeting and doing some research. We got to talking about the town and she recalled knowing you in college."

"That's right." Lizzie wasn't about to go into any details. "Did she mention any specifics about the meeting or what she was researching?"

"Well, she spent several hours in here going through our files of old *Ashton Corners Colonist*s. We're still pretty basic here and have back issues bound in big red covers. Nothing as updated as fiche or even digitized. The ones she wanted were fairly old."

Lizzie couldn't imagine what would spark Ashley's interest in the *Colonist* unless it was local news. Maybe a clue as to what her future intentions were. "Did she say what she was looking for?"

"No. I asked but she didn't share. She did ask if I'd ever been to the Huxton Hotel, though, but didn't elaborate. I told her I'd been to their dining room many times and also attended a few weddings there, too. In the past, it was always the first choice for anything major going on, like a reception or a cotillion." She smiled. "In fact, my own coming-out party was held there. I won't mention how many years ago that was."

"I'll bet it was quite wonderful." Lizzie thought back to the last time she'd visited the hotel. She'd been a teenager, and although she'd been impressed, she hadn't spent much time thinking about the hotel's past.

"Oh, it was. All the beautiful ball gowns. Mine was white satin with lots of crinolines helping me float along. And the flowers. My daddy and mama had ordered in every white gardenia they could get their hands on." She laughed and added, "But that's not what you want to talk about." She straightened. "But back to Ms. Dixon, that's all I remember from that day. She had left by the time I came back out on the floor late in the afternoon."

"Well, that's certainly interesting. Do you have a record of what dates in particular she checked?"

"No, but I remember she did ask for the files from 1982 to 1984."

"Do you think I could take a look at them?"

Ethel looked at Lizzie, her face filled with curiosity. Lizzie thought she deserved an explanation.

"I want to see if she found anything significant in them."

"How will you know what that is?"

Lizzie shrugged. "I'm not really sure. Just hopeful."

"And what do you think this significant information will tell you?"

"Well, for starters, why she was planning to spend time in Ashton Corners, which is what she'd told me. And if I'm lucky, maybe something that will lead to the identity of her murderer."

"Oh dear," said Ethel, looking distressed. "Shouldn't the police be doing this in that case?"

"Don't worry. I'll be sure to tell Chief Dreyfus all about what I find, if anything."

Ethel thought about it for a minute. "All right then, follow me."

As they were walking to the back of the library Lizzie said, "What I'd really wanted to talk to you about, though, is the Ashton Corners Garden Club, if you can spare a few minutes."

"Happy to. What did you want to know?"

Lizzie paused, wondering just how to put it. She should have thought it through more thoroughly, she realized. She didn't want to blurt out anything about the phone calls.

"I know that both Nathaniel Creely and Lavenia Ellis are members," she started.

"Oh yes, they are and isn't it so sweet? We have a romance right in our midst."

Lizzie smiled. *Great opening.* "It is great. Nathaniel is my landlord and it's wonderful to see him so happy. I think it's such a dreamy story. Are there any other blossoming romances in your group?"

"Why? Are you thinking of joining?" Ethel laughed. "I can tell you right now to set your sights elsewhere. They're all a bit too old for you, darlin', but I will tell you that several women have had their eyes on Nathaniel for some time now." She leaned toward Lizzie, really getting into it. "We have one bachelor but I think he's far too set in his ways. None of the ladies have kept the pursuit going after a date or two."

"Sounds like the garden club is dating central in town," Lizzie said with a chuckle.

"Oh, they are all serious about their flora and fauna, believe you me, but when you get to be a certain age there are only so many venues to find eligible men."

"I'd say that applies to anyone out of high school."

Ethel laughed. "You may be right."

Lizzie decided that by asking for the names of the other women interested in Nathaniel she might be setting off alarms. She'd find another way around it. The membership list must be published somewhere or else she'd just ask Lavenia for a copy and see who might have been away or recently returned. Like at the beginning of the fall session.

They had reached a small room off the reference section. Ethel indicated a large table near the window. "You just take a seat and I'll bring those newspapers right over."

By the time she'd finished reading through all the relevant issues of the *Ashton Corners Colonist*, Lizzie felt like she was going cross-eyed. She'd skimmed the pages for the most part, reading mainly the headlines. She hoped she hadn't missed anything vital, but of course, she couldn't be positive. She'd made a list of all the articles in which the name Huxton had appeared, either a family member or the hotel. Had Ashley found something in one of those stories? Lizzie hadn't taken the time to read them all through but it seemed like the usual stories—mainly social items and city council matters, since Ross Huxton had been a councilor.

She stretched, gave the cover a pat, and then waved at Isabel on her way to the door. She took a deep breath and turned her face to the sun. She'd never make it as a researcher. She decided to turn her attention to the Huxton Hotel and she knew just the person who might have some answers.

She parked in front of the newspaper office on Main

Street and spotted George Havers, the owner, editor and publisher of the *Ashton Corners Colonist*, through the window, in conversation with someone she didn't recognize. Lizzie glanced over at the police station parking lot next door but didn't see Mark's Jeep. With a sigh, she went to get her information from her old friend.

Chapter Twenty

∾∾∾

I will ride my luck on occasion, but I like to pick
the occasion.

MIGHT AS WELL BE DEAD—REX STOUT

George Havers greeted Lizzie with a haggard grin and
turned his attention back to the two women standing in
front of him at the counter. Lizzie walked over to the wall
and glanced at the numerous awards and certificates the
paper had won over the years. She could hear George discussing the merits of the *Colonist* running an exposé on
obese cats in the town. Lizzie wondered if the two women
might be from the Humane Society but an exposé didn't
seem up their alley.

George finally saw them off with the promise to send a
reporter out to interview them both at length. He was grin-
ning as he leaned on the counter waiting for Lizzie to walk
over to him. His thick, wavy brown hair seemed to have
more visible graying in the sunlight that cut a swath through
the front window. Of course, the black-rimmed glasses
added extra contrast. He straightened up and his six-foot-five

height made Lizzie feel like a little girl again, which is what she was when she'd first met him working for her daddy.

"Nicely done," she said. "I doubt they even realize you didn't promise a story, much less an exposé."

"You noticed. Those two busybodies, uh, excuse me, ladies come in at least once a week with another suggestion of an exposé for the paper to run."

"Where did obese cats come from?"

"Seems there was a case up north of a woman being charged with animal cruelty or some such thing after her cat was found to be too obese to be healthy and had to be put down." He shook his head. "They believe the same thing is happening right here. They could be right but it's not something I'm going to spend time or resources on. Now, murder is much more like it. What body has your attention this time? Wait, don't tell me. There's only one murder in town. That must be it."

Lizzie sighed. "Busted. Or actually, I hope I won't be."

"Yeah, I've heard that you are possibly the only person in town whom the victim knew and that you two weren't on the best of terms."

"Is that the gossip?"

"Young lady, I do not deal in gossip. It's straight from the police chief's mouth but strictly off the record. He wanted my help but I made him tell all first."

Lizzie was immediately suspicious. "Just what kind of help did he want?"

George switched his weight from one foot to the other. "Well, he knew I'd be digging for a story, so he told me the facts and asked that for now, until he had real evidence, that I leave out all mention of you."

"And you went along with that?" Lizzie tried to sound incensed although she was secretly surprised and pleased. "My daddy would not have done that."

"You're probably right but I'm no Monroe Turner. Never will be. I figure the bar is held higher for a renowned journalist than for a small-town newspaper editor. And I also figure it's the least I can do for him. And you."

Lizzie blushed. "Thank you, George. For the record, I didn't do it."

"Well, I know that. Otherwise, I wouldn't have caved so quickly when Dreyfus asked. But, I would like to know all that you can tell me about Ms. Dixon."

"You've been wanting to ask, haven't you?"

"I figured, all in good time. I knew you'd be in one day, so here you are and you have some questions of me. I have some of you. I won't use anything that might taint a story until I'm given the go-ahead."

"I trust you, George. Maybe I can ask my questions first?"

He nodded and motioned her to the back section of the building that housed his messy desk and a couple of chairs. She sat across from him but perched on the edge of her chair.

"I just learned that Ashley was asking about the Huxton Hotel and that she spent some time going through old issues of your newspaper to gather information. I, too, just looked through those same papers at the library, trying to find out what she was after. I can't figure it out, though, aside from the fact that there was a lot of press about the Huxton family in those days. I need to know what her interest in them or the hotel was."

"Can I ask why?"

"Well, she told me she expected to be spending a lot of time in town from now on. I'm trying to find out why that was. If there's someone else in town she knows, that could be her killer."

George leaned back in his chair, thinking. It took him several minutes to answer. "I suppose that's possible. I assume the chief is following the same lead?"

"Only if he found this out himself."

George smiled. "I see. Okay. I'll tell you what I know but I don't know how it's tied in." He held up his mug, asking if Lizzie wanted a cup. She shook her head. He got up and poured himself some from a carafe on a table at the end of the space.

When he sat down, he began. "I remember the Huxton Hotel well from my childhood. It was the place with the large flowing lawns where the pony rides were held each summer." He nodded at her surprised look. "They brought in ponies for a week each summer and sold boxed picnics to everyone. My parents brought our own blankets, bought the food, and we kids got free rides. It was quite special. I think we went for several years until I outgrew that sort of thing. I can remember my folks having special dinners there and attending a big dance at the end of each summer season. It was that kind of place, catering to tourists, the rich locals, and then, something special and affordable for everyone."

"Sounds like it was run by nice people."

"Oh, Herbert Huxton and his wife were just that. However, they were finally talked into taking a vacation by their then-grown kids, and unfortunately, they were in a plane that went down in stormy weather. No one survived."

"Oh, how terrible for the family. How many kids did they have?"

"Two, a boy, Ross, and his younger sister, Fay. Of course, Ross took over running the hotel, although he was only in his early twenties at that point. Fay got married at the tender age of nineteen to one of the Parson boys, and believe me, there wasn't a family in town more inaptly named. Anyway, Ms. Huxton-Parson has a financial part in the hotel but has never been involved in running it."

"It was always there, when I was growing up," Lizzie

said. "We went to the dining room a couple of times maybe, but aside from that, I don't really remember much about it."

"It became more upper class very quickly. You know, originally it was called Huxton's Dream because, as the story goes, that's what it was to Herbert. His lifelong dream. But Ross Huxton had very definite ideas about the type of clientele he wanted and the locals, except for a few whom I know you would recognize by name, weren't included. And so, he changed the name. Thought the Huxton sounded more upscale and trendy."

"That's a shame. But that doesn't give me any idea as to why Ashley was interested."

"Ross Huxton died last month."

Lizzie sat back. "He did? I can't remember if I heard that or not."

"He was in Boston for cancer treatment when it happened. I did a fairly big spread on it." He looked pointedly at her.

She shrugged. "Sorry. Last month was very busy with school starting up and Teensy's promotional stuff and . . . well, I guess I just skimmed the headlines. But even so, what did that have to do with Ashley?"

"I don't know. Maybe nothing. But you asked what was new about the hotel. Fay Huxton-Parson is now the sole owner. She and her, shall we say, money-grasping husband. And their two kids."

"Hmm." Lizzie sat there thinking but didn't know where to take it. "Maybe Ashley knew someone who used to work there and she was trying to find her. Maybe a relative she hadn't seen in a long time."

"Anything's possible. Now, I have some questions for you." He raised his eyebrows.

"Shoot."

"How did you know Ashley Dixon?"

Lizzie went through the whole explanation about college and their unhappy sharing of a room. She finished by admitting she hadn't been happy when Ashley appeared at Molly's the night before the fair.

"Sounds like a flimsy but possible motive for murder," George said. He held up his hand before Lizzie could speak. "Flimsy. Hold that thought. I can see why Dreyfus needs to appear unbiased here but I also don't believe for a minute that they'd charge you with that evidence. However, in order to ensure that doesn't happen, I'll look a bit deeper into the hotel connection and see if there even is one."

"Thank you so much, George." Lizzie rose quickly but prevented herself from flinging herself at him. She would appear dignified and un-suspect-like as she left his office.

But she had to figure out what Ashley was snooping around the hotel about. Despite his protestations as to not knowing what was going on in his fiancée's life, Nick Jennings had to know something. Lizzie was sure of it. You couldn't be engaged to someone and not know things like that. Could you?

She hoped he was still in town. Rather than call Mark to find out, and in the process alert him to the fact that she was sleuthing, Lizzie headed straight for the Ashton Inn.

She spotted Nick sitting at the bar in the lounge. She glanced at the clock in the lobby. Twelve thirty. Perhaps not too early, after all. She sat down on the next stool, startling Nick, who appeared to be in deep thought while holding what looked like a martini in his right hand. He looked very New York editor today, striped long-sleeved shirt with white collar and cuffs, dark pants with a matching jacket slung over the stool on his left side. Lizzie felt positively dowdy in her green cotton blouse and beige cargo pants. She tried for a New York attitude.

"Hi, Nick. Remember me? Lizzie? I hope you don't mind if I join you for a few minutes."

Nick looked amused and smiled. "Please do. No man should have to drink alone, especially at this time of day. What would you like?"

"An iced tea would be just great."

Lizzie waited for her tea to appear before starting in. Nick seemed content to just sit and stare at his drink. Lizzie couldn't get over the change in him. He no longer seemed the suave guy she'd talked to before, but more of a lost soul.

She sipped her tea when it arrived and then said, "I wasn't sure if I'd find you here. Did the police ask you to stay? Is that why you're still in town?"

Nick sighed. "No. Well, they did initially, but then the chief told me I could leave. But to tell you the truth, I'm hiding out for a bit." He finished off his drink and signaled for another. "This thing with Ashley has sort of left me wrung out. I'm actually surprised at how much she meant to me. I thought it might help me get some perspective on things . . . on my life, if I stayed awhile longer."

"What are the funeral plans?"

"I don't know. I spoke briefly to an uncle of hers who said he'd have her cremated and buried back home, someplace in New England, I think. Anyway, he didn't want to include me in his plans. I guess that about sums up our relationship."

"That's not how you'd sum things up, is it?"

"No, it's not. I understood Ashley's need to live the good life, which is what I could give her. She liked money and what it could buy. It was almost like a craving."

"So if you could give it to her, why did she break the engagement?"

"I also think she had a deep fear of a serious commitment.

She probably couldn't picture herself being tied down to one person for the rest of her life." Another drink arrived and he took a sip. "Of course, this is me in my Freud mode. I didn't really know Ashley because she wouldn't let anyone too close. Does that make sense?"

Lizzie was quiet a moment. "I think it might explain a lot of things about Ashley. Do you mind if I ask you something?"

"Go ahead."

"Did Ashley ever say anything about the Huxton Hotel?"

"Not that I recall. Where is it and what does it have to do with Ashley?"

"It's here, in Ashton Corners, and she seemed to be asking a lot of questions about it."

"Can't think why. She never mentioned it to me anyway. Maybe she was going over to the dark side?"

Lizzie looked puzzled.

"Decided to become a writer. Maybe she was looking for a good location to set a book and your small town with its historic hotel might have been it." He cocked an eyebrow.

Lizzie didn't know what to say. She'd never thought of that. Could it be true? Or had Ashley thought about it? Might that be the reason Ashley had planned to spend time there in the future? She couldn't think why else Ashley had the interest in the hotel.

Chapter Twenty-one

Do act mysterious. It always keeps them coming
back for more.

NANCY'S MYSTERIOUS LETTER—CAROLYN KEENE

The sound of the phone ringing startled Lizzie as she was
opening the back door. She sprinted for the phone, careful to close the door first so the cats wouldn't escape. She
got it on the final ring before going to message.

"Ms. Turner?" She recognized Principal Charles Benton's voice and almost hung up. It might not be good news.

"Yes, Mr. Benton. What can I do for you?"

He cleared his throat. "It's come to my attention that you
have not been arrested and the police have not bothered
anyone at school for the past few days. I talked it over with
the superintendent and we agree that you should be in school
doing your job. Can you be back here Monday morning?"

Lizzie bit back what she'd prefer to be saying to the two-
faced moron. He was taking credit for dropping the suspen-
sion when she knew it was probably due to the petition. And
that the superintendent probably initiated the decision.

However, she did need her job and she was relieved to no longer be considered a pariah.

"I'll be there."

"Right. We'll just carry on as if nothing has happened." He cleared his throat again and mumbled what sounded like a good-bye before hanging up.

Lizzie didn't respond. She stood looking at the phone for a few minutes before dialing Mark on his cell phone. He picked up on the second ring.

"Is everything okay?" he asked.

"Yes, it's all good. I just wanted to tell you about my phone call." She talked about the call but didn't mention what she'd been up to that morning. She needed to be checking out some more details before doing that. It just struck her that she should be talking to the authors, asking if any of them knew of authorial aspirations of Ashley's.

"Well, I'm sure glad to hear that," Mark answered.

"I am as well. Now, if you could just tell me that you're closing in on the killer, I'd be really thrilled."

"Sorry."

"Well, can you tell me how much longer the authors will have to hang around? After the events we've planned, I mean?"

"Well, technically they're good to go, although I admit, I haven't actually told them that. I do have all their information so I can track them down if more questions arise, if they change their minds and decide to leave. But as you see, no one seems in too much of a hurry to leave now. You've done a fine job of keeping them occupied and promoting their books, which seems to be the most important thing in the world to them," he added with a chuckle.

"Does that mean you think the murderer is a local?"

"That's a possibility."

"Tell me you have more suspects."

"Nobody definite, or who I'm willing to name, but I'm still looking."

"So why do you think it's a local?"

"Just one of those assumptions investigators sometimes make after nosing around, you know. And I've come across some interesting things about our victim. It seems Ashley Dixon was asking a lot of questions around town. It may be nothing but it could lead to something. That's where the focus is right now."

"Not on me?" She had her fingers crossed.

"Much less on you. In fact, I'm awfully tempted to take some time off tonight and visit my gal. That is, if she's up to it."

"That would be a yes."

"Good. I'm looking forward to it. See you later."

Lizzie heard the sexy tone his voice had taken on and it sent a shiver down her body. She was smiling as she hung up.

Brie came sauntering into the kitchen and rubbed against her leg, getting serious about a head rub against her sandals. She bent down to scoop her up, grabbed the brush and sat on a chair to give Brie a good grooming session. She could hear Edam come running down the stairs, and in a moment, he had leapt up on the next chair and rubbed his head against Lizzie's arm.

She found the motion involved in brushing very relaxing and she felt the tension begin to leave her shoulders. After a long while, her mind started to focus again on the murder at hand. She wanted to talk to the authors and see if any of them knew about Ashley having plans to join their end of the business. She could go over to the bed and breakfast on her own right now, on the off chance someone would be around. She glanced at the clock. Almost time for the sherry hour. She gave Molly a call, explained her plan and said she'd pick her up in an hour.

* * *

Caroline and Lorelie were almost finished with their drinks when Lizzie and Molly arrived. Molly had called Patsy ahead of time to make sure it was okay for them to join in. Molly went into the kitchen carrying something that looked suspiciously like a wine bag. Lizzie helped herself to some sherry and sat down with the two women.

"So, what have you been up to today?" she asked pleasantly.

Caroline walked over to the tray of shortbreads and chose another before answering. "Oh, let's see, we went on a picnic, the three of us, out at the Fairview Picnic Grounds. It was so pleasant to be there by the water. And there was a game of bocce going on, so Lorelie and Carter joined in. I read and dozed some."

"A.J. Pruitt wasn't with you?"

"Oh, goodness no. As much as we love A.J., we seldom do much with him when we're out on these tours. In fact, we've seen even less of him this time," Caroline said. She looked at Lorelie. "I wonder what he's been up to."

Lorelie shrugged. "Something about an old school chum. Whatever."

"And what about Gigi? Does she do things with you all while you're here?" Lizzie asked.

"She says she's busy doing research," Lorelie smirked. "Why she'd want to set a series in a funeral home sure beats me."

"Well, we have another event for y'all if you're interested," Molly said as she rejoined them. "It's a local talent show put on by the Ashton Corners Service Club, next Wednesday. It's a really important charity event in town here. There'll be a large audience, a chance to sell more books and it should be fun, too."

Caroline perked up. "A talent show? What do we do, read?"

"Exactly. Writing is a talent, and y'all are such entertaining presenters I'm sure it will be a big hit."

The divas looked at each other. Lorelie spoke first. "I'm all for it. I can't imagine anyone being against it since it's what we do, after all. That is carrying our stay over somewhat longer than I'd first imagined, though."

"I do hope you can adjust your schedule." Lizzie noted that Molly sounded very sincere. "It would also mean a lot to my bookstore to get another opportunity to get new fans and sell a lot of books."

"Of course we'll do it," Caroline said, all sweetness. Lizzie noted the sour look on Lorelie's face that quickly changed as she said, "Of course. As you said, we are good at it."

"Change of subject," Caroline said, "but I'm wondering how the investigation into Ashley's murder is going."

Molly fielded the question. "As I understand it, the police are making some progress. Now, may I refresh your drinks?" She picked up the decanter and did so as the women held their glasses out to her.

"I was wondering," Lizzie said, thinking this would be a good time to get them on track, "do either of you know if Ashley was planning on writing a book?"

"Ashley?" Lorelie looked as shocked as she sounded. "Why, she was a publicist, not a writer. You don't just decide you want to write a book. It's a passion, something you are at a loss to resist. There was none of that with Ashley. She would have been talking about it all the time, if that's what she planned."

Lizzie caught Caroline with a slight sneer on her face but she nodded in agreement when she realized she was being watched. "Oh, Lorelie is so right, for a change. She would have told us for certain. We could have given her invaluable advice. Besides, she had a very busy schedule planning all our tours and the like. I don't see how she would have found time to write. Why do you ask?"

Lizzie tried to make light of it. "It's just that a friend of mine who works in the library mentioned that Ashley was in doing some research into a hotel that's near here."

Carter joined them before either could answer.

"I thought I heard a lot of voices in here. Nice to see you both again." He nodded at Lizzie and Molly.

"Yes," Caroline told him, "we were just talking about Ashley. Lizzie wanted to know if she was writing a book. We told her how ludicrous that was."

Carter stopped in the process of grabbing a piece of shortbread. "I would have thought she'd tell you gals if that's what she was doing."

"She was doing some research in town, though," Caroline sounded almost whiny.

Carter seemed to reconsider. "Well, maybe she was and that's what got her killed. You know, she unearthed something she shouldn't have. Every small town has its secrets, you know." He chuckled.

"Oh, you don't think that's what happened, do you?" Caroline sounded surprised.

"I have no idea, my dear. But I'm going out for my constitutional. I shall return in good time for dinner. Ladies, it's been a pleasure seeing you again." He did a small bow in Lizzie and Molly's direction before leaving the room.

Lorelie stifled a yawn. "This here sherry is making me even more tired. I would so like to have a little nap before eating." She glanced at her watch. "I really must run over to the pharmacy, though, and pick up some more allergy pills. I'd better do that now and then I'll still have time for a nap."

"We could do that for you," Molly said. "Just tell me the brand and we'll drop them off back here."

"Oh, don't you go bothering yourselves," Lorelie said. "Although that's very kind. Caroline, you look like you could do with a rest, too."

"Really? Oh, maybe you're right. I didn't sleep too well last night." She glanced at her watch. "Yes, it is nap time."

"Well, we'll be going, too," Molly said, standing. "I do hope you are planning to come to my place for dinner after the reading on Sunday."

"Why, that's very kind of you, Molly. We'd love to."

"Yes, we would," Lorelie said as she grabbed her handbag and made for the front door. "See you then."

Caroline started up the stairs.

Molly went to say good-bye to Patsy so Lizzie wandered out to her car, noticing Lorelie speed off in her rented yellow Focus. She wasn't headed toward the pharmacy and Lizzie hoped she wouldn't get lost, although it wouldn't take long to find one's way in Ashton Corners. She started up as Molly got in and drove in the same direction Lorelie had gone. As they passed the turn-in to the baseball park, Lizzie noticed Lorelie's car parked partially behind the field house. Or was it? Farther off in the field there were two figures standing awfully close to each other. The colors of their clothes looked very much like those worn by Lorelie and Carter.

Couldn't be. Or could it?

Chapter Twenty-two

◇◇◇

All I have to do is prove it.

UNLEASHED—DAVID ROSENFELT

High C seemed much higher at choir that evening. Lizzie realized she wasn't giving her full attention to the rehearsal and therefore wasn't preparing for the runs as she should. Shoulders back, chest high, deep breath, shoulders relaxed. Was that really Lorelie Oliver and Carter Farrow she'd seen embracing in the park? If so, what did it mean, other than he was yet another two-timing lowlife? She hated to think that of him, though. Oops, that time she was definitely flat.

Fortunately, the director, Stanton Giles, called for a fifteen-minute break and Lizzie chugalugged the remainder of the water she'd brought in her stainless steel bottle. She looked around the room at her fellow choristers, realizing she was missing her weekly chats with Lucille Miller, Bob's sister. Lucille had decided she needed a few weeks away from all the stress and strain that had ensued when Bob had recently been wrongly imprisoned. A few weeks at her sister's home in Seattle had turned into a month, and there was no word on when she'd be back.

Lizzie spent the remainder of the break talking to a teacher from her school and when the sound of fanfare being played on the piano brought them back to their seats, she vowed to pay strict attention to the rest of the rehearsal. She took a deep breath and tried to center herself. She listened with eyes closed to the opening lines that Tommy McCann played on the piano and then quickly found her place in the music score before the sopranos' entry.

It wasn't difficult to immerse herself, as she loved the *Gloria* by Vivaldi, the main piece that Musica Nobilis would present at the annual Christmas concert on the third Saturday in December. The second half of the program would be Strauss waltzes sung in German.

Part of her mind, contrary to what she'd vowed to do, thought the waltzes reminded her of the cotillions Ethel Lee had mentioned. She could picture the white gowns swaying in a wonderland of lights and flowers. And of course, that reminded her of Ashley.

M ark showed up just as Lizzie finished getting ready for bed. He had already called twice that evening to say he'd be later than he thought. She'd given up hope he would be able to make it over.

"I'm sorry. I should have called first," he said when she opened the door, but the look he gave her as he eyed her from head to toe said otherwise. She felt that familiar tingle in her toes, although they were covered in old socks, and since she'd chosen to wear her shapeless but brightly colored pajamas, his obvious interest delighted her.

"Don't worry about it." She grabbed his hand and pulled him into the living room. "Can I get you something to drink?"

He tossed his hat on the love seat. "I'd like to say yes but I'm dead tired. I just took Patchett for a quick walk and was hoping to at least share some closeness for the rest of the night." He pulled her to him and she wrapped her arms around his waist. She could feel his body start to relax.

"I'm all for that. Tell me what you want."

"A quick shower and a comfy bed."

"Done. Just go ahead and I'll lock up down here." She watched him trudge up the stairs, favoring his left leg. Whenever he overworked to the point of physical exhaustion, as he obviously had now, his leg was the first obvious indication. An old war injury, she knew, although he had never spoken about it. She kept meaning to ask him about his time in the army in Iraq but always decided to let him bring it up, when he was ready. Trouble was, he never seemed ready and that, she realized, was what she pegged the future of their relationship on. When he felt ready to let her totally into his life, she would be there. Or would she? As much as she thought she loved him, and she was ready to admit this fact to herself, Lizzie had been wondering lately about his true feelings for her.

Silly, she often admonished herself, because it had only been a year since they'd started seeing each other. One year. Boy, a lot had happened in that time. Her life had changed and Mark, along with the members of the book club, were totally responsible for that. She readily admitted it was a good thing but a year wasn't a long time. She realized she shouldn't let herself get such high expectations. Not yet.

By the time Mark had showered and dried off, Lizzie sat in bed, with the cats perched warily by her feet. When Mark came in, they jumped off the bed and leapt up to the bureau, watching Mark and Lizzie.

Mark slid under the sheets beside her and wrapped his

arms around her. He nuzzled her shoulder and said, "Tell me about the rest of your day."

Oh boy. What could she say? She didn't want him to know that she'd talked to George Havers about Ashley, had questioned Nick Jennings or the authors. No, that was wrong. She needed to tell him what she'd found out about the research Ashley was doing. If that merited another lecture, so be it.

She snuggled down closer to him, fitting her body in with his. And then she told all. She could feel him reacting to her various revelations, especially when she said she'd visited Nick Jennings. But, to his credit, he didn't comment until she finished with the ladies at the bed and breakfast. She did leave out the two figures she noticed on the way home. She couldn't be positive about their identities but she would try to figure it out.

"And if Nick Jennings turns out to be the murderer, do you think it was a good idea to go question him? Alone?"

Lizzie propped herself up on her elbow. "Is he?"

"Not that I can say for certain either way."

She slumped back down. "I want this to be over."

Mark started running his hand up and down her back. "You are going back to work, that's a start. And, you haven't been reinterviewed by the police. I'd say things are going in the right direction."

"Of course, you're right. But it's still unsettling not knowing."

Mark took a deep breath.

"What?" Lizzie asked.

"What do you mean, 'what'?"

"That silent sigh. What's up?"

Mark pushed himself up to lean against the headboard. "That cell phone Yost found in your car? It belonged to Ashley Dixon."

"What?" Lizzie screeched. "How did it get there? I did not put it there, Mark. I have no idea how it got there."

"Relax," he said, reaching out to her. "It's a plant. I'm sure of it. The stolen change from your car was just a diversion. The real reason for breaking in was to plant the phone."

"That makes sense. You believe it?"

"Of course. Like I said, you haven't been pulled in for another interview. But even with the money being taken, it's still a bit too obvious."

"Who would do that? Who wants to frame me? Or rather, being so obvious, who now wants to unframe me?"

Mark stared at her. "Is that even a word? What do you mean by that?"

Lizzie shook her head. "I don't know. I'm so totally confused. I just thought the only reason you searched my car was because of the broken window. But on the other hand, it is a bit obvious, breaking the window to draw attention to the cell phone that had been intentionally left in my car. Therefore, the killer is either dumb or trying to make it look like I was being framed. So, if it looked like I was being deliberately framed, you wouldn't think I was the killer."

Mark grinned. "Huh. You've lost me but I'd say we have a very amateur and very confused murderer on our hands."

"Well, that doesn't really sound like an author you know. They specialize in murder so you'd think they could pull it off. How long can you keep them around here?"

Mark sighed, "I see we're not going to get much sleep or anything else until we talk. I'll make you a deal. I have a splitting headache, so if you rub my left temple, I'll tell you where we're at."

"Deal." She pushed back up on her elbow and with her free hand started gently massaging his temple. After a few minutes she gently punched him on his shoulder. "Uh, we have a deal here. Talk."

"Mmm. That feels good." He sighed. "Okay, for starters, all the authors appear to be hiding something."

"They are?" Lizzie momentarily stopped the massaging, as she was dumbfounded. "I didn't get that from talking to them. In fact, they're very eager to talk and point the finger at one another."

"They deal in fiction, Lizzie. I think you're getting their version of what's going on but it may not be the whole story or even the right one." He gently bumped her with his elbow. "My head."

She started the soothing rubbing action again. "Do you think one of them is the murderer?"

"It's possible but I don't have a motive for any of them, at the moment. That's why I've asked them to hang around until next week at least. They don't have to, you know. In fact, I find it sort of curious that they all agreed to do so. I'm just hoping one or all of them doesn't have a sudden change of mind. And that's why I asked you and Molly to organize some more events for them."

"Yes, and we came up with some good ideas and the authors are most enthusiastic. Who's your most suspicious author?"

Mark chuckled. "Most suspicious? I told you, no motives other than arguments that can be classified as petty."

"Mine, too, in that case."

Mark grimaced. "So to finish answering your question, they're equally suspicious at the moment."

"Okay. Let me rephrase. Who gets your spidey senses tingling?"

Mark sat up quickly and rolled Lizzie onto her back. "Now we're into entirely different territory." He gave her a long, deep kiss that sent her own senses a-tingle. "I suggest we continue this conversation tomorrow."

Chapter Twenty-three

<small>◇◇◇</small>

Which left me wondering: what was the liar?

TOPPED CHEF—LUCY BURDETTE

The thing about conversations left for the morning is they never seem to fit at that point. Lizzie and Mark finished a breakfast of eggs, bacon and toast with a second cup of espresso while Patchett sat at the back door, slobbering on the screen while watching them. The cats had retreated back upstairs after vacuuming up their breakfasts while the dog searched the backyard.

"Are you coming to Molly's for dinner tomorrow?" Lizzie finally asked.

"For sure. All the suspects in one room. Rather Poirot-like, wouldn't you say?"

"Now you're starting to sound like Molly. I hope you're not including me in that bunch."

Mark stood and kissed her on the top of her head. "Not you. That would mean I'm sleeping with the enemy. I'd better get going, though, or I might not get out of the office in time to eat."

"What about Patchett?"

"He's coming with me today. I need to drive out in the countryside later and he can have a nice long walk out there."

"Countryside. You mean to the Huxton Hotel? You do think it's suspicious that Ashley was so interested in it?"

Mark sat back down for a minute. "Interesting, not necessarily suspicious. I want to talk to Richard Huxton-Parson and see if Ms. Dixon actually visited out there and maybe had a meeting with him."

"What would her reason be? We were wondering if she was planning on writing a book and wanted to set it there, for some reason. Do you have her computer? Have you checked what she's googled?"

Mark shook his head. "You don't quit, do you? Yes, to both. She did google the hotel and the family several times but that doesn't tell us much more. Do you know for sure she was going to write a book?"

"No, in fact, the divas think not. What about checking with her publisher?"

"I'll do that. Now, I'd better get going. Thanks for . . . everything." He pulled her out of her chair and kissed her lightly.

"Entirely my pleasure," she murmured as he walked out the back door and whistled to Patchett.

Lizzie was dying to drive out to the Huxton Hotel and ask some questions of her own but she knew better than to try it with Mark likely to show up there at any time. So, he did have his suspicions about the authors. They'd all be at the library this afternoon. She needed to think of how to approach each of them to find out what they were hiding.

Because she was now pretty certain they were all hiding

something. Maybe it was only petty arguments, as Mark classified them. But often that could mean something bigger was lurking far deeper. The other question was, were they all in on it and hiding the same thing? She couldn't for a minute imagine what that would be, though.

The fact that her sandals were sticking to the kitchen floor next to the fridge made her realize it was time to wash the floor. She devoted the next couple of hours to giving the house a thorough cleaning, an especially good idea since she'd be back at work the next week. She also found the repetitive motion, which did not require a lot of thought, gave her brain time to wander through various scenarios.

She decided to start with the most outlandish thing she could think of as a reason for Ashley moving to Ashton Corners. Love. It had to be love. She was jilted by one of the Huxton family and never got over him, that's why her engagement to Nick hadn't worked. And that's why she'd finally given in to her desires and followed Mr. X to town. That would explain her interest in the hotel and the family. She wanted to know her enemy before approaching because she was certain that family was at the root of the failed relationship, them not wanting him to marry a Northerner. She made contact and they killed her. *Ha*. The plot for a romantic-suspense possibly, but how probable in reality?

Okay, next up. She did, in fact, have the promise of a book contract for a series set in a small Southern hotel. She made contact, got her information and what? They'd have no reason to kill her. So maybe it was one of the authors after all. Here again, what was the motive?

Third scenario. That was the problem, she couldn't think of another one but certainly neither of the two she had so far seemed likely.

One thing Lizzie did realize is that she had to talk to someone in the Huxton family as well as someone who worked at the hotel. She had to take a chance on running into Mark. She'd done it before and eventually his anger would subside. It was just a chance she had to take. This was too important and she couldn't afford to lose any more time.

She quickly changed into a pale orange sweater set and tan pants, spotting the cats curled up next to each other on her bed, obviously catching up on the sleep they'd lost keeping track of Patchett overnight.

The drive took half an hour by the time she'd waited for a funeral procession of about twenty cars to slowly make their way through an intersection and out toward the Memorial Gardens cemetery. She found a parking spot just a few steps from the main entrance. No sign of Mark's Jeep or a police car in the parking lot. A good start. It was only as she entered the massive lobby that the thought hit her. What if no one from the family was working today? Well, she'd start with the front desk person and work her way through the staff until she found someone who had talked to Ashley.

She paused at the end of the front walk and took a slow look around. The Huxton Hotel still retained the charm of its plantation house beginnings, helped along with a recent fresh coat of paint. The wraparound porch was dotted with groupings of dark green wicker chairs, love seats and coffee tables. Virginia creeper wrapped along the porticos at either end of the porch. The fact that it was open to the lawn, without any railings, made it look all the more welcoming. Lizzie could imagine herself lounging for many hours on such a porch, an iced tea close at hand and a book in the other.

The grounds around the hotel hadn't changed much since her last visit, about sixteen years earlier. It had been for a Sunday lunch, with her best friend Paige Raleigh and her parents. But Lizzie had been too busy as a young teenager gossiping with Paige to take much notice of where they actually were.

The double front door was opened for her by an elderly man dressed in brown pants and a crisp beige shirt with the hotel logo in green on the pocket. She looked around her while she waited patiently for the young man at the desk to finish with a customer. The lobby, done in shades of rose and mint green, was set up in two sections. To the right of the front door were four large sofas, two facing the front lawns and the other two at right angles. Three smaller chairs in a coordinating striped microfiber fabric were in a small grouping to one side.

To the left were six chairs around a coffee table. These were placed close enough to the entrance to the restaurant, the Essence, to be of use if guests were waiting for tables. A combination of enticing smells drifted from that direction.

Finally, the fellow turned to her. His name tag said Dillon. "How may I help you today?" he asked, with a smile that Lizzie knew ensured he was never without female company. Maybe he was the guy. He could be the new generation of Huxton learning the family business. He looked a bit on the young side but that wouldn't stop Ashley, not if he appealed to her.

"I'd just like to ask you a few questions about a friend of mine, Ashley Dixon, who stopped by the hotel sometime in the last week, or maybe longer ago." She smiled what she hoped was a nonthreatening smile. "I know it's a long shot that anyone will remember her, but it is really important."

"Of course. But I can't really give out any information about our guests."

"That's all right. She wasn't a guest, at least I don't think she was. She was probably just asking some questions about the hotel for a novel she's writing."

His smile grew wider. Did he envision spin-off increased bookings for the family business when the novel became a bestseller? Perhaps it was a starring role in the movie adaptation he had on his mind. "Yes? Well, that should be all right then. What was her name, or better yet, do you have a photo?"

Lizzie thanked her stars she'd thought to pull one out of her college photo album. It showed Ashley and her sitting on a park bench out front of Auburn U. In early days, before Ashley had shown her true colors. She handed it over to Dillon.

"It's a few years old but I'll bet you'd remember her if you spoke to her."

He let out a soft whistle. "Cool. You two were sure something to look at."

Were? Lizzie suddenly wanted to grab a mirror for a close look at the new her. Dillon looked like he was giving it a lot of thought. At least he didn't say no right off the bat. She saw the light dawning.

"Say, isn't that the name of that body that was found at the funeral home?"

Lizzie nodded but he shook his head.

"Sorry. But I never saw her here. Of course, I've been off for a couple of weeks." He stood a little straighter. "Was in New York for a modeling gig."

Lizzie made the appropriate admiration noises. "Can you suggest someone else I should talk to?"

He gazed around the lobby, held up his index finger in the universal "one moment" sign and went into the office behind the counter. A couple of minutes later, he reappeared followed by an older woman, probably in her late fifties, with silver streaks in her dark hair, carrying a large green binder. The smile she gave Lizzie was pleasant but inquisitive.

"May I help you?" she asked, placing the binder on the desk and now openly curious. "Why, you're Evelyn Turner's daughter, aren't you?"

"Yes, I am."

"I'm Delilah Yates. I knew your mama in high school. How is she doing?"

"About the same. Thank you for asking." Lizzie felt a little less comfortable proceeding, now that someone could put a name to her face, in case a police officer or such should ask. *Oh well*.

"I'm asking about a friend of mine who had probably stopped by the hotel sometime within the past month, asking about its history. I think she might have been planning on using it as a setting in a book. Does that sound familiar?"

"Dillon said she's the person whose body was found earlier this week? That's such a shame. She was such an inquisitive young woman and very personable. Such a tragedy to die so young and violently, too." Delilah shook her head. "I did speak to her but not for very long."

"When was that?"

"Early last month. She said she was from New York and in town for a few days. I was very surprised to see that she'd been killed here. I assumed she'd come back again but I hadn't seen her a second time."

"Do you mind telling me what she was asking about?"

"I suppose it doesn't really matter if I tell you. Excuse me, one minute." She turned to take the phone receiver that Dillon passed to her after answering.

When she hung up and turned back to Lizzie, her eyes were kind but she shook her head. "I'm sorry but that was Police Chief Dreyfus on the phone telling me he was on his way out here and not to answer anyone's questions, especially from, and I quote, 'a beautiful nosy woman who is bound to come poking around.'"

Lizzie felt her face turn the shade of the fuchsia in the vase at the far end of the counter. "Oops, I don't want to get you in any trouble with the law."

"Well," Delilah said, patting Lizzie's hand that was

resting on the counter, "if you don't ask me any more questions I think I should be able to have a polite conversation with you and maybe suggest that you talk to Bertha Redding. She's the head housekeeper and it's her day off, but I'll bet you'll find her at the folk museum over on Penrod Street. She's a volunteer there most of her days off."

Lizzie grinned. "Thank you so much, Ms. Yates. It was a real pleasure not asking you anything." She winked and turned to walk hurriedly to her car. Best to avoid seeing Mark at the moment and she wanted to get to the museum before he did. She knew a hot lead when she heard one. She drove out the long sloping driveway and turned right onto Sheridan, rather than retracing her earlier route out to the hotel. It wouldn't add too many minutes to cut over at the junction and take another road into town.

Chapter Twenty-four

◇◇◇

Right now all I had was a whole lot of nothing for a whole lot of trouble.

KILLER IN CRINOLINES—DUFFY BROWN

The parking lot at the museum was jam-packed, not a surprise since it was a small lot and the museum café served the best pumpkin and sweet potato pie in town. Lizzie chose one of the few remaining spots at the rear, next to a very familiar black Porsche. What would A.J. Pruitt be doing here, she wondered as she took a final look around before entering. She asked the woman sitting at a small round glass table that doubled as the information desk where she might find Bertha Redding. Following the directions, Lizzie chose door number two on the left side of the hall and knocked briefly before opening it. She wasn't quite sure what she'd find inside but she was certain nothing could have prepared her for the bright display of colors that drew her eyes to the large black desk to the left of the doorway.

"Are you Ms. Redding?" Lizzie asked when the aged woman finally looked at her.

She squinted and leaned forward a bit, giving Lizzie a thorough once-over before answering. "I am, and who might you be?"

"My name is Lizzie Turner and I wondered if I might ask you a few questions." She kept her fingers crossed. The woman's face gave nothing away. Lizzie took her to be in her mid-seventies, her face more greatly lined than Molly's, with a nose that looked too big in the space provided and eyes that were too small but such a piercing blue that she felt mesmerized. Her jet-black hair, pinned into a bun at the nape of her neck, looked like it was straight out of a 1950s magazine. The lace collar on her long-sleeved white blouse, which stretched to bursting over her large frame, completed the time-warp look.

After a few minutes, which seemed more like hours to Lizzie, Bertha nodded. "About what?" She indicated a comfortable-looking chair to the left side of her desk.

Lizzie breathed a sigh of relief and took a quick look around the room while sitting down. The cream walls were covered with a variety of sizes of posters of quilts. Flashes of color leapt out from an American quilt poster from the Metropolitan Museum of Art that almost filled the entire left wall of the small room. Behind Bertha, three posters from various exhibits over the years livened the wall. And to Lizzie's right, there were ten posters, different sizes that, upon second look, focused on different parts of the same quilt.

"A friend of mine visited the Huxton Hotel early last month. She was from New York. I'm wondering if she spoke to you? Her name was Ashley Dixon."

That got a reaction. Bertha looked startled then quickly composed herself. "You mean the young woman who was murdered. Yes, I spoke to her but I'm not sure what business that is of yours."

"I don't mean to be nosy and I wouldn't ask you to say

anything you're not comfortable telling me, but I'm trying
to find out what she was doing here and why she died."
There, it was out. She was officially poking her nose into
police business.

Bertha seemed to be giving it much more consideration
than Lizzie had hoped. Perhaps she wouldn't get any information after all. She had a moment's regret for even coming.
What good could come from this? Would anything she
might hear have any bearing on Ashley's murder? And Mark
would hear about this, for sure. She steeled herself for any
consequence.

"She did come to see me but only the one time, about a
month ago. She had a lot of questions about the hotel in the
old days. Her mama was working there the summer of 1983
in the housekeeping department. She wanted to know about
that time."

That was within the time frame Ashley had researched
at the library, Lizzie thought.

"Did you know her mama?"

"Yes." A warm smile lit Bertha's eyes. "The girl had a
picture of her mama and I recognized her immediately. She
was such a warm, friendly young thing, full of energy. She'd
always bring me a tea midday, without being asked. I was
in charge of the girls, new in my role and trying hard to be
friendly with my staff but still strict enough to gain their
respect. I think Joan sensed that. That was her name, Joan
Allen."

"So, Dixon must be her married name."

"I don't know anything about that. Anyway, the mama
had a lot of questions, just like her daughter."

"What were her questions?"

"She was really taken with the hotel. She wanted to know
all about its history and the Huxton family. She told me she
would daydream a lot and imagine living here. She loved

the stories of the cotillions in the old days, when the ladies would arrive in their long finery and the men were dressed in white tie and tails. Of course those were the early days of the hotel, when it was called Huxton's Dream. I've been working there a long time." She sighed. "Those were fine times. A lot of elegance around. Yes, fine times."

"And the mama was there for only one summer?"

"Yes. She left rather suddenly before her work time had ended. She told me she had to get back home because her mama was ailing. I never heard from her again although she did tell me she'd write."

"Mmm. Do you know the Huxton family well? Do you think I could talk to one of them?"

"The grandson manages the hotel these days. Richard. I don't think his mama goes out much anymore. You know, of course, that her brother, Mr. Ross, died just last month?"

"Yes, I'd heard that. It must have been quite a blow for the family."

"I expect it was. Although Mr. Huxton and his sister were at odds over the hotel. She'd said it in public just after their daddy had died and left the hotel to the both of them, that she didn't want anything to do with the running of it but I heard the odd row she'd have with her brother, and she sure as shooting wanted to tell him how to do things." Bertha paused a moment, as if visualizing the two. "I understand she's still as feisty as ever, too. Lives with her husband on a large estate, Falling Meadows, out near Brymar."

Lizzie couldn't think of anything else to ask. "Thank you, Ms. Redding. I appreciate you sharing your memories."

Bertha smiled. "I always enjoy taking my memories out of storage. You take care now."

Lizzie nodded and left. She wanted to talk to Richard Huxton but knew that Mark would be at the hotel by now. Maybe his mama would be the wiser choice. Obviously, next on her to-do list. She left the building and had almost reached her car when she noticed A.J. Pruitt standing behind a hydrangea bush, not far from a window at the side of the museum. Aha, she finally had her chance to ask him some questions.

He was so intent on staring at the building, he didn't notice Lizzie until she'd almost reached him. He started and then gave a nervous twitter. "My, my . . . you do know how to sneak up on someone, don't you?"

Lizzie wasn't sure if he was upset or teasing her. "It wasn't deliberate, A.J. It's just hard to be noisy on grass." She smiled her most charming smile.

He responded and his shoulders relaxed. "So it is. What lovely grounds these are."

"Very. I'm surprised to see you here."

He coughed and quickly glanced back at the building. "Someone had recommended this as a must-see while in town."

"Oh, who?"

"I'm not sure. Can't really remember. I've had so much advice over the past few days. You know, what's too touristy and what's really got the feel of the old town." He looked around suddenly seeming bewildered.

"Do you mind if I ask you a few questions?" Lizzie asked, kindly.

"About what?"

"Ashley Dixon."

"Oh yes. Very tragic. She was such a charming young woman. Of course. Let's just wander while we talk, shall we?" He started walking away from the building without waiting for her.

Lizzie had to scramble to catch up. "I was just wondering if Ashley had said anything to you about having another reason for being in Ashton Corners?"

A.J. looked surprised. "No. Not that I can remember. No, I'm sure she didn't. Why, is it important?"

"It could be. Do you know if she had plans to write a novel?"

He shook his head. "Can't say. She was charming, as I mentioned, and friendly but we didn't really chitchat. Not the way she did with the girls. You should ask them." He glanced behind them and then veered toward a fountain, sitting abruptly on a bench in front of it. "You know, I think the girl had a bit of a devious or mean streak in her."

"Why do you say that?"

"Well, both Caroline and Lorelie could be demanding at times but they were both downright venomous about her. That's not like them. Catty with a bit of trickery thrown in. But not venomous. Good word, that. You should ask them."

Lizzie joined him, glad to stay put for a few minutes. "I will. You know, I'm just trying to figure out who had a motive to murder her."

A.J. gave a small chuckle. "I certainly hope you're not querying me hoping I'll give away the fact that I did it."

Lizzie smiled. "No, I doubt you're a killer."

A.J. had a wry look on his face. "Not in any way, shape or form." He glanced at his watch. "Goodness, look at the time. I think we both should be heading home now. The library event starts in just a couple of hours."

Lizzie sat at the back of the room, trying to count the number of people in front of her in the somewhat uncomfortable folding chairs. She'd bet there had to be about forty eager readers crowded into what she'd thought was one of the larger activity rooms in the library. The walls were painted a lemon yellow as if urging everyone who entered to be happy or at least welcoming to the authors. She realized there were no windows and figured that was just as well. Organizers would not want attendees sitting there, staring outside and daydreaming in case things got too boring inside. She'd often found herself doing just that as she sat reading in one of the comfy stuffed chairs in the main rooms. Although the library was in the center of town, it backed onto some of the prettiest green space in town.

She glanced over at Molly, standing at the bookseller tables placed at the left of the door. Molly looked particularly impressive in her cream jersey-knit pantsuit and white silk blouse. A lime green scarf tucked under the collar gave her a flattering splash of color. Stephanie sat at one of the tables and Andie staffed the other. Both looked keyed up and eager for the event.

Isabel Fox walked to the front of the room and the noise level visibly lessened. Her lightweight quilted navy and white jacket paired nicely with the pale green pants and dark green blouse. She smiled at the audience until the chatter had died to a few whispers.

"I'd like to welcome y'all here to this very special afternoon at the Ashton Corners Public Library. We're so pleased to have four well-known and very entertaining mystery authors with us today. I know firsthand that it will be an enjoyable time as I was honored to be a part of the recent Mystery Book Fair held by our wonderful bookstore, A Novel Plot. And you'll notice that Molly Mathews and her pleasant staff have brought some books to make it easy for you to purchase and get autographed copies, right on the spot.

"This afternoon we'll start with a reading by each of the authors and then finish off, say, the last half hour with questions for them all. Now, let's get right to it with, and we're going to do this in alphabetical order, Caroline Cummings reading from *Dishing Out Murder*."

Caroline stood from her seat in the front row with the

other authors, turned slightly and gave a little bow then walked to the lectern at the front.

"I'd like to first off thank Ms. Fox and the library for having us all here. It's so much fun getting to stand in front of so many avid fans and pour out our humble writings and innermost thoughts to y'all." She cleared her throat and looked slowly around the room before speaking again. "I want to start by telling a little story about how I came to write this, the seventh novel in my Southern Caterer series."

Lizzie tuned out for a moment, glancing around the room to see just who was in the audience. She spotted Carter sitting at the back of the room, arms crossed, a look of disgust on his face. No wonder Caroline kept her eyes focused on the first few rows of seats. Not the type of reaction one would want from their loving spouse, Lizzie thought. She wondered what had brought that on, or did he just dislike attending the readings? Or maybe all was not well in the Farrow household. Carter suddenly looked over at Lizzie. His face transferred instantaneously to its usual friendly smiling self. Lizzie felt a tinge of embarrassment but smiled back.

A.J. read next and delighted the ladies in the audience, which amounted to about three-quarters of the crowd, with his use of voices for different characters and his many asides. Lizzie was certain he'd just managed to enlist some new fans from this group. A.J. probably shared her views, from the look of pure delight on his face.

A hush fell over the crowd as Gigi Briggs took her turn in front of them. Lizzie wondered if the reaction was because of her age, compared with her compatriots, or if it had something to do with her outfit. This time she'd chosen all black, leotard, tights and ballet slippers, to suggest perhaps an acrobat. Her first words, a reading that introduced the main character, a circus acrobat, confirmed her vision of her outfit. Of course, thought Lizzie, she certainly had the figure for it. And also, the dramatic reading. It seemed that each time she read in public, her author persona blossomed even more.

Lorelie took her turn next, and after a significant pause, possibly for a mental cleansing of palate, gave a slow and dramatic reading with beseeching glances at the audience when she reached the romantic parts, a sinister scrunching of eyebrows for the mystery and sweeping gestures throughout. When she'd finished, the floor was opened up to questions and that kept the authors busy for over twenty minutes. Finally, with a gesture to the clock hanging at the front of the room, Isabel thanked everyone for coming and suggested they visit the bookselling table to stock up for signatures. Most did as asked, crowding around the table where Stephanie and Andie sat selling books, moving over next to the signing table. By the time Isabel ushered the final attendee out the door, the authors had fallen silent. A.J. stood and stretched.

"I'm totally wiped out. It's been a long day and I, for one, am looking forward to a quiet evening. But what a great response, Ms. Isabel. I do thank you."

"Why, it's my pleasure," Isabel beamed.

Carter collected Caroline, who left with a muted "Thanks," leaving Lorelie to beg a lift from Molly.

"I'm passing right by there," Lizzie said. "I'd be happy to drop you off." *And get a chance to ask more questions.*

"Why, that's nice of you, Lizzie."

They said their good-byes and left. Lizzie didn't waste any time once they were on the road.

"I was just wondering if you'd given any more thought to what you told me about Caroline and Ashley." Lizzie said, as she turned left onto Bishop out of the parking lot.

"No. Should I?"

"Perhaps not but I did hear that you and Ashley had clashed about a missed award submission."

"Whoever told you that?" Lorelie sputtered.

Lizzie didn't answer the question but said instead, "So you got over the fact that Ashley neglected to send your book in for the Cozy Lovers awards this year?"

"Yes," Lorelie said in a tight voice. "Ashley admitted she'd made a huge mistake and I graciously forgave her."

"Why would she make such a mistake? I've been hearing how great she was at her job."

Lizzie caught Lorelie's shrug out of the corner of her eye. "She said she'd been preoccupied with something more important in her life. Although that was her job. What could be more important than making sure your top writers are entered in awards?" Lorelie's voice had turned shrill. *So, not so forgotten. Maybe not even forgiven.*

"Is that why in your new book you had the publicist as the victim?"

Lorelie turned sideways to face Lizzie. "I don't know what you've gotten into your head. Are you insinuating I murdered Ashley or something equally crazy? I'll bet Caroline put you up to this. You've seen how she can get. Caroline Cummings is on a downward spiral. Her sales are plummeting, she's losing her fan base."

Lorelie said something under her breath that Lizzie didn't hear, except for the word "loser."

"Is she losing her husband?" Lizzie asked.

Lorelie gave her an icy stare. "How would I know?"

Lizzie thought it best to let Lorelie believe it was an innocent question. Lizzie shrugged instead. "I don't see them together much. And Carter seems at loose ends much of the time." Lizzie glanced over at Lorelie, who had shifted back and sat staring straight ahead. "Do you think Carter Farrow knew Ashley very well?"

Lorelie's head gave a slight jerk. "Carter? Why, I don't know. I hardly know the man. He doesn't say much when we authors get together, although he's always an angel and willing to run errands for us all."

Lizzie wondered if that were the truth. Had her eyes been playing tricks on her when she thought she'd spotted the two of them together? Of course, Lorelie was a writer. Perhaps she was spinning out some of her own lines.

Lizzie pulled up in front of the Quilt Patch and Lorelie quickly opened the car door.

"Thank you for the ride, dear," she said, her voice on the frosted side. She shut the door without waiting for Lizzie's response.

Chapter Twenty-five

◇◇◇

And sometimes, they were to be feared.

WRITTEN IN STONE—ELLERY ADAMS

Sunday morning dawned as one of those days that comes just when you think you've escaped summer, and it surprises you with a great gust of humidity and sunshine. Not that Lizzie would complain. She knew the rains would soon be coming. Not a lot, but enough to give all the fall plants a growth spurt.

She rolled over slowly in bed, careful not to displace the cats that had decided sometime overnight to abandon the crooks and nooks of her body in favor of stretching out, head to head, the length of the bed. They knew the concept of overheating.

Lizzie eyed the clock. Seven. She debated about going for a run but caved to the small voice telling her that taking a day off was actually a good thing. Besides, she wanted to get over to see her mama midmorning before the heat became oppressive. Even in the air-conditioned comfort of Magnolia Manor, Evelyn Turner tuned in to the outdoor heat and would often spend such an afternoon napping.

The phone rang as she stretched and wiggled her toes.

"Good morning, beautiful. I hope I'm not waking you," Mark said before she had a chance to say anything.

"No way. I've been up for hours, done a long run, mowed the lawn and washed my car already."

"Hah. No way. I'm sorry I didn't make it over last night but it was a rowdy night at one of our more formidable drinking establishments."

"Are you at the office right now?" Lizzie asked.

His voice lowered and took on a cozy, caressing tone. "Yes, but my thoughts are elsewhere."

"Right along with mine." Lizzie sighed. "You didn't spend the entire night there, did you?"

"No. I got a few hours sleep at home and then walked Patchett before coming back in. I'll finish up some paperwork and then thought you might be free after seeing your mama?"

"Umm. I'll be back after lunch. But then we've got the author readings at the band gazebo in the town square, remember? A certain police chief asked us to set that up?"

"That does ring a bell, now that you mention it."

"And then, we're invited to Molly's for dinner with the authors. I hope you can still come to that."

"Wouldn't miss it. How about you give me a call when you get home from the afternoon excitement and I'll give you a ride to Molly's. Service with a smile."

"Hmm. Sounds too good to pass up."

"Good. See you soon."

Lizzie hung up, a smile on her face, and got up to start her day.

* * *

Evelyn Turner sat on a three-seat swing out on the back patio, a light breeze keeping her cool in the shade. Lizzie sat down beside her and started the swing moving back and forth. After about five minutes, Lizzie could feel Evelyn's feet helping with the propulsion.

"It's such a beautiful day, Mama. I'm so glad you're taking advantage of the good weather even though it's a bit hotter today. And I just love this swing. We can get a bit of a breeze on it. I wonder if I'd have enough room for one on my back patio. Probably, but only if I didn't want anything else out on it." Lizzie kept up the monologue until she realized she was really reaching for things to say. Nothing had elicited a response but Lizzie felt they'd shared a good visit.

They went back inside and Lizzie waited until Evelyn went into the dining room for her lunch. Lizzie knew how important routines were in Evelyn's life. The visits were every bit as important to Lizzie, even knowing she wasn't recognized most times. She glanced at her watch and realized she'd have just enough time to grab something to eat at home and then head over to the band gazebo for the author event.

When she arrived at the town center, she noticed that the four authors were all seated in the gazebo and a respectable number of attendees were getting settled on the large lawn in the center square. Many had brought fold-up garden chairs and some were even seated on blankets. The number should make the authors happy.

Molly acted as host of the day, doing the welcome at the start and a short intro before each author read. Lizzie sat at the bookselling table set up close to the parking lot and enjoyed just lazing with the sun shining on her face, fanning herself with a book. At the end of the event, she roused herself and helped with the selling. As the authors made their way over to the table to sign books, Lizzie wondered if Lorelie would still be upset with her. A gracious smile from Lorelie assured Lizzie that, at least in public, all was forgiven.

M ark arrived just as Lizzie pulled the iced tea from the fridge. She'd made a fresh pitcher that morning before heading out. Mark came up behind her at the counter as she poured them each a glass and wrapped his arms around her.

"And how was the grand event this afternoon?" he asked, nuzzling her neck.

"It was a big hit. I was amazed we got such a huge turn-out. I think Molly's going to be doing this again real soon. And it's all thanks to you."

"Hmm. Wish that keeping them here longer could have paid off more."

"Uh-oh. I don't like the sound of that." Unfortunately, Mark wasn't very forthcoming with an explanation on the drive over to Molly's.

When Lizzie and Mark arrived, A.J. Pruitt and Gigi Briggs were already seated in the sunroom, nursing cold mint juleps. Sally-Jo, Jacob and Stephanie, along with baby Wendy, came through the door next followed by Bob, and then Andie, whom he'd given a ride to. Andie rushed over to Wendy and spread out a blanket on the floor, along with the tote bag of toys Stephanie had brought along, and started playing with the baby.

Molly, who'd decided to cook the dinner herself, kept watching the clock, hoping the other authors would arrive before long. She let Lizzie and Sally-Jo help serve the hors d'oeuvres of crabmeat on crackers and stuffed endive but shooed them out of the kitchen when they tried to lend a hand with the main meal.

"Too many cooks," Molly told them, laughingly. "Now shoo. Get back in there with your beaux."

"Yoo-hoo. I'm here," Teensy announced in a singsong voice as she sashayed into the kitchen. "You know, Molly, your front door is unlocked. Who knows how many unwanted guests you might be attracting. Myself excluded, of course."

Molly laughed. "I thought the divas might let themselves in, just in case we don't hear the bell. You didn't happen to see them, did you?"

"No, I didn't but I'll bet my new red garters they'll appear anytime soon. Those gals have radar and can tell just the right moment to make an entrance."

Lizzie bit back a smile. Teensy would know.

Right on cue, they heard the front doorbell followed by an entrance by the divas, similar to that made by Teensy.

"I'm so sorry if we're late," Caroline said as she accepted the drink Bob held out to her. "The hours just fly by."

Lorelie, not to be outdone, sat grandly on one of the wicker chairs, her hand outstretched to Bob. "Y'all know that a Southern belle cannot be rushed in any circumstances. I hope we haven't ruined your schedule, Molly."

"Not at all, but I'm afraid you won't have too much time to linger over your cocktails," Molly answered with a light tap on Bob's arm. "Now, I'll just check on the food and be right with you."

Carter had followed the two women in and nodded a hello around the room, although he hadn't said anything. He walked over to Bob, standing by the drink cart. "I could do with a cold beer if you have any there."

Bob grinned. "Right up my alley." He pulled a Coors from the small cooler on the bottom shelf. He looked over at Mark, who shook his head. "Molly is always prepared for any emergency."

The meal was ready before they knew it and they retraced their way to the seats they'd taken just a short week earlier. *Was it really only a week ago all this started?* A lot had happened in that week's time. No one would have imagined it all. Or had someone? Lizzie looked around the table at each of the authors and Carter. No one had an obvious motive to kill Ashley.

Lizzie believed that if her argument with Ashley needed to be recognized for what it was, nothing major, then the others deserved the same benefit of the doubt. Besides, she didn't believe that anyone in real life would commit murder because she felt his or her book needed more exposure. A dead Ashley meant a momentary lapse in publicity, except for that which surrounded the actual murder. And a new publicist could choose to go either way. In fact, she or he could turn out to be worse. No, not a good motive.

"Lizzie, honey, would you pass along the roasted butternut salad, please?" Molly must have been asking a few times from the look on her face.

Lizzie shrugged an apology and passed the plate to Jacob on her left. She thought she'd bypass the extra calories this time.

"So, Chief," A.J. asked, leaning slightly toward Mark, "who's your number one suspect in the murder? I don't believe that Lizzie should hold that spot for one minute."

Lizzie grinned at him and quirked an eyebrow at Mark, who sat across from her. He finished chewing the forkful of pork roast in his mouth before answering.

"That spot is wide open at the moment. I can tell you,

though, that we're seriously looking into Ashley Dixon's connections here in town, aside from Lizzie that is."

Lizzie noted that Mark had been closely watching each of the authors in turn as he spoke. She wondered if he'd been enlightened any.

"The puzzler," he went on, "is how Lizzie's cell phone happened to be at the scene of the crime."

Lizzie could hear the sound of the large mantel clock at the end of the dining room ticking away. No one had any comment on that topic, she was sorry to note.

"Surely you were able to pull some fingerprints from it, other than Lizzie's?" A.J. asked, leaning on his elbows. Lizzie noticed he seemed to be relishing the discussion. Of course, she reminded herself, he did write police stories.

"Funny thing about that," Mark answered. "It had been wiped clean. There were no prints on it, not even Lizzie's." He finished the last of the roasted potatoes on his plate but Lizzie could tell he was alert to what was happening around him.

Gigi made a squeaking sound. "Oops, excuse me," she said and cleared her throat. "Isn't that really odd?" she asked.

Mark looked at her a few seconds before answering. "Very. Why wipe your phone if you're just carrying it? And why plant a phone with no prints if you're wanting to frame someone?"

Gigi shifted in her seat. "That would make a good plot."

"A plot involving your funeral home?" Lorelie asked in a voice registering her disapproval. Lizzie wasn't sure of what, though.

Molly cleared her throat and asked, "Can I get anyone anything else? More roast? More veggies?"

Everyone was in agreement on one thing anyway, and that was they were quite full.

Gigi glared at Lorelie and then said, "Well, I saw you put your cell away in your purse, Lizzie, at the book fair in the morning just as it was getting started. You must have lost it later in the day or evening."

"Probably," Lizzie answered and wondered why that would stick in Gigi's mind anyway.

"Well it sort of sounds like a plot in one of Margaret's books," Carter said, then looked startled. He turned to his wife and said, "Sorry, that's Caroline's books. Do you remember? The one about the guy who murdered his wife?"

Caroline looked miffed. "Most of my plots involve the husband murdering the wife." She turned slightly to look at Carter. "Or the wife murdering the husband."

Lorelie snorted in a very unladylike manner. She excused herself and dabbed at her mouth daintily with her napkin.

"I must admit," Molly said in a loud voice, "to having cheated with the desserts. We have a marvelous bakery in town, LaBelle's, and I've chosen two of their most delicious offerings."

She started clearing the table with the help of Andie and Lizzie while Sally-Jo noted everyone's preferences for coffee or tea. Gigi brought into the kitchen a couple of serving dishes while Lizzie was stacking the plates.

"I'm pretty amazed that you can remember me with my cell phone last week," she said to Gigi.

"Well, I am a writer. I'm very observant. It's like doing research all the time." She left the room and was back in with two more dishes in a few minutes. "You know, though, on second thought, I may have seen you put the Nokia down on the registration table. Hopefully it wasn't tossed in the trash. Or perhaps someone picked it up."

"As in the killer?"

"Oh no, I didn't mean that," Gigi said hastily. She left again and when Lizzie went back to the dining room, Gigi was deep in conversation with Jacob. And Lizzie was left thinking that Gigi really was very observant to know the make of her old cell phone.

Chapter Twenty-six

◇◇◇

Sticking my nose where it didn't belong was never healthy under any circumstances. I knew that from personal experience.

KILLER IN CRINOLINES—DUFFY BROWN

Lizzie had no idea if she should report to the principal's office on entering the school the next morning. She debated with herself on the walk in from the parking lot. He hadn't asked her to; she should just to show she was there; he could still say something demeaning; she needed to show she was powerful and in control. Her decision was made for her as Charles Benton came out of the main office just as she entered through the front doors. He looked at her a few seconds before nodding. She summoned her brightest smile then shrugged as he turned away and headed down the hall.

Welcome back, Lizzie. She approached the staff room with less caution but still some hesitation. No need. The handful of teachers grabbing their coffee greeted her with enthusiasm. Sally-Jo rushed over and threw her arms around Lizzie, whispering in her ear, "So glad you're back. Knock 'em dead."

Lizzie grabbed her own coffee and then headed to the library to try to sort out her agenda for the remainder of the week. She'd attempt to reschedule the missed appointments without shortchanging anyone in the time department.

After attending to her already booked in-class time with a third-grade teacher followed by a testing period with a young sassy girl in sixth grade, she made the necessary phone calls to parents and managed to fit everyone in for the remainder of the week. By lunch, Lizzie felt she'd accomplished a full day's work but knew she was in for a long afternoon at a full meeting of special education teachers at the school board office.

Glancing at her watch as she left that meeting, she was surprised it was only three o'clock. It felt like at least two hours later. Maybe a good time to visit Fay Huxton-Parson. She'd bet Mark would not be there at this hour of the day.

She'd shared her thoughts about Gigi and her cell phone with Mark when he took her home after dinner the night before. He said he'd look into it and then the discussion had turned to a romantic parting of ways for the evening. Maybe she should follow up with Gigi just in case. After a visit to the Huxton family.

It didn't take her long to find the estate, just fifteen minutes out of town. The antebellum mansion rivaled Molly's but the vast surrounding grounds seemed to go on forever. A great place for privacy. Lizzie rang the doorbell and a black woman dressed in a traditional maid's outfit, black dress and white apron, opened the door. She made Lizzie remain out on the door stoop until she returned a few minutes later. She asked Lizzie to follow her to a darkened sitting room just off the main hall and wait for the lady of the house.

Fay Huxton-Parson swept into the room, a vision in pales. Her short whitish blonde hair, obviously colored, was the same color as her cashmere sweater set and skirt. Cream-colored pumps completed the look. She held out her hand to Lizzie, an inquisitive look on her face or at least Lizzie assumed that's what it was. What it looked like to Lizzie was that Ms. Huxton-Parson had had several visits to a plastic surgeon or perhaps a series of Botox treatments. The wrinkle-free face did not match her age or the frail appearance of the rest of her body.

"I'm sorry to intrude without calling first," Lizzie said and explained who she was. "I was hoping you might spare me a few minutes. I have a couple of questions I'd like to ask you."

Huxton-Parson eased herself onto a straight-backed arm-chair sporting a brocade slipcover. It looked more suited to the dining room, but from the way she sat, Lizzie figured the chair was ideal for a bad back. Lizzie sat on the other side of the massive carved oak coffee table.

"About what? You have my curiosity piqued, I must admit."

Lizzie wondered just how forthright to be but decided it would be best to just get it out there. "I'm wondering about a friend of mine, Ashley Dixon, who had been making enquiries about the Huxton Hotel. I wondered if she'd been here to speak to you."

Huxton-Parson looked as if she'd been slapped and then quickly recovered her composure. "And what business is it of yours, if she had?"

Lizzie took that to mean yes, so she forged ahead. "You may have heard that she was murdered last week. I'm trying to find out more about what she did while she was in Ashton Corners. She was visiting from New York."

Lizzie knew she was being sized up. She sat perfectly still, hoping to present a nonthreatening persona. Huxton-Parson stared a couple of minutes and then stood abruptly and walked to the window. She spoke, her back to Lizzie.

"And just how much do you know and want, Ms. Turner?"

"What?" Lizzie wondered if she'd heard correctly.

Huxton-Parson whirled to face Lizzie, her face a sneer.

"Oh, come on now. You said you were friends with that woman. Surely, she confided in you. In fact, I'll bet since you're local, you put her onto us. To me."

Lizzie shook her head. "No. No, I didn't. I had no idea what Ashley was up to. She only told me that she planned to stay on awhile."

"I think you should leave." Huxton-Parson's voice was stone cold.

Lizzie stood shakily. "I'm sorry if I've upset you. I only want to find out the truth about what happened to Ashley."

"And you think my family murdered her? For what reason? She was a nobody and she had no claim whatsoever. She was never a threat. Now, leave."

Lizzie left quickly, wondering if the maid had been hovering and heard, since she appeared at the front door, opening it quickly and closing it firmly behind Lizzie.

Lizzie sat in her car a few moments, hands shaking. What was all that about? She glanced at the house and felt eyes on her. She started the car and drove slowly down the driveway, turning left toward town. As she passed Glendale Park, she turned into it and pulled over at the far end of the parking lot. She needed to think.

She got out of the car and walked toward the Tallapoosa River, sifting through the conversation in her mind. What claim had Huxton-Parson been talking about? That seemed to be the crux of her reaction. Lizzie kept walking, slowing her pace as she turned onto the walkway that paralleled the river. She passed several joggers going the other direction, and an elderly couple, leaning on each other as they slowly made their way along.

Lizzie knew that Ashley had been asking questions about the hotel. No, more specifically, about when her mama had worked at the hotel for a summer. How did that translate to a claim of some sort?

Lizzie stopped in her tracks, almost causing a cyclist to collide with her. Had something happened to her mama? Bertha Redding had told her that Ashley's mama had left before the summer was over. Had she witnessed something and maybe tried her hand at blackmail and now Ashley had picked up the same trail?

Had she witnessed something and run away, afraid for her life? And had Ashley finally found out about it and tried to get the whole story? Or was she trying to get even more? Had Ashley tried to blackmail the Huxton family? But why? What had her mama seen? Or done? *Too many possibilities*.

Lizzie did some quick math. If she remembered right, Ashley was about a year younger than she, which meant she was born in 1983. What summer had her mama worked at the hotel? Lizzie had it written down at home. She dared not trust her memory. She wanted to be certain of her facts before she took this any further.

If she was right, she needed to talk to Mark right away. She knew she'd get no further with Fay Huxton-Parson, and by now, the entire family had probably been alerted. At the very least, told not to speak to Lizzie. Of that she was certain.

Secrets. Indeed.

Chapter Twenty-seven

◇◇◇

I put my head back and closed my eyes. There had
to be some way to fix this. I just wished I knew how.

GRACE INTERRUPTED—JULIE HYZY

Lizzie phoned Mark as soon as she had checked her
notes at home. It took several tries before she connected
with him on his cell phone. She asked if he could come
to her place as soon as possible, refusing to discuss it with
him on the phone. He made it to her place in less than ten
minutes.

"Are you all right? What's wrong?" he asked as he burst
in through the kitchen door.

"Yes, I'm fine. I just need to tell you something and I
thought it was better to discuss it in person."

Mark heaved a sigh of relief and then glared at her. "I
thought you were in trouble. I was on my way to a meeting
with the mayor. This had better be good."

"It is. I'm sorry. I didn't mean to worry you."

"I worry about you all the time, Lizzie." He walked over

to the fridge and pulled out the Brita, pouring himself a glass of water, and turned to face her. "Now, what's up?"

"I had a little chat with Fay Huxton-Parson this afternoon."

"You what?"

Lizzie knew the signs of Mark's breaking point quickly approaching. She hurried on. "Have you talked to her about Ashley yet?"

"Yes."

"And?"

"And, nothing. You are not part of this investigative team. I tell you nothing."

Lizzie stamped her foot. Now she was getting angry. "That's not fair. I need to know if you have any reason to suspect the Huxton family is involved in Ashley's death."

"You need to know? I need you to keep out of this investigation. We go through this every time there's a murder, Lizzie. I am the cop. You are a civilian. It's my job to solve this. It's your job to stay out of it. I can't let you get involved just because we're in a relationship. And besides all that, it's too frigging dangerous. Now will you please back off?"

Lizzie just stared at him. She hadn't seen him that angry with her before. She knew she had to calm herself before saying anything.

Mark finished the glass of water and then took a deep breath. He sounded more like his old self when he spoke. "I don't want to argue with you, Lizzie. Look, I know you're worried about being a suspect and I know that you're naturally nosy." He held up his hand as she was about to object.

"But I can't share details of the investigation with you because you are a suspect, even though an unlikely one. So, please don't ask."

"Okay, then let me tell you what I suspect." She waited a few seconds and when he didn't object, she continued. "I asked Fay Huxton-Parson one simple question, namely had Ashley been around to talk to her, and she blew up. She wanted to know what I knew and how much I wanted. And then she ordered me out of the house."

She let Mark think about it. He started pacing and then finally sat at the table. She followed suit.

"What do you think she meant by that? I know you have an idea," he finally said.

"It had something to do with Ashley's mama working at the Huxton Hotel one summer in the early 1980s. She left her summer job earlier than planned, before summer was over. And I'm pretty certain that Ashley was born in 1983."

"You think her mama was pregnant? Don't tell me you think by a Huxton?"

"Well, doesn't it add up?"

"It could or it could mean something entirely different. I don't want to go jumping to conclusions." He ran his hand over his head. Lizzie could see he was almost due for another shave, small hair growth beginning to show in places.

His next question sounded more like a statement. "You think a Huxton killed Ashley Dixon?"

Lizzie nodded. "I know it sounds a stretch but doesn't it make sense? Ashley said she planned to stay on for a while. She'd been asking questions at the hotel about the family and about her mama. I wondered if she had been planning to write a novel with the hotel as a setting. Maybe she still was but it would be her mama's story. Or, she could have been trying to blackmail them."

"Ross Huxton did die just a couple of months ago."

"Maybe that's what spurred her on. All that money going to his children, who wouldn't want a breath of scandal, especially not about the newly departed Ross Huxton."

"Ashley's father?"

"Could be."

Mark stood abruptly. "I need to think about this and do some digging. And I want you to stay out of it. Do not, I repeat, do not contact any members of the family. The next thing you know, you'll be sued for harassment. Promise me, Lizzie."

She nodded.

"Show me your hands and say it verbally."

She did as told.

He gave her a quick kiss, grabbed his hat and opened the door. He glanced back at her before leaving. "Good work."

Lizzie walked over to the front window and watched him back his Jeep out of the driveway just in time to see Lavenia pull up in front of Nathaniel's place. She felt a short stab of guilt. Aside from asking questions at the library about the garden club, she hadn't done anything to try to track down the malicious gossiper threatening to spread rumors about Nathaniel. Mark wanted her to back off the Dixon case; maybe she should take his advice, for now, and try to track down the garden club membership list.

Although she was reluctant to ask Lavenia and possibly have to admit she hadn't done much yet, she knew that had to be her next move. Not only would she know the members, she'd also be attuned to any other women in the group who had their eyes on Nathaniel. A woman in love can sense those things.

Lizzie flung open the door and ran across the lawn, catching Lavenia as she exited her car.

"Do you have a minute? I need to talk to you."

Lavenia looked over at Nathaniel's house. "Is it about . . . you know? I don't want to alert Nathaniel and he'd probably think it awfully strange if I went to your place first."

Lizzie nodded.

"I'm just dropping of this bag of preserves I'd promised him. He knows I won't stay long because I have a piano student coming at four." She glanced at her watch. "Perhaps we could meet at the Cup 'n Choc for a quick coffee in about twenty minutes? I really could use one."

"Fine," Lizzie answered. "I'll see you then. I'll just walk down the block so it doesn't look like I came out specifically to see you, in case he's watching."

Lavenia smiled a secretive smile. "And I'll be sure to keep him away from the windows so you can turn around and come right back."

Lizzie had already been waiting at a corner table for ten minutes, taking her time enjoying an iced cappuccino, when Lavenia walked in. After ordering hot tea at the counter, Lavenia carried it over to the table.

"Thanks for meeting me," Lizzie said.

"No, thank you, my dear. I appreciate your help and your discretion. Now, what is it you want to know?"

"First of all, I'd like a copy of the membership list of the Ashton Corners Garden Club."

"Certainly. Why don't I email you a copy?"

Lizzie appreciated this tech-savvy woman, probably in her mid to late seventies. "I was also wondering if you'd noticed any women at the garden club who'd been flirting with Nathaniel prior to the two of you going out?"

"You think it's someone from the club? I hate to think that. We've had some very good meetings over the years and everyone seems friendly enough."

"I could be way off base but it's a place to start. No stone unturned and all that."

Lavenia smiled tentatively. "Hmm. Well, Ursula Nesbitt certainly had her eye on him at one point, just as she's eyed every male who walks in a room, even if he needs a cane to do so." She chuckled and Lizzie smiled. "I don't think she ever asked him out but I could check with Nathaniel. If she did, I'll let you know."

"Good. Anyone else?"

"Not so overtly but Maude Drummond and Bernice Waller always are talking about the men in their lives and eyeing the poor souls in the club. Not that that necessarily means anything."

"This is good information. And who knows where it will lead. By the way, have you received any more calls?"

"A couple of hang-ups when Nathaniel has been over. You don't think it's the same person, do you?"

Lizzie shrugged. "I'm not sure what to think at the moment. It's a good sign, though, not receiving any more threats." *Unless the culprit's gearing up for the grand finale, the unveiling to the world.*

They finished their drinks, chatting about Lavenia's students. She'd been teaching piano for over forty years, but at this point, had only a couple of students still with her. "I'm so proud of them. They're both hard workers and even if neither wants to pursue a career in music, it will stand them good in the future."

"I know," Lizzie said. "I had about four years of piano and wish now that I had continued."

Lavenia patted her hand. "I could take on another student, my dear."

Lizzie smiled. Something to ponder. Lizzie Turner, touring concert pianist. *Not.*

She checked her email when she got home, having stopped by the Piggly Wiggly for some fresh chicken breasts. She was delighted that Lavenia had taken the time to send the list. She printed it out and studied it while grilling the chicken and pulling the remainder of a three-lentil salad out of the fridge. She planned to make a green salad and use up some of the pears she'd bought earlier in the week, along with dried cranberries, pecan and feta cheese.

She found the names and addresses she was looking for

but what she needed was a pitch. She couldn't very well go up to them and ask if they were threatening to spread a rumor that Nathaniel had killed his wife. But maybe she could ask if they'd heard anything about someone spreading rumors about all the eligible men. If taken off guard, surely she could spot the liar.

That was a plan. But maybe she could do better.

Chapter Twenty-eight

◇◇◇

At any other time she might have found that thought
amusing, but now it only served as an unsettling
reminder that she was about to set sail on a vast,
uncharted sea.

SKETCH ME IF YOU CAN—SHARON PAPE

Lizzie finished preparing her meal and ate while studying
the membership list. Her thoughts then turned to possible motives for Ashley's murder as she washed up the dirty
dishes. Molly phoned just as she finished drying.

"How are things going, honey?" Molly's calm, concerned
voice made Lizzie feel happy.

She quickly filled Molly in on all that had happened
that day.

"Oh my goodness. Who would think Fay Huxton-Parson
would act in such a way. She must be stressed way beyond
her endurance. I should probably drive over there tomorrow
and have a little noncommittal chat with her."

"I'd suggest you don't ask her about Ashley."

"Oh no. I wouldn't do that. I was thinking more like she
might want someone to confide in these days. I know she
doesn't have many friends and she's not that close to the family.

Hmm. I'll take her a caramel chocolate pecan pie, too. She always had a sweet tooth."

Lizzie chuckled. "Pastry to the rescue. If anyone can help her, it will be you. Any news from the Quilt Patch? Did you see the divas today?"

"I did stop by after spending a couple of hours at the store, just in time for afternoon sherry. I get the feeling they're starting to get restless so I got them talking some more about the upcoming talent show. I think they're looking forward to it, at least enough to quell any thoughts of leaving for the time being. And you might be interested in my observations during the sherry hour."

"For sure."

"Well, Caroline and Lorelie seemed to be at outs. They talked but not directly to each other."

"I wonder what that's all about?"

"Could be nothing more than they both wanted to use the dining room table for their writing at the same time. But I sense a storm brewing."

"Or it could be that Lorelie got in Caroline's face. She, Lorelie, thought that Caroline told me about her earlier argument with Ashley. That may have been bugging her." Lizzie thought that fit.

"Hmm. I'll try a drop by tomorrow, too. Maybe if they get into it, something about Ashley will be said."

"I hate to admit it and decrease the names on the suspect list, but I really can't see either of them being a killer. Only with words. And more than that, what would be their motives? It may be a moot point if the killer happens to be a member of the Huxton family."

Molly caught her breath. "That would be a real shame. Such a well-known and respected family. But as I know, respect has nothing to do with what's going on underneath it all. I'll let you go now, honey. Have a good night."

"You, too, Molly." Lizzie wondered if Molly would ever be able to forget what her dead husband, Claydon, had wrought in secret.

Lizzie glanced at the clock. Only seven thirty. The evening was still young, at least young enough for her to be making some house calls. She looked at her list of garden club suspects again. Bernice Waller lived about four blocks in one direction; Maude Drummond lived on the other side of town. She might as well start with the one farthest away. She quickly changed into a tangerine long-sleeved pullover sweater and camel cords, very casual and friendly looking.

On the drive over, Lizzie noticed the streets lined with tall maples and poplars showing off their autumn colors, not the brilliant reds of farther north, but an array of oranges and yellows. She did love this time of year, as much for the display as for the crisp evenings when the heat and humidity of summer became another memory.

A late-model cream-colored Chevy Impala took up most of the short driveway in front of Maude's picture-perfect house. The two-story white Cape Cod style sported deep blue shutters and the iron-framed love seat on the front porch had matching pillows. A mixture of late-blooming colors provided contrast in a border running in front of the house.

She parked on the street directly in front, feeling there was no need to surprise her, and noticed the front sheers flutter closed. By the time Lizzie had her hand on the doorbell, the door was being opened and a tall, slender woman who looked to be somewhere in her seventies stood in the gap. She had a hesitant smile on her face but waited for Lizzie to speak first.

Lizzie had rehearsed her lines on the way over and was prepared to watch Maude's face very closely. She wanted a way to get these ladies talking candidly. She'd toyed with the idea of saying she was planning a surprise party for Nathaniel and Lavenia but then realized she'd have to follow through with it. And things might get too uncomfortable for Lavenia if they knew she'd been receiving phone calls.

She'd tell them she was writing a feature article for the newspaper. One thing she knew, she could count on George Havers to back her up if need be.

"I'm Lizzie Turner," she said, doubting that would mean anything. "I'm writing a story for the *Colonist* about the garden club and I wondered if you might have a few minutes to talk to me?"

"Why, I can do that." Maude stepped back to open the door wider. "Would you like some tea? I was just fixing to have some myself and then we can take our drinks out to the back patio and enjoy this ending of a day."

Lizzie nodded and followed her, waiting for her glass to be poured, and then out to the back patio. Here the color of the front gardens doubled in size and provided an amazing border to the patio stones. They sat in dark green wicker chairs facing the garden that was obviously the showpiece of the property.

"I had no idea there'd be a piece on us," Maude said once she'd taken a sip of her tea. "Nobody has said anything but I think that's an excellent idea. What would you like to know?" She settled back, managing to keep her spine straight.

"It's just a short piece, in fact, it might not even get printed. I'm pitching this idea to the editor about an article that takes a brief look at different groups and clubs that give Ashton Corners such character. And of course, the people who make these clubs what they are. Does that sound like something you'd agree to being interviewed for?"

Maude preened a little at that. "Of course."

"First of all, could you tell me how long you've been a member?"

"I guess about thirty years. I was one of the founding members."

Lizzie nodded. "I've noticed that most of the members are, shall I say, of retirement age?"

Maude tittered. "We are that. We did try to interest the young folk but to no avail, so we're content with what it is. Unfortunately one day there might not be enough of us still around to keep it going. But that's life, isn't it?"

Lizzie nodded again. She had to admire Maude's attitude. "Given the ages, I'm just wondering if this might be a hotbed for romance? That's the angle I'd like to take, finding something that makes it a bit unique or quirky."

Maude had paled slightly at the question but gave it some thought and was soon chuckling. "I think that's very clever of you, Ms. Turner. Sort of a garden club that's also a dating service?" She tried to control her laughter while she took another sip. "Forgive me. I don't mean to laugh at your idea but the club's not doing so well in that department. We have, let me see, one active romance going, although several hopefuls are in the wings, shall we say."

"Who would the happy couple be?"

"I don't know if they'd want this in print, so you'd better check first with them, all right?"

"Of course."

"Their names are Lavenia Ellis and Nathaniel Creely and they've got to be on the later side of seventy, I'd think."

"Are you very good friends with them?"

Maude gave it a moment's thought. "Not really good friends, good acquaintances is more like it." Lizzie gave her points for sincerity and nonchalance.

"How does this affect the group? Are there any jealousies aroused?"

"Oh, I might have had a tinge of the green stuff when it became apparent Nathaniel had eyes only for Lavenia but I'm old enough to know when not to waste my time or energy. My Wilbur died eight years ago and while I'm not desperate for a companion, I wouldn't say no if the right man came along. By this stage, though, most I can hope for is someone to play nursemaid to. Nathaniel at least is in good health, has his own teeth, I hear, and has a sense of humor. But although we have had some pleasant conversations, it wasn't meant to be more than that. As for others in the club, I will say there are a couple of very competitive females who are not above going to funerals to scout out the widowers."

Her eyes were twinkling as she said this and Lizzie felt herself smiling.

"Care to share any names?"

"I think it's best if I don't, although . . ." She paused. "You might get some very interesting interviews from them. All right, their names are Bernice Waller and Ursula Nesbitt."

Lizzie finished her tea and felt a bit abashed as she thanked Maude and left. She felt badly about tricking her. She was certain this was not the rumormonger and was, in fact, one very nice lady. But she had confirmed what Lavenia had said. Were the two women that obvious? She glanced at the clock in the car. Too late to pay any more visits. She'd try them both tomorrow after school.

By the time she reached home, she'd come up with a different angle of attack. She called Andie, hoping to bypass a conversation with her mama. Their short words in passing these days were just that, short. Lizzie put it down to the fact that Andie had fled the family home this past summer and stayed at Lizzie's. Fortunately, Andie answered the phone.

"Yo, Lizzie. What's happening?" Andie asked, her voice buoyant and filled with a residue of laughter. Lizzie wondered what she'd interrupted.

"I'm sorry to bother you but I have a task for you, if you don't mind. Although, I'm a bit worried about what I'm about to ask you to do." Lizzie paused. She really had second thoughts about getting Andie involved. What if this was illegal?

"Out with it," Andie begged. "I'm dying for something exciting in my life."

"Okay. All I can tell you at this point is that someone sent a nasty email to Lavenia Ellis, Nathaniel Creely's good friend. I'm wondering if we can figure out who it's from?"

"Oh, goody," squealed Andie. "I'm so into that. Do you have the email? I'll need to see it. Can you send it to me?"

"Yes, I can, but I want you to promise not to share its content with anyone. Okay?"

"Yes, fine. But what if I have to bring my friend in on it? He's a computer whiz and lets nothing stand in his way."

Nothing? Uh-oh. "Who is this guy? You've not mentioned him before."

"He's uh . . . a friend. A guy I met on the computer."

"Online dating?"

"Yeah. Sort of. Not really. I guess. Does that bother you?"

Lizzie thought fast. She didn't want to put Andie off but she did want her to be cautious. "No. I know that's how people are hooking up these days. You will be careful, though, won't you? What do your parents say?"

"As if they would care. Anyway, we've been texting and sending emails and then we met about a month ago. He's goth and, like I said, a computer genius."

Oh no. And we'd just gotten her away from her goth styling, too.

"Thanks, Andie. And, thanks to your friend, too."

"Spike. That's his name."

Lizzie felt a mixture of apprehension and relief as she hung up. If they could track down the sender, she wouldn't have to do more interviews and risk arousing suspicions.

She spent some time getting ready for school the next

day and then phoned Mark before going to bed. She wanted to know if he'd talked to Fay Huxton-Parson yet. He answered on the fourth ring.

"I hope I didn't get you away from something," she started out.

"Just bed but I'm happy to share this time with you." She could hear the smile in his voice. She hated to change the mood.

"Me, too. But you can guess what I'm calling about. Have you talked to Ms. Huxton-Parson yet?"

She heard his heavy sigh. "Yes. I called as a courtesy to tell her I was on the way over and I met with her and her lawyer."

"She'd called him?"

"Yes. Has him on speed dial, I imagine. I asked a few questions which she answered, with a slightly different version of facts from yours, I might add."

"Well, you knew that would happen."

"Yes, I expected it. The upshot is, her lawyer threatened to sue you and the city for harassment if I or anyone else continued this line of questioning with her or any member of her family."

"Can she do that?" Lizzie was indignant.

"It's a good threat and she can probably do that to you, but I'm not taking it too seriously. If I find evidence that ties a member of the Huxton family to the death, I'll be talking to them all, over and over, as long as it takes to get to the bottom of it."

Go get 'em, tiger.

Chapter Twenty-nine

Next time you hatch a plan like that, however, it would be better to hear it from you first.

GRACE INTERRUPTED—JULIE HYZY

Lizzie had several spare minutes before her first appointment at school the next morning, so she spent them going over her notes for the literacy class that night. She wanted to get the students thinking about description, and while she had been trying to come up with a different approach this term, mainly for her own interest's sake, she ended up back at the tried and true. She thoroughly enjoyed teaching the classes, but aside from the variety of students and all the new views they'd spring on her, she needed to keep things juiced up to prevent falling into routine patterns, which could eventually lead to routine responses. She needed to keep herself revved up in order to ignite these kids.

She knocked over the lists of suspects she'd been working on at dinner the night before and when she leaned over to pick them up, she hit her head on the side of the table.

"Oww." She stood up moaning and sat down quickly. *Take some deep breaths. One issue at a time. Do not let your brain get scattered.*

After a couple of minutes she felt sufficiently calm to start all over again.

Her klutziness had traveled to school with her, she realized, as she shut the door to her shared office on her scarf. She grinned to herself as she freed it. At least she hadn't pulled an Isadora Duncan. No death by strangulation here, yet.

Her first appointment canceled at the last minute, which left her free to get caught up on workshop preparations for the next teachers' professional development day. She looked forward to these sessions, a time when she felt she got as good as she gave. The comments from her colleagues were most useful in developing new techniques to interest young readers, and the thanks she always received was most gratifying. The rest of the day proceeded as planned and she waved a cheery good-bye to Charles Benton as she passed him in the hall.

She pulled into her driveway after school and felt a moment's apprehension when she spotted Andie sitting on her back doorstep, lounging against the door. Had she changed her mind about living at home?

"Yo, Lizzie. I've got some info for you," Andie said with a smile as Lizzie exited her car. Lizzie let out a sigh of relief.

"That was fast."

"Told you he was good. Anyway, it's not much, really." She followed Lizzie into the house, talking the whole time. "Turns out it's one of the public computers at the library. You know, whenever you use it, you have to sign in and out. So we went to the library but they wouldn't show us the records. Real bummer."

Lizzie poured them each an iced tea without asking. "That's good, though."

"I know. So if you and me go over there right now, I'm sure they'll show them to you. I know they're pretty straitlaced over there and I can be sort of off-putting to look at."

Lizzie looked at Andie. Today she was wearing a plain black T-shirt, without holes or skulls, and jeans, again without any holes, not at all off-putting. She wondered what her friend had worn. She glanced at the clock. She had time.

"All right. I'll just top off the cat's dry food and then we'll go."

Lizzie looked for Isabel as they entered the library. She figured she'd go with who she knew and maybe that would work. Isabel was pleased to see them but not so engaging when she heard the request.

"I'm sorry, I can't show you that, Lizzie. We do have a sign-in and we also track usage, hoping to get a better idea of how many computers we need and also maybe some ideas as to how to allocate space." She indicated the spiral notebook at the edge of the desk within Lizzie's reach. "But it's a matter of privacy. I could get the library into a lot of trouble. Now, if the police chief came with a warrant, that's a different matter."

"It's not a police issue, Isabel. Something personal I'm helping a friend with. And it's important." Lizzie tried not to plead too much.

"I really am sorry, Lizzie." Her phone rang and she excused herself to answer. After a short conversation that had Isabel mainly listening, she hung up. "I'm sorry, I'm needed in the reference section." She squeezed Lizzie's hand and walked off.

"That's a real bummer," Andie groused. She looked

around slowly. "Just turn to the right and look over at the window, Lizzie."

"Why? What are you up to?" Lizzie asked but turned anyway.

"Shh." A few pages rustled. "Hmm. Ursula Nesbitt logged on at exactly eleven for a total of five minutes on October seventh. And Rosaline Vernon was on from ten fifty for an hour. That's it. Let's get out of here."

Andie grabbed Lizzie's arm and steered her out of the building. "Whoopee. That was so cool. Just like on *Castle*."

Lizzie glanced at Andie. That look of satisfaction on her face. What had she just validated? "Thanks for your help, Andie, but I have to say, I'm wishing it hadn't come to this."

"Why?"

"I've just encouraged you to snoop, maybe even break the law."

"First of all, we're all snooping, trying to find out who the murderer is in order to save you. And we've done it before. And now we're snooping to help another friend. Now, no more feeling guilty."

Lizzie smiled at the complete one-eighty the lecture had taken. She nodded and grabbed Andie's wrist to check out her watch. "Oh, boy . . . gotta get a move on. I teach literacy tonight. Want a lift home?"

"Nah, I'm meeting some friends at the Big Boa."

"Is everything okay at home?"

Andie nodded. "So far so good. We're in sort of a no-man's-land here. My folks aren't too sure just what sorts of rules to use and I'm not sure if I like that. But I'm sticking with it, if that's what you mean. No, you won't be stuck with me. For now."

Lizzie smiled. "Take care." She gave Andie a quick hug and walked over to her car, thinking about what they'd learned. Ursula Nesbitt had been on Lizzie's to-visit list. This as good as confirmed that she was the mystery caller, in Lizzie's mind anyway. The right day and time and for only five minutes. Just enough time to send a warning. What to do now? Make that visit or tell Lavenia all she'd learned and see what action she wanted to take?

Chapter Thirty

◇◇◇

I stared at him. My mouth was probably open, which
I know is not acceptable for a lady.

NAUGHTY IN NICE—RHYS BOWEN

Wow. Full class tonight, Lizzie thought as she handed
out the new batch of Rapid Reads that had finally
arrived. She'd chosen a mystery by Canadian author Gail
Bowen, *The Thirteenth Rose*. She'd had a quick read and
was certain the plot would appeal to them all. After giving
instructions for the short essay she wanted in return, Lizzie
spent the remainder of the time going over the previous
assignment, encouraging discussion. Although Tyler
Edwards remained silent and slumped in his chair most of
the class time, he did appear to be listening. She supposed
that was the most she could hope for at the moment. But she
felt determined to find out what would grab his attention
and get him involved.

At the end of two hours, Lizzie watched the last of her
class leave and then went to join Molly in the kitchen. Molly
handed her a glass of fresh lemonade and pointed to the

sunroom where A.J. Pruitt sat nursing his own glass. "He's been waiting a while for you. Said he needed to talk to you."

Lizzie joined him and waved him to stay seated when he started to stand. "I'm surprised to see you here, A.J."

He smiled sheepishly but the tapping of his finger on his glass belied his calm exterior. "I sure hope you don't mind, Lizzie, but I told Ms. Molly that I needed some private time with you."

Lizzie settled back into the deep cushion back of the white wicker chair facing A.J. "Not at all. What can I do for you?"

She hoped it was nothing too much or too long as she was dead tired and longing to head home to bed. And most of all, she hoped it was not a murder confession.

A.J. played with his glass, rolling it back and forth in his hands, holding the cold up against the side of his face and then finally setting it on the coffee table between them. "I guess it's best if I just out and say this."

He cleared his throat and Lizzie's curiosity grew, wiping out earlier feelings of impatience. It was obviously something major that he had to share. She sat silently, letting him choose his own way of telling her. He stared out the window into the darkness, fingering the edge of his brown cardigan.

"It's about the other day when you saw me on the grounds of the museum. I wasn't quite truthful with you." He shifted in his seat.

Uh-oh, not a confession. Surely he didn't kill Ashley. But they hadn't talked about Ashley that day. Or had they? Lizzie couldn't remember.

"I was there trying to get up my courage to go inside and talk to the director of the museum. You see, I once knew him, in college. We were roommates to start with and then we became much more than that." He told his story staring out at the backyard, which was highlighted by strategically placed lights. He cleared his throat.

"I got spooked at the end of that year and transferred to another college. I didn't even so much as say good-bye to Quentin. That was probably the biggest mistake of my life. I have never gotten him out of my mind and I've tried to keep track of his career over the years. So when I got the opportunity to come here to Ashton Corners, I jumped at it. I've been driving around for several days now, almost stalking him, if truth be told, trying to get up the courage to approach him. I have no idea what I'll say, except that I'm deeply sorry for hurting him. But those are the hardest words to say."

He stopped talking but continued staring out the window.

"Why are you telling me this?" Lizzie asked gently.

"Because I know you're asking a lot of questions trying to find out who killed Ashley Dixon and I'm just worried that something might lead to my being exposed to Quentin before I'm ready to approach him." He looked over at Lizzie. "I didn't murder Ashley, you know."

"I know," Lizzie answered.

They sat in silence for a few minutes. Finally, Lizzie said, "I won't do anything to blow your cover, A.J. I'm sorry if I gave you cause to be even more distressed. But I think you'd be wise to just approach Quentin and get it over with. Putting it off won't make it any easier. And you have to know how he'll react before you can move ahead with your life." She smiled hesitantly. "And that's my Ann Landers talk for the evening."

It took so long for him to answer that Lizzie was sure she'd offended him. When he did, he looked at her and his smile seemed more relaxed. "You are so right. I thank you, Lizzie." He stood and straightened the collar of his mint-colored golf shirt, picked up his glass and walked into the kitchen.

When Lizzie finally did the same, Molly was sitting at the banquette with a glass of wine in hand.

"I won't ask what that was all about but he sure looked mighty happier than when he came here."

Lizzie gave a tired smile. The exhaustion had returned. "Good. Now, I'm heading home and to bed or I'll never make it to school tomorrow." She leaned over and kissed Molly on the cheek. "Have a good sleep."

"You too, honey. And think happy thoughts. This will soon be over."

Chapter Thirty-one

◇◇◇

Yeah, I'm the fly in the soup. I don't like it any better
than you do. Flies don't like being swamped in soup,
especially when it's hot.

CHAMPAGNE FOR ONE—REX STOUT

Lizzie escaped the school just after the lunch bell rang.
She had no appointments nor any classroom visits
booked and had meant to spend the time at her desk in the
library, working on that teachers' workshop.

She tried calling Lavenia Ellis to fill her in on what she'd
learned at the library. She wondered if Lavenia actually
wanted Lizzie to talk with Ursula or if she would be the one
to confront her. She let the phone ring until it went to message and then hung up after saying she'd call again.

Lizzie decided the afternoon could be better put to use
visiting the Huxton Hotel and talking to Richard Parson, if
he were there working today. She shoved aside any unease
she felt at the thought of his mama and her threats. Lizzie
felt determined to either confirm or dismiss the Huxton family connection to Ashley's death today.

Fortunately, Richard Parson was at the hotel and had a

spare half hour before a scheduled meeting. He welcomed
her into his office, leaving Lizzie wondering if his mama
had not gotten around to warning him off talking to her. His
first words gave flight to that notion.

"I want you to know that Mama has already ordered that
no one in the family talk to you, Ms. Turner." He leaned
back in his chocolate brown leather swivel chair, an amused
look on his face.

"She did say that's what she'd do," Lizzie admitted. "So
may I ask why you agreed to see me?"

Parson snapped forward and sat upright. "Because I do
not always see eye to eye with my mama. This being one of
those times. I believe you have questions about Ashley
Dixon and her possible connection to the Huxton family."

It was a statement. He already knew but would he cooperate, Lizzie wondered. She waited for him to continue.

"I spoke to Ashley Dixon the week before last, on Friday
afternoon."

Lizzie was surprised. She hadn't realized Ashley had
been so busy the day she arrived. "What did she want?"

"Apparently I'd been out of town when she'd come last
month but she had made up for that by talking to the staff and
to my mama. She went back to New York, did some more
research and then demanded to see me. You see, Mama had
given her the brush-off, same instructions as you, not to bother
the family or there'd be charges." He settled back again.

"I don't know how much of the story you know, but you
see, she was convinced that her mama had an affair with
my uncle Ross the summer she'd worked here and that Ashley was the result. Since Ross died last month, she felt she
was entitled to part of the estate."

"No wonder your mama was upset."

"I'm not sure what bothered her more, the scandal or the

money. Ross was married at the time, although his wife died about ten years ago. They didn't have any children so his estate reverted to my mama. And she wasn't about to share any of it with Ashley Dixon."

Lizzie wondered how to phrase her next question or if she should even ask it. But he had been forthcoming. "Do you think it's possible your mama might be responsible for what happened to her? I know there's no way she could physically pull it off but could she have hired someone?"

His eyes turned shrewd. "I really don't know. It's a terrible thing for a child to say, but Mama is an anomaly to all who know her." He glanced at his watch and pushed away from his desk. "I'm sorry but I have to be going. It's a very important business lunch. I've told you everything I know. What are you planning to do with it?"

Good question. "I'll have to tell the police, unless you have already."

"Part of it. I hadn't decided on total candor when the chief paid me a visit yesterday."

"And why did you today?"

He stood a little straighter. "I'm tired of the subterfuge. I have a hotel to run and all this going on in the background is interfering. It's time to air our scandals and get on with life." He walked to the door and held it open for Lizzie.

She thanked him again as she left, deciding her next move would be finding Mark and sharing what she'd learned.

She was still puzzling over the information, questioning why Richard Parson would share it with her, when she noticed a yellow Ford Focus approaching her and then making a left turn into the Dewdrop Motel. She knew that car. She slowed and passed by just as Carter Farrow held the passenger door open for Lorelie. Lizzie realized she was driving with her mouth hanging open.

* * *

Mark closed the door behind Lizzie after she'd entered his office. He smiled but then looked at her speculatively when he noticed her face. "This is not a social call."

She shook her head. "Sorry, I just saw something that threw me for a loop but that's not the reason I'm here. I want to tell you what Richard Parson and I just chatted about."

She noted the tug of disapproval at the corner of his mouth but he remained silent, opening his notebook and picking up a pen from his desktop.

She filled him in on her visit and what had been said. When she finished, he made a few more notes, then closed the notebook with a thud.

"Didn't I tell you to stay away from the Huxton family?"

"But if I had, you wouldn't know all this, would you? Richard admitted he hadn't told you everything."

"What if you're being set up?"

"How?"

"Parson tells his mama you were by and she calls her lawyer. Simple as that."

"But I only asked questions. I didn't imply anything." She thought a moment. "Much."

"What did you say?"

"I asked if he thought his mama might be responsible for Ashley's death. But only after he told me all the other stuff."

Mark sighed.

"You don't really believe what you said, do you?" Lizzie asked. "You were just saying that to warn me off, right?"

"I already tried warning you off and look how far that got me. Now, is there anything else I should know?"

Lizzie shook her head.

"Good. Now please go home and stay out of trouble."

As she reached out for the door, Mark asked, "Maybe we can have a late supper?"

"That would be nice."

"I'll call."

Lizzie stopped in at A Novel Plot, hoping to find Molly there. Stephanie was her first point of contact, at the main desk.

"Hi, Stephanie. Busy day here?"

"It's been fairly busy. In fact, I haven't had time to open the deliveries that already came in, so Molly's in the back doing so. I don't know, I seem to be not too organized these days. I come in with good intentions and then all it takes is a customer, and even after she's gone, I stand around here daydreaming. Do you think I'm starting to show signs of aging?"

Lizzie laughed. "Not quite yet, Stephanie. At least I hope not. I'm well over the hill if that's the case. I'll bet you're just tired out. It must be hard to work here during the day and then go home to the baby, even if she is a sweetie pie like Wendy."

Stephanie nodded. "You've got that right. She's an angel but there's a bit of the devil in her, too. She seems to know when I've just sat down and am relaxing. That's when she wants my attention the most. Mrs. Sanchez is so good with her, but I'm wondering if my little girl wants her mama at home with her. But even though I feel badly, Lizzie, I just can't do it. I have to be out working to support us both." She sighed. "And that's not going to change anytime soon. I'm sure lucky Molly's such an understanding boss and doesn't mind if I don't always do a full shift."

"Molly totally understands and she's delighted that you're working here."

"Well, I am, too, and you know, she's an awfully generous employer. And I do so like being around the books. I owe that to you, you know."

Lizzie was puzzled. "Why do you say that?"

"Because you helped me get my GED and at the same time, got me interested in reading, and then had me join the book club. Why, if none of that had happened, I can't bear to think where I'd be now." She looked and sounded like she was near tears. Now Lizzie really knew she was one exhausted mama.

"Look, why don't you take a break for a few hours. Go home and have a nap and keep Mrs. Sanchez there to watch Wendy? I'll stay here and work."

"Oh, I couldn't do that, but I do thank you, Lizzie. Besides, if I went home and Wendy saw me, she'd surely want to be playing with me. Believe me, there'd be no resting." She paused in thought. "I would appreciate it if you'd take my place selling books tonight, though. A quiet evening might just do me some good."

"Done."

"Lizzie. Come on back here and have a look," Molly called from the back room.

"Enjoy your evening," Lizzie said to Stephanie and gave her a warm smile. She walked to the back of the store and found Molly with a stack of hardcover books on the table and three empty boxes on the floor.

"Looks tempting, Molly, but I'm hoping you might be able to get away for now. I'm heading over to the Quilt Patch and I think I need some support."

"Why, whatever is up?"

"I'll explain in the car."

Molly went into the back room and grabbed her handbag. "Stephanie, dear . . . I've got to go on an errand with Lizzie. If I'm not back in time, you'll just close won't you?"

Stephanie was about to answer when the front door swung open and Teensy charged in.

"I was pretty certain I'd find you here, Mopsy, since you weren't answering your phone."

Stephanie burst out laughing. They all looked at her.

"I'm sorry but I just can't get used to your calling her Mopsy all the time. I know that was her nickname when you were kids but she's just not a Mopsy to me." Stephanie covered her mouth with her hands and tried to compose herself.

Teensy tried to look stern but her face broke into a smile. "So happy to provide the help with some mirth. Now, what's going on here? Are you two going somewhere?" She looked from Molly to Lizzie.

"We were just heading over to the Quilt Patch," Lizzie said.

"You're welcome to join us," added Molly, with a glance at Lizzie, who nodded.

Teensy turned back to the door and pulled it open. "I'd love to, ladies, especially if we're on some kind of mission. Now lead the way."

Lizzie drove to the bed and breakfast and on the way over filled Molly and Teensy in on her afternoon, ending with her spotting Carter and Lorelie at the motel. "I want to talk to Caroline before they get back and try to figure out if she knows anything about this."

Teensy gasped and then chuckled. "Why, the old dog. I'm not at all surprised. Well, I am about Carter Farrow. He seems like such a lifeless bump on a log, but that Lorelie, she's got her eyes open for a man, all right. I can tell just by looking at her."

"I never noticed anything like that," Molly said.

"You wouldn't, sugar."

Lizzie turned onto Tay Street and pulled up in front of the house. "I think I saw them together the other afternoon, too. The day we'd come over to talk to them, Molly. Remember, Carter went for a walk and Lorelie went to the pharmacy?"

"Oh my, I do remember. I wonder how long this has been going on? Maybe it's just started."

"Or maybe not."

"But what does it have to do with the murder?"

"I'm just thinking back to what Gigi said about Ashley's comment that someone's secret was another's pot of gold. Doesn't that sound suspiciously like blackmail? What if Ashley had tried her hand at blackmail and that someone happened to be an author?"

"You mean, Lorelie?"

"Could be." Of course, Lizzie thought, it could also have referred to the Huxton family, but why would Ashley mention that to Gigi?

"Oh my. A motive."

They found Caroline out on the patio, a sherry in her hand. "Ladies," she said. "Care to join me for a drink? It's well past noon, you know."

"Nice to see you, Caroline, but I'm wondering if Carter happens to be in." Molly asked in her friendliest Southern voice. "I hear he's a whiz at accounting and I do need some advice."

Lizzie glanced at Molly. Where had she heard that? Molly was certainly the last person to need that kind of help.

"Oh Carter, Carter, Carter," Caroline exploded. "I'm not his keeper."

Patsy had come out the door as this was being said and stopped abruptly in her tracks. None of the other women dared to say a thing.

Finally, Caroline said in a small voice, "Oh, that's bad Caroline speaking out of turn. I do so apologize." She sat up straighter and looked at each of them. "If you'll just excuse me, I think I'll just go lie down for a short while. I seem to have a splitting headache."

She stood with a bit of a sway and left before anyone could come up with an answer.

"Oh my," said Molly as they heard Caroline's heavy footsteps up the stairs.

Patsy sat down and fanned herself with a serviette. "I do declare, that just came right out of the blue. I wonder how much she's had to drink." She picked up the sherry bottle and held it up to the window. "Well, that does explain it."

Lizzie grimaced. "I sure hope she recovers before the talent show tonight."

Molly gasped. "That went right out of my mind. Let's just hope her husband can get her there in good shape."

"Sounds like he's the reason she's in such rough shape," Teensy mused. "Maybe you shouldn't count on him for anything."

Patsy made a tsk-tsk sound. "This is not at all what I meant when I said they should make themselves at home." She tucked the empty sherry bottle under her arm. "I guess I'd better break out a new one for the real sherry hour. If you'll excuse me."

"No problem, Patsy. We'll just be going. See you later," Molly said, pulling Teensy out of her chair and following Lizzie around to the front of the house. "We should have tried to keep her downstairs and talking."

"That was quite a surprise. We've just seen the other side of Caroline. Maybe that side was willing to commit murder," Lizzie mused.

Molly shook her head. "I'd say from what we suspect, it's Lorelie who should be the victim, in that case."

"Unless Caroline was being blackmailed and she killed Ashley, rather than pay to keep the news about an affair quiet. She may not have wanted to be known as the woman scorned," Lizzie said.

Teensy snorted. "Tosh. I'm sure Caroline could dish it with the best of them. She'd just make sure to muddy Lorelie's name so that none of the other facts would matter."

Lizzie stopped and looked at Teensy. "That's a downright cynical thing to say."

"Realistic, you mean. Now, you knew Ashley," Teensy continued once they were in the car. "Who do you think she'd target with the blackmail?"

"If she did try to blackmail someone. We only have Gigi's word that's what happened."

"Do you think Ashley was capable of it?" Molly asked.

Lizzie paused. "I'd like to say yes because she certainly didn't have any scruples about the other stuff but blackmail is really in a different league. I'm not sure."

Teensy replied, "You are going soft, girl. Think the worst until proven wrong."

Molly burst out laughing and Teensy soon joined in. Lizzie shook her head and started the car.

Caroline sported sunglasses even though the talent show was indoors, in the basement of St. John's Evangelical Church and at seven at night. She also walked gingerly up to the second row of chairs and took her place next to A.J. and Lorelie. They sat facing the stage. The first row had been reserved for the musical talent, those with instruments in particular. Gigi had bowed out saying she had a viewing to attend. Research and all.

Even the colors Caroline wore were muted, green and shapeless, while Lorelie dazzled in bright orange from her lipstick to her sandals. A.J. was his usual dapper self in a cream suit with pale blue shirt and polka-dot bow tie. He looked a lot more confident than the last time Lizzie saw him, as he nodded to her. She hoped for the best.

Lizzie sat at the back of the room, along with Andie, at a table displaying the authors' books. The entire back wall had tables set up along it, some with CDs being sold by family members of participants, some artwork and needle-point, even a variety of pottery. Lizzie checked the program.

Judy Ginn, listed as number seven, would demonstrate pottery techniques. *Hmm, that could be odd but interesting.*

The master of ceremonies, the newly elected mayor, Harlan Tucker, welcomed everyone on behalf of the Ashton Corners Service Club, explaining all the proceeds from the tickets, and part of the money from the sale of items, would be going to the scholarship fund for children of fallen military personnel. Everyone applauded with enthusiasm.

The first two slots on the program belonged to an accordionist, ten-year-old Mikey Mason. Lizzie remembered him from last year at school, a kid with absolutely no interest in reading even though he had the ability. It seemed this was where his interest lay. After a piano solo, A.J. Pruitt stepped up to the stage. He searched the crowd and seemed to focus on someone near the back. Lizzie tried to figure out who it was but couldn't from her position. He read an action-filled scene that included a lot of witty dialogue and the audience cheered enthusiastically when he finished. He gave a gentlemanly bow and returned to his seat.

By the time Caroline's turn came around, she seemed to have perked up somewhat, at least Lizzie thought she had. Lizzie looked around the room and spotted Carter at the far side, last row. He looked none too pleased. She wondered what had been said between the two earlier in the day. Oh, to have been a fly on that wall.

Lorelie seemed quite pleased to be the final participant. She'd shared her strategy with Lizzie earlier. This was new territory, a totally untapped source of new readers, and she planned to wow them. After ten minutes of background about her career and the Southern Fashionista series, she ended with another dramatic reading. That sent the audience rushing to the back to buy her books and after signing for a good fifteen minutes, Lorelie left with the mayor and his wife.

Lizzie started packing away the unsold books, did a quick tally of sales and gave the cash to Molly. Bob appeared at the right moment and loaded the boxes into his SUV.

"I think that went very well," Molly said as she gathered up her lightweight pashmina. "The authors all seemed happy, even poor Caroline. That must have been a chore for her."

Bob nodded. "If ever someone needed the hair of the dog, I'd say it was that woman. Now wouldn't that have been a performance?" They left chuckling.

Lizzie thought about Caroline all the way home. Something must have happened to push her over the edge earlier in the day. Was it the pressure of having to remain in Ashton Corners while the investigation continued? Was she guilty of murder and finally got blindsided by guilt? Or did it have to do with Carter?

That was a possibility. Given what Lizzie suspected, it was quite possible that Caroline also had her suspicions, had seen a half-hidden touch or embrace somewhere along their touring. But somehow, Ashley didn't ring true as her target. It should have been Lorelie. Or maybe even Carter.

Lizzie pulled into her driveway and turned the key. She sat in silence, thinking. Carter had a lot to lose, too. And from what she'd witnessed, pleasant and bland Carter had a hidden side. He'd looked like he wanted to throttle Caroline earlier in the evening.

But if so, she should be dead and Lorelie should be consoling Carter.

Did anything make sense?

Chapter Thirty-two

◇◇◇

Fresh kills or cold case, the pursuit of killers had to
be relentless. It was the only way to go and the only
way Bosch knew how to go.

THE BLACK BOX—MICHAEL CONNELLY

Lizzie finished her second espresso while waiting for her
waffle to finish cooking. She'd hardly slept all night and
had decided to abandon any pretense at five A.M. The cats
followed her down to check out their dishes but had disap-
peared upstairs as she pulled her running shoes on. She'd
had a long run followed by a refreshing shower and now had
enough time to savor a leisurely breakfast.

She knew Lavenia was an early riser so she tried giving
her another call. This time she answered on the third ring.

"Good morning, Lavenia. It's Lizzie. I wanted to update
you on what I've learned."

"Good morning. I'm so glad you called. I was wondering
what was on your mind after your message."

Lizzie quickly brought her up to speed. "I know it's all
on the circumstantial side but it does point to Ursula Nesbitt.

Would you like me to confront her with this information and see if she admits it?"

Lavenia was quiet for a few moments. "No, dear. I think I should be the one to do that. I do thank you and want you to know that I really appreciate all you've done. Nathaniel will, too."

"Are you going to tell him now?"

"Yes. I think he has the right to know, especially since we know who did it. She is the person, isn't she?"

"I'm pretty certain," Lizzie said.

"Good. I'm glad that's all over. It's been causing me many sleepless nights. I can't thank you enough."

"I'm just glad I could help. Good luck."

After hanging up, Lizzie took her now-cold waffle out of the waffle maker and decided that was as good a way to eat it as any. She topped it off with almond butter and jam, thinking all the while about how love, or rather lust, made people do irrational things.

Ursula wanted Nathaniel for herself, or so it seemed. To get him, she tried at first to make it seem like her warnings were for Lavenia's own good, then quickly progressed to good old-fashioned blackmail when that didn't work. You drop him or I tell on him.

She bit into her waffle. Was love at the basis of Ashley's demise? Had her mama's indiscretion ended up with the daughter's death? She finished her waffle, trying to make some sense of the thoughts flitting through her mind. Fay Huxton-Parson had intimated that Ashley tried to blackmail her or, rather, the family. Had Ashley tried the same trick with someone else? The Huxtons weren't the murdering type. Why would they be when they could buy their way out of any scandal? Or as Richard Huxton-Parson had said, just move on.

But had Ashley latched on to another someone who

wouldn't pay? Or couldn't? And if so, what was she black-mailing this person about?

Lizzie quickly rinsed off her plate, her mind spinning. Forbidden love. What better motive for murder? The phone rang, snapping Lizzie out of her thoughts. She answered but was anxious to get out the door.

"Lizzie, it's Patsy. I thought you'd want to know that Caroline is standing in the front hall, her bags packed, demanding that I call a cab for her. She's in a real state and determined as all get-out to leave here."

Uh-oh. "Thanks, Patsy. Maybe you should call the cab but ask him to come in about twenty minutes. I'll give Chief Dreyfus a call and get right on over there."

It sounded like Caroline had reached her breaking point. Would that change anything? She dialed Mark as she headed out to the car and passed the message along.

She beat him to the bed and breakfast but didn't get a chance to question Caroline before Mark entered through the front door.

"Ms. Farrow, I understand you're wanting to leave," he said without preamble.

Caroline glared at Patsy who hastily backed out of the hall and went to the kitchen.

"Yes. I'm leaving right now." She almost stamped her foot as she said it."

"Well, as I told you right from the start, I'm not holding you here against your will. You're free to leave at any time. However, you might wonder how that would look to me just as I'm about to wrap up this investigation. It might even make me think you had something to hide. Maybe even a murder."

Caroline huffed, "I don't. No. It's not me. I'm no murderer."

"I'm just saying." He stood his ground and stared at her. She was giving it some thought when Carter stumbled down the stairs. He completely ignored Caroline and the others, making a beeline for the dining room. Caroline glared at his retreating back.

If looks could kill, Lizzie thought.

Caroline opened her mouth to speak but instead, grabbed her suitcase and headed back upstairs, brushing past Lorelie who was also fully dressed and coming down.

"Oh, Chief Dreyfus, just the person I wanted to see. Tell me, dear," she said, hooking her arm through his as she reached his side, "is it all right for me to leave town today? I've got so much to do, so many fans to be seeing. I really do have to get moving."

"Well, ma'am," Mark said, "like I was just saying to Ms. Cummings, it might just look a bit suspicious to me if you were to leave town just as I'm about to make an arrest."

"An arrest. Do tell. Who is it?" Lorelie was all sugar and sweetness.

"I will tell. When I'm ready."

Lizzie thought that if the "ma'am" didn't make Lorelie a bit worried, Mark's tone should. Lorelie sniffed then disentangled her arm and stomped back upstairs, saying nothing.

Mark looked at Lizzie and raised his eyebrows.

"Interesting morning," was all she said.

He followed her outside. "How about a coffee and you can fill me in before you head to work?" he asked.

"Make that breakfast and you're on. I had to bypass a second waffle to get over here."

"I always knew that food was the way to your heart," he said, walking her to her car. "Oscar's Diner?"

She nodded, got in and headed to the restaurant. When she checked her rearview, Mark's Jeep was right behind her. Lizzie took the last parking spot in front of the restaurant and watched while Mark pulled a U-turn and parked across the street. They found a table for two in the far corner, away from the tables overlooking Main Street, always the first to fill up at any time of day.

As soon as they were seated and fresh cups of coffee placed in front of them, Lizzie said, "Are you serious? You're about to make an arrest?"

"Well, I may have been exaggerating a bit but I didn't want them skipping out just yet and I don't have enough evidence to hold any of them here."

"But you have some evidence?"

Mark took a long sip of his coffee and just stared at Lizzie.

"You at least have some idea of the murderer's identity?" she demanded.

"I have my suspicions."

Lizzie held off quizzing him some more until they'd given their orders to the server. When Mark seemed disinclined to share any more information, she filled him in on the previous day's events. He let out a slow whistle after hearing all about it.

"So, are you saying the Huxton family is now off your suspect list and someone being blackmailed by Ashley Dixon is on it?" he asked.

"When you put it that way, I haven't crossed anyone off but after what Gigi told me and after seeing Lorelie and Carter, I'm wondering." *And then there's A.J.*

"Two people you thought were Lorelie and Carter."

"Huh? Uh, there is that. I didn't get a clear look, but how many people are there who look like them?"

"Let me see, two people in their late sixties, gray-haired male, red-haired female, obviously a dye job."

"All right. But what's all this behavior about if there's not some hanky-panky going on?"

"Hanky-panky?"

Lizzie made a face. "You know what I mean."

Mark waited until their breakfasts had been served before continuing. "Yes, I do know and you may very well be right. But there's got to be more than someone suggesting a motive and a possible extramarital affair."

"Evidence."

"You got it."

"So why haven't you told me about your suspicions?" Lizzie asked as she pushed her cup to the edge of the table, hoping for a refill.

"Because as I've said before, I am the cop. You are not. There are certain things I cannot tell you while an investigation is active."

Lizzie frowned, not quite sure where to take the conversation.

"However," Mark finally continued, "I'm not fully satisfied with their alibis and I'm equally satisfied that the murderer was not a local person. I had a long talk with Ms. Huxton-Parson and am convinced she's not a murderer nor did she hire one."

"Huh. And you let me go through all the telling about what I'd discovered?"

"It's always good to have confirmation, and remember, I told you I don't have to share my information with you."

Their food arrived and Lizzie eyed her mushroom omelet and tomato salsa with anticipation. "What about Nick Jennings? He didn't have an alibi, either."

"There are security cameras at the Ashton Inn and he couldn't have left his room without being seen. While the B and B does not have any such cameras."

Mark reached for the pepper grinder at the same time as Lizzie. She let her fingers rest on his for a moment.

"Am I still on that list?"

He put the grinder down and squeezed her hand. "Are you trying to seduce an officer of the law?"

"Yes."

"Hmm. Fine, and you're not really on it."

"Not really, what does that mean?" She added the pepper to her omelet with vigor.

"It means I can't officially remove you from the list, but you're at the bottom and not a serious contender."

She thought a moment. "Good. Later tonight?"

His eyes lit up as he dug into his steak and eggs.

Lizzie was glad she'd thought ahead and brought her school supplies with her earlier. She slid into a desk at the back of a fourth-grade class just as the teacher was about to start with the reading portion of the morning. Lizzie had been asked by the teacher to observe a couple of students whom she felt were having difficulties but were trying to cover it up by acting out. Nobody but the teacher and the kids sitting next to Lizzie noticed she'd arrived. She sat silently throughout the next hour, making a few notes that she'd turn into a work plan for the teacher by the end of the day.

She slipped out and went to her desk to start working on it. By noon, she'd referenced some extra reading materials for the teacher and was well on her way to sketching out a few tricks to get the two kids in question more involved. Her cell phone rang as she was about to head to the lunchroom. She hadn't realized she'd forgotten to turn it to vibrate.

It was Molly. "Lizzie, honey, I'm so sorry to bother you at work but I'm hoping you might take a few minutes of your lunch hour to meet me at the Quilt Patch. Caroline Cummings just called me and said she has a confession to make."

"Really? About what? Do you think she was being blackmailed by Ashley? Or is she the murderer?"

"All I know is that's what she said," Molly said, anxiety in her voice.

"All right. Do you want me to pick you up?"

"No, I'm on my way. I'll see you there." She hung up without saying good-bye, a sure sign she was distressed.

Lizzie reversed her direction and headed to her car. She pulled up behind Molly's Audi about six minutes later. She grabbed her handbag and was about to exit when she noticed Carter leaving by the side door of the B and B looking like he was taking great care not to make any noise closing the door. She watched as he got into his car, backed out and headed in the opposite direction. This looked interesting.

Why was Carter leaving when his wife was obviously in emotional distress? Was she about to rat him out? Lizzie felt her pulse rate accelerating as she threw the gearshift into reverse, deciding to follow him. She hung back as far as she dared, hoping not to lose sight of his Sebring. He turned left and then right on Broward, heading out of town. By the time she'd rounded the first curve, Carter had turned into the parking lot at the White Haven Funeral Home. Lizzie stopped on the verge behind a tree and walked the rest of the way, wondering what he could be doing here, at the scene of the crime?

He'd pulled in next to a black Toyota Verso and held its passenger door open, talking loudly as he slid in. Lizzie couldn't get much closer without being seen so she hung back and pulled out her cell phone to call Mark. And tell him what? That she had now fixated on Carter Farrow as a suspect and she decided to follow him?

The thing was, this did look suspicious. He was meeting with somebody in a strange car and it wasn't Lorelie this time. So what was it all about? Maybe something totally private and not associated with the murder, which is what Mark would probably tell her.

It did seem odd they'd be meeting here, though. The funeral home was usually closed on Wednesdays except for emergencies. What was so private that it needed to be said away from everyone? She switched her cell to vibrate, shoved it in her pocket and looked for some way to angle around to get a better look at them both. She had to dive for cover when Carter abruptly got out of the car, but she was close enough to hear him yelling.

"I don't care what you think you have. I'm not going to be a part of this again. Just remember, it's a dangerous game you're playing." He slammed the door and stomped back to his car.

Lizzie felt a stinging along the side of her arm and realized she'd landed on a small honey locust tree. She tried to reposition herself but it only scratched her more.

The driver door of the Verso opened and Gigi Briggs leapt out. That was a shock. Lizzie struggled for a better view, hoping to hear all of the conversation, too. Whatever was going on, she'd bet her last jar of almond butter it had something to do with Ashley's murder.

"You don't think I'll go to the police? I've got news for you, mister. I'm teed off at you enough to do just that. Ashley Dixon was my ticket to the bestseller list and now that's ended." She rushed up to Carter and pounded on his chest. "You men are all alike. You can't keep your pants on and everyone around you gets hurt."

Carter grabbed her wrists, yanking open his car door, and pushed her. "Get inside," he snarled. He pushed her in and toward the passenger side, slamming the door after he'd slid in behind the wheel. Lizzie heard the car start as she scrambled through the tight underbrush back to her Mazda. She stumbled and twisted her right ankle. She plopped on the ground and gingerly probed her ankle and foot. Nothing appeared to be broken despite the pain. But how would she make it back to her car? She had to try. She couldn't let them out of her sight. Gritting her teeth, she struggled to stand

and somehow managed to make her way back. She caught sight of Carter's Sebring turning right just as she stuck the key in the ignition.

She ignored the throbbing in her ankle and her arms that felt on fire, while digging to get her cell phone out of her pocket. She tried calling Mark's number while keeping in her lane and not losing sight of the quickly disappearing Sebring.

She had to give up when Carter veered to the right and down a small dirt road. Lizzie knew the destination was the banks of the Tallapoosa River. Surely Carter wouldn't do anything stupid. It was his very own car, after all. How would he explain any evidence of a violent act?

She slowed down and opened her window, trying to hear the car ahead without making too much noise or gaining too fast on it. She could once again hear voices as she came to a spot where the road curved around a gigantic rock. Lizzie remembered this place from high school, not that she'd frequented it. Etched on that rock, along with hundreds of painted versions, were the names of couples, bragging rights of school teams and assorted other adolescent memories.

She backed up and steered into a small clearing at the side of the road, slid her cell phone back into her pocket and eased out of the car. Her foot hurt when she put pressure on it and she stifled a yelp. *Oh boy, what could I do?* Maybe she'd better stay put and just call Mark.

Suddenly Gigi screamed and Lizzie dropped her iPhone. *Get going, girl.* She shoved the phone in her pocket and hobbled down the road toward the sound. Her heart pounded as she rounded the corner in time to see Carter raise his hand and punch Gigi on the left side of her head. She staggered back but didn't go down.

Lizzie looked around, searching for something to use as a weapon. She glanced back as Farrow pushed Gigi toward the river and bent over to grab a thick branch that had dropped from a tree. Carter raised it over his head, aiming at Gigi. She stood staring at him, mesmerized. The silence chilled Lizzie to her core. *Do something.*

Lizzie started yelling and charged through the shrubbery, ignoring the sharp pain that shot up her leg. Carter turned toward her in surprise, lowering his arms. Lizzie slammed into him and they toppled into the river.

The cold waters of the Tallapoosa shocked Lizzie for a couple of seconds and then she looked around for Carter. He'd landed a bit downstream and pushed through the water toward her. She tried touching the bottom and eventually her foot landed on a sunken limb.

Gigi had gotten down on her knees and was screaming at Lizzie to grab her outstretched hand. They connected at the same moment that Carter grabbed the back of Lizzie's blouse. She kicked backward at him and felt her blouse rip but she was freed from his grasp. She scrambled up the riverbank, falling beside Gigi, feeling her lungs ready to explode. Almost immediately, Gigi stumbled to her feet, pulling Lizzie up, too. This time she cried out as pain shot through her ankle. Carter had reached the riverbank but had trouble getting a foothold to climb out.

Lizzie gritted her teeth as she desperately scanned the clearing. She spotted the branch Carter had dropped, grabbed it and held it like a baseball bat, poised to whack him if he lunged for them after climbing out.

She could hear her name but it came from a long way off, then hands grabbed the branch from behind her, easing it to the ground. She could hear Mark's voice in her ear.

"It's all right, Lizzie. We're here. We'll get him. You're going to be all right." His arms wrapped around her from behind and she started shaking. She heard Officer Craig's voice as she joined them. Mark pulled away and wrapped a blanket around Lizzie's shoulders.

Gigi started babbling about Carter going berserk and trying to kill her; Carter kept yelling at her to shut up. Officer Craig handed another blanket to Carter after two other officers helped him get ashore. He quieted for a moment and then pointed at Gigi.

"That bitch tried to blackmail me."

Gigi fell silent. Mark looked from one to the other and asked, "For the murder of Ashley Dixon?"

Gigi nodded and looked down at the ground as Craig went over to her and placed handcuffs on her wrists.

"She did help me, Mark," Lizzie said, still shaking.

Mark nodded and told his officers to take them both in, then picked up Lizzie in his arms and carried her to his Jeep.

"My car . . ." she tried saying between chattering teeth.

"I'll get it later. Right now, you're going to the hospital."

"Not necessary. A hot bath would be good, though. Oh, shoot." She reached into her pocket. "My new phone," she wailed, pulling out her waterlogged iPhone.

Chapter Thirty-three

◇◇◇

Adrenaline is a truly remarkable thing. It can take you from comatose to Marathon Runner before your wits have anything to say about it.

THE TANGLEWOOD MURDER—LUCILLE KALLEN

Molly and Teensy were waiting at Lizzie's house when she limped downstairs wrapped in her old terry robe. She had a sore ankle and was covered in scratches and bruises but aside from that, felt just fine.

"Mark called as soon as Officer Craig brought you home," Molly explained. "I just used my key to get in. Thought you might need some TLC."

Bob let himself in through the front door as each of the ladies wrapped an arm around Lizzie's waist and led her into the living room. On the side table was a pot of hot tea along with a plate of buttermilk biscuits, Lizzie's favorite, that Molly had brought.

Teensy passed a glass of bourbon to Lizzie as she sat down on the love seat. Lizzie looked at it, then at Teensy.

"I thought it was called for. I always have some on hand

for medicinal purposes," Teensy said with a smile. "Now, sugar, do you want to tell us what happened?"

Molly held up her hand. "Maybe now's not the time. You're looking a little peaked, honey. Why don't you just finish your drink and then go lie down."

Lizzie nodded, grateful to not have to relive it quite this soon.

"Well, sugar, Molly's right, of course, but you know we're just so happy and relieved that you're fine," Teensy gushed.

Molly sat next to Lizzie, holding her hand, and Bob couldn't seem to sit still. He paced and finally stopped in front of Lizzie, saying, "I cannot believe we let you get in danger's way again. I'm feeling pretty useless right now. An ex–police chief who can't even protect you."

Lizzie smiled. "It's not up to you to protect me, Bob, but I do appreciate the thought. It's all worked out, the killer has been caught, and I'm dying to know the whole story."

Molly shuddered. "Perhaps you could rephrase that last bit, honey. I'm also very pleased that it's turned out all for the good. Who would have thought that a simple book fair could bring so much turmoil to our town?"

The doorbell rang and Nathaniel walked in, holding Lavenia's hand. They looked shocked when they heard the story. Teensy poured out more glasses of bourbon all around. By the time Mark called, the house was filled. The other members of the book club had rushed over when they'd heard what had happened and everyone tried to coddle Lizzie. *So much for that nap.* She finally went into the kitchen to look for her cats, knowing they'd be upset by all the to-do.

Nathaniel followed her and told her that Lavenia had finally admitted what had been going on.

"I just wanted to thank you for all you've done," he said and gave her a hug. "I can imagine that Lavenia was going out of her mind about this. I'm glad she thought to talk it over with you."

"I'm so glad I could help."

He held her at arm's length and looked her in the eye. "Thank you for being a good friend, and for not believing it."

"I know you, Nathaniel. It was easy to discount the rumor."

"Now, I must take care of something. I'm glad to see you're healthy and surrounded by your friends. I'll give you a call later."

Lizzie saw Nathaniel and Lavenia out the door and then limped upstairs after saying good-bye to the others, knowing they'd lock the door as they left. The cats were huddled together next to her pillow. She lay down beside them and they cuddled up to her body. It didn't take her long to fall asleep, for a change.

Chapter Thirty-four

◇◇◇

It wasn't clear to me what had just happened. On the other hand, it often wasn't, and I'd gotten used to it.

THE PROFESSIONAL—ROBERT B. PARKER

Lizzie took a final look in the mirror and smoothed her hair back behind her ears. The peach long-sleeved cotton pullover and long black pants she wore covered the bruises and scratches on her arms and legs. She made her way gingerly down the stairs, favoring her right ankle.

"I'm ready," she told Mark, who pushed out of his chair and walked over to her.

"You're gorgeous."

"And you're just saying that." She knew there were still some ugly red marks on her face.

"Uh-uh. A police officer always tells the truth."

"So, tell me what's been happening." She grabbed her handbag as Mark held the front door open for her.

"Why don't we save that until we get to Molly's, since I know all your book club cohorts will start pumping me for information, too." He held the passenger door of the Jeep open for her.

Lizzie grinned as she got in. "Cohorts? Catchy. Sure, that's a good idea. It was nice of Molly to invite us all over for dinner, yet again."

"She's quite the lady. And cook." Mark started the car, paused and glanced at Lizzie. "There is something I should share before I go into all the other details, though."

Lizzie turned in her seat to look at him.

"I spoke to Richard Huxton-Parson, who said his mama finally told him she'd tried to pay off Ashley so she wouldn't make a claim on the estate. The family seems to believe she was indeed the daughter of Ross. In fact, that's about what Ms. Huxton-Parson had already admitted to me."

Mark stopped at a traffic light. "He, Richard, seems to have taken more control of things now and, in fact, has invited you and me to dinner at the hotel. I can't accept, but of course, you can."

"And I imagine you can come as a guest."

"That would be a yes." Mark grinned.

"Hmm. Quite the family." Lizzie turned to face forward again.

"You sure you're feeling all right?" Mark asked.

"Of course. There was no major damage done, except to my poor iPhone." Lizzie watched a group of kids playing soccer on a front lawn and smiled. Everything was fine.

Even Nathaniel's problem had been settled. He'd called earlier that day to say he'd talked to Ursula Nesbitt and she'd admitted what she'd done. Seems she'd been jealous about his relationship with Lavenia and also that Lavenia was standing for president of the garden society and would surely win. Nathaniel told her he would not press charges if she left the club and promised never to do anything like that again. She'd agreed.

The front door swung open as Mark was parking the Jeep next to Jacob's red Ford Escape in Molly's driveway. Sally-Jo gave Lizzie a big hug as they entered and Molly came out of the kitchen to do the same.

"I'm so happy you're getting around so well, honey," Molly said. "Now, come in to the living room. Everyone is here and I've just put some appetizers out."

Lizzie went through another round of hugs as she made her way to the love seat in front of the window. Mark sat beside her and chose a tuna-apple mini-melt from the tray of food that Andie had snatched up and brought over to them.

Molly took a seat next to Stephanie on the second love seat in the room and said, "We've been hoping you'd be willing to share what all happened with Carter after his arrest, Chief."

Mark finished his mini-melt before telling them. "Carter Farrow has been charged with the murder of Ashley Dixon. Now, y'all know this still has to be proven in court, but he did admit that the victim had been blackmailing him about his affair with Lorelie Oliver. It seems they've been carrying on for several conferences now, but if his wife had found out, she'd divorce him and she had all the money. Lots of it, from her family."

"Huh. Some love story," Lizzie said. "And he admitted to framing me?"

"Well, backing up just a moment, he said he hadn't planned to kill her. It was an accident. They argued, he pushed her and she fell, hitting her head on a large rock. She was dead when he checked."

Jacob snickered. "I hear a defense coming on," he said.

"But didn't you say it looked like she'd been hit with something?" Lizzie asked.

"That was the initial finding, especially since we hadn't

found anything to suggest otherwise at the scene. However, Farrow also admitted to stashing the rock in his trunk. There wasn't much external bleeding so there was nothing else to clean up." Mark shrugged. "She's still dead and he tried to hide the body. So, deliberate or not, it's murder in my book."

"Why were they at the funeral home?" Jacob asked.

"Apparently, Ashley Dixon had suggested they meet there for a little talk, saying it was a bit out of the way and they wouldn't be disturbed. She wanted more money and he decided to stop paying."

"What about planting Lizzie's phone at the scene?" Bob asked. "That looks premeditated to me."

Mark sat forward in his seat. "The way Farrow tells it, he hadn't planned to frame Lizzie at the outset. But he'd noticed Gigi Briggs pocket Lizzie's phone at the book fair, so he took it from her, thinking it might come in handy. Seems he'd also seen Ms. Briggs steal some small items at the B and B when she thought no one was looking." Mark looked at Lizzie. "He left your phone with the body and at the last minute, took the victim's phone to incriminate you even more. He then broke into your car and left it there."

"But why did he try to kill Gigi?" Lizzie felt even more confused.

"Now, this is where the story gets convoluted. It seems Ashley Dixon knew about Gigi Briggs's propensity to steal things, so Dixon asked her to take Farrow's cell phone. Ms. Dixon said she needed to check on some calls he'd been making. Gigi Briggs put two and two together and came up with blackmail."

"She figured out that's what Ashley was up to?"

"Exactly. By this time, Farrow realized his phone was missing and suspected the light-fingered Gigi, so he asked her to meet him at the funeral home. She admitted she had it. In fact, she hadn't even given it to Ashley Dixon, and added that she needed ongoing financial support so she could quit her day job and spend all her time writing."

Andie did another pass with the appetizers. "Blackmail. Didn't she worry that he'd kill her, too?" she asked.

"She had his cell phone so felt safe."

"Wow. How dumb." Andie plopped down on the floor beside the car seat that held Stephanie's sleeping daughter.

"You can say that again," said Bob with a snort. "I've come up against some pretty stupid thinking in my time on the job. Which is darn fortunate for the cops. That's good police work, Mark."

Mark grinned. "I'd like to take all the credit but Molly alerted me when she saw Lizzie drive off without even going into the B and B."

"I tried calling you, Lizzie," Molly added, "and got real worried when you didn't answer."

"I tried with the same result," Mark said. "I was, however, thanks to your new iPhone and the Find My Friends app you'd installed, able to track you and get close enough so that even when your phone took a swim, I was able to locate you."

"Cool," said Andie, clapping her hands. She stopped abruptly and looked at the baby, hoping she hadn't awakened her.

"I'd set it to vibrate, so I never even heard the calls," Lizzie explained with a slight shudder.

Mark squeezed Lizzie's hand. "It's all over."

"What about the divas?" Stephanie asked.

"A.J. phoned to say he was driving Caroline to her home," Molly explained. "He thought she needed some company. That's so nice of him. But he'll be coming back and promises to stop by. And Lorelie left without saying good-bye to anyone, except for Patsy. What will happen to Gigi?"

"I'm leaving the charges up to the DA but she's being released on bail as soon as her parents arrive from Seattle."

No one said anything for a couple of minutes. Lizzie sat thinking about how she'd misjudged Ashley all this time. It hadn't been about Lizzie at all. It was all Ashley. The money, the popularity. She'd been craving it all these years and she thought Nick Jennings, and then the blackmail plans, would get it for her. "Desperate" was the word for Ashley.

Jacob finally stood and left the room, followed by Sally-Jo. Molly watched them, then said to the others, "You must be thinking I'm slipping in my hostess duties." They heard a loud pop but Molly continued as if nothing had happened, even when a second pop followed. "I haven't yet supplied you with liquid libation, as my daddy used to say, but there is a good reason for my lapse."

She stood as Sally-Jo entered the room carrying a tray of empty champagne glasses, followed by Jacob holding two bottles of Mumm Napa Brut Prestige. He made a big show of filling the glasses, which Sally-Jo then passed around.

Lizzie accepted one and looked at Sally-Jo. "What's up?"

Jacob walked over to stand beside Sally-Jo, slipped his arm around her shoulder and asked for everyone's attention. "We have an announcement to make. Sally-Jo and I are getting married."

Reading Lists

Lizzie Turner

1. Duffy Brown—*Killer in Crinolines*
2. Lucy Burdette—*Topped Chef*
3. Victoria Abbott—*The Sayers Swindle*
4. Tess Gerritsen—*Last to Die*
5. Julie Hyzy—*Grace Takes Off*

Sally-Jo Baker

1. Leslie Budewitz—*Death al Dente*
2. Jacklyn Brady—*The Cakes of Wrath*
3. Shelley Costa—*You Cannoli Die Once*
4. Peg Cochran—*Iced to Death*
5. Victoria Hamilton—*Bran New Death*

Molly Mathews

1. Rhys Bowen—*The Twelve Clues of Christmas*
2. Kate Kingsbury—*Mulled Murder*
3. Mathew Prichard, editor—*The Grand Tour: Around the World with the Queen of Mystery*
4. Margaret Maron—*The Buzzard Table*
5. Louise Penny—*How the Light Gets In*

Bob Miller

1. Brad Smith—*Shoot the Dog*
2. Michael Connelly—*The Black Box*
3. James Lee Burke—*Light of the World*
4. John Sandford—*Storm Front*
5. Steve Hamilton—*Let It Burn*

Stephanie Lowe

1. Janet Bolin—*Night of the Living Thread*
2. Kylie Logan—*Mayhem at the Orient Express*
3. Lila Dare—*Wave Good-bye*
4. Susan Boyer—*Lowcountry Boil*
5. Elaine Viets—*Fixing to Die*

Andrea Mason

1. Janet Evanovich—*Takedown Twenty*
2. Bailey Cates—*Charms and Chocolate Chips*
3. Heather Blake—*A Potion to Die For*
4. Ali Brandon—*Words with Fiends*
5. Juliet Blackwell—*Tarnished and Torn*

Jacob Smith

1. Craig Johnson—*Junkyard Dogs*
2. Robert Crais—*Suspect*
3. Harlan Coben—*Missing You*
4. David Baldacci—*King and Maxwell*
5. Rick Mofina—*Into the Dark*

Turn the page for a preview of Erika Chase's next
Ashton Corners Book Club Mystery

Coming soon from Berkley Prime Crime!

I'm telling you right now, sugar, I'm leaning toward bumping off Clyde Worsten rather than having to deal with him one minute longer," Teensy Coldicutt said with a dramatic sigh.

Lizzie Turner almost dropped the mini Triple Chocolate cupcake she'd just rescued from the serving tray on the wicker patio table next to her. She shot a glance at Molly Mathews who started laughing, much to Lizzie's surprise.

"Don't look so distressed, Lizzie," Molly said between chuckles. "Teensy's talking about her new book, aren't you?" She shifted her glance to her childhood friend of over sixty years.

Teensy looked around at the three other women in Molly's sunroom and burst out into her own deep belly laugh. "Oh, my. Of course your mind went straight to the worst, Lizzie. Being such a great fan of mysteries, and I might add, a dynamite crime fighter, I can see as that would happen. But Mopsy is right. Clyde Worsten was going to be the hero on my latest novel, *Divine Secrets of Desire*, but he's not cooperating at all, at all. So, he's either going to be the victim or, if he gets me really riled, I'll turn him into a murderer. Serves him right if he has to spend the rest of his life in jail."

"*Mopsy*," Sally-Jo Baker stated with a grin. "It still takes me by surprise sometimes when I hear you use Molly's childhood nickname."

"And I didn't know you were writing a mystery, Teensy," said Lizzie.

"Goodness gracious, of course not. My forte is romance and I'm into another hot plot, I want you to know, but that doesn't mean I can't throw in a dead body or two if the characters don't shape up and cooperate."

Lizzie shook her head. "I'd heard that writers talk about their characters taking over a story."

Teensy leapt up from the white wicker love seat with more energy than many women her size. Her new hairstyle, a dramatic wedge, had also changed from a bright orange-red to a vivid dark red with a broad white streak sweeping across her brow since the last time her friends had seen her. The black leggings, smock-necked orange and green long-sleeved blouson and four-inch-heeled sandals contrasted with Molly's classic cream ensemble of casual pants and silk blouse. Lizzie marvelled at the many differences between the two long-time friends.

"Oh, believe me, they do," Teensy said. "And, I'm just bursting to tell you both about my news."

Molly looked up from the *Wedding Bells* magazine she was perusing. "You have a publisher?"

"Right in one, Mopsy. Remember poor Nick Jennings, the editor at Crawther Publishing? Well, it looked like he needed someone to talk to when he was in town after that tragedy last fall, so I befriended him, and one thing led to another."

Molly wasn't able to suppress her gasp. "No."

"Oh, Molly. There's hope for you yet but that's not what I meant. We starting talking about writing and I told him of the great success my first book had garnered around here and he said he'd take a look at my new manuscript. So, maybe it's not a done deal but I know that when he reads the first three chapters and synopsis I just sent him, I'll be signing on the dotted line."

Lizzie fervently hoped that would be the case. Of course, she knew nothing about Crawther Publishing and their lines, except for the mysteries they had showcased at the book fair held in Ashton Corners last fall. But, she had read Teensy's first book, which had been copublished with a local printer, and Lizzie wondered if it would have met the criteria of an established publisher like Crawther.

"We're wishing you loads of luck with that Teensy," said Sally-Jo, choosing a pecan swirl from the tray of sweets. "This is really a nice idea, Molly, having us over for a girls' afternoon while the guys are out fishing."

"I thought so," Molly agreed. "It's a wonder, though, that Bob, Jacob and even Mark were all able to find a free weekend in common to get away."

Lizzie nodded, knowing only too well that her significant other, Mark Dreyfus, didn't often take an entire weekend off from his job as police chief of Ashton Corners, Alabama. She was pleased he'd decided to go, knowing how hard he'd been working for some time now without a real break.

Teensy walked over to the table and chose a sugar cookie. Rather than eating it, she held it in her hand and started pacing. "Well, let's just hope they have lots of luck and we can indeed have that fish barbecue they're promising when they come home tomorrow."

"What has gotten into you today, Teensy?" Molly asked. "You've either got ants in your pants or you've had way too much coffee."

"I have all these ideas floating around in my head and I'm just trying to shake them into some sort of order," replied Teensy, waving her hands in emphasis. "I need to harness all this energy and do something."

"I thought writing was taking up most of your time."

"Oh, it is, but that doesn't mean I can't do others things also. I think I write best if I'm under pressure and a deadline."

"You also have the writing course you're running, I might remind you. How much more do you want on your plate? And how is the course going, by the way?"

Teensy perched on the edge of the love seat. "As well as it should, I guess. There are mostly women enrolled, although I do have one elderly male. He's a bit too old for my taste, must be at least seventy-five if he's a day, but he does have a good sense of humor. Anyway, to most of the others in the class it's a social afternoon out. Oh sure, they do the homework exercises I give them, but not many are trying their hand at writing anything else. And that's what this whole course is for. I wanted to help others find themselves and explore their inner writers."

Sally-Jo leaned over to touch Teensy's hand. "I can see that you'd be frustrated, Teensy. I'd bet there's a lot of preparation time that goes into it, too."

"Not really," Teensy admitted, with an embarrassed grin. "I put the outline together by looking at other courses and then I found tips and suggestions from a whole slew of books on writing. It was easy, really. I think I'm even learning a few things, too."

"Why that's just great," Molly said with enthusiasm. "And even if you don't turn out a Pulitzer winner, at least they're all doing something they must be enjoying."

"Oh, for sure." Teensy sighed. "I guess I'm just being silly. There is one gal, though, who has lots of promise and she's working her way through writing a novel. I'm trying to help her as best I can."

"Well, that's all to the good," said Molly. "Now is there anything else that's got you so bothered?"

"That's just it, I do not have an iota of an idea why I'm so antsy these days. Maybe it's a touch of spring fever. But I feel like I need something else to be getting involved in. You don't have another body hidden away somewhere that needs a heaping of justice, do you?"

Molly shuddered. "Heavens no. And don't you go jinxing us now, Teensy Coldicutt. Things have been nice and quiet with the Ashton Corners Mystery Readers and Cheese Straws Society for a while now, aside from the occasional verbal fracas with a certain stubborn retired police chief, that is."

"Pshaw. I do believe you enjoy the sparring just as much as that old dog does, Mopsy."

Lizzie turned away from them quickly before Molly could see her face. Teensy had hit the nail on the head but Molly was still in denial. Bob Miller and Molly had known each other since childhood and although their lives had taken such different paths, the ties were maybe even stronger. Much as between Molly and Teensy. That was the wonderful thing about small towns.

"What about doing some volunteer work?" Lizzie asked. "I'm sure you'd fit right in with the reading program the school board promotes in elementary schools. You go in and read to various groups of kids. Usually they're ones having trouble with their reading skills or maybe they have short attention spans. And, you can choose the days and times you'd like to be involved. I think you'd be really good at that, Teensy."

Sally-Jo nodded. "You'd certainly be able to hold their attention, Teensy. I think you'd give very colorful readings."

Teensy's face lit up in a smile. "You could be right, girls. I'll look into that. Thank you."

"You're welcome," they answered in unison and broke into laughter.

Molly reached for the empty pitcher of iced tea. "I'm betting y'all would like some more." She paused before going into the kitchen. "Now don't say anything important until I get back."

"We'll just talk about you behind your back, Mopsy," Teensy called out. "Nothing important, though."

Molly made a face at Teensy as she came back outside. She offered to refill Sally-Jo's glass. "I know I'm real anxious to hear where you're at with your wedding plans, Sally-Jo."

Sally-Jo flipped the cover shut on the magazine on her lap and held it up to them. *Premier Bride*. "This is about as far as I've gotten. Thumbing through all these magazines. Who knew there were so many focused on wedding planning? Jacob and I are thinking small but my folks are thinking big. I'm not quite sure what to do."

"Well, I'm enjoying looking through all these here magazines," Molly said. "It sure brings back memories, although we didn't go searching through catalogs for a wedding dress in my day."

Lizzie looked at her with interest. "What did you do? Go to a big city for a day of shopping?"

"Not at all. My mama had wanted me to wear her dress but it had gotten damaged over the years, despite her careful packing away of it. So, she had a local dressmaker come in, suggest a style and take my measurements. We agreed on the material and a few months later, I had my dress. And I just loved it."

Lizzie nodded. "It looks wonderful in your photos. Maybe that's what you should suggest, Sally-Jo."

Sally-Jo had her finger marking a page in her magazine. She opened it and showed it to the others. "So tell me truthfully, what about the style of this dress?"

Lizzie leaned closer for a better look. She tried not to sound too critical. "I don't really think it's you, Sally-Jo. I somehow can't picture you in a mermaid look. I'd think something more elegant and flowing. Sorry."

"That's quite all right. In fact, I was hoping you'd say something like that. My mama, however, loves this dress. She told me to go out and buy this magazine and have a look at this particular one." Sally-Jo sighed. "It's not me but I know just how pushy Mama can be. And I'm afraid I just might end up walking, or rather waddling, down the aisle in this."

"Can't you just go out shopping and buy a dress on the sly?" Teensy asked, a devilish twinkle in her eye. "We'd all be as happy as a puppy with two tails to go with you."

Molly glanced at Teensy. "That's not being very sensitive to her mama's role in all this. It's as important a day for her as it is for Sally-Jo." She raised her glass toward Sally-Jo and smiled. "But, honey, we would be very pleased to help you out with this."

"Oh, no. Mama wants me to come home some weekend soon and she'll book appointments in all the bridal salons in Fort Myers. She'll summon the sisters, too. She's even offered to pre-shop for me to narrow it down and make the decision easier."

Sally-Jo looked so gloomy and defeated that Lizzie wanted to give her a big reassuring hug. "What do you want?"

A small smile crept across her face. "I'm sort of leaning toward a strapless dress on the shorter side, maybe falling just below the knees and with an empire waist."

"I think that sounds like a wonderful choice for you." Molly's voice rang with enthusiasm.

"Thanks, Molly. Maybe I can get you to brainwash my mama."

"It's early days still. You've got until next spring, a whole year off."

Sally-Jo shrugged. "You don't know Mama. There'll be no resting until I have a dress chosen and tucked away in my closet."

Lizzie's started to say something but was interrupted by the ringing of the front doorbell. She looked at Molly who had settled back in a lounge chair, and said, "I'll get that for you."

"Thank you, honey."

Lizzie went through the foyer to the front door and peered through the peephole to see a young woman standing there. She pulled open the door.

"Hi. May I help you?"

The girl with the Miley Cyrus hairstyle looked to be in her early twenties. She wore trendy skinny jeans and a silver distressed-style leather jacket along with a black shirt and multicolored beads around her neck. She tried to peer past Lizzie.

When that didn't work she crossed her arms and stated, "I'm looking for Bob Miller."

It sounded like a challenge to Lizzie.

DON'T MISS THE FIRST NOVEL IN
THE BOOKS BY THE BAY MYSTERIES FROM

Ellery Adams

A Killer Plot

In the small coastal town of Oyster Bay, North Carolina, you'll find plenty of characters, ne'er-do-wells, and even a few celebs trying to duck the paparazzi. But when murder joins this curious community, writer Olivia Limoges and the Bayside Book Writers are determined to get the story before they meet their own surprise ending.

M769T0910